HER DARK VIKING

ASHE BARKER

Published by Stormy Night Publications and Design, LLC.
www.StormyNightPublications.com

Cover design by Korey Mae Johnson
www.koreymaejohnson.com

Images by Period Images, 123RF/Iakov Kalinin, and
123RF/Danny Smythe

1st Print Edition. May 2017

ISBN-13: 978-1546686446

ISBN-10: 1546686444

PROLOGUE

Scotland, 1105

The tall Viking spun on his booted heel, alerted by an innate sense of danger that he had honed finely over the years. A Celt materialised from the forest at his rear, let out an animalistic snarl and charged, raising the roughhewn branch he was using as a makeshift club high above his head. The man brandished the weapon, his intent clear—to fell the Nordic invader who threatened his home, his family, all he held dear.

Gunnar's nostrils flared. He narrowed his eyes and smiled, an expression he knew well would accentuate the grim severity of his features. The scar, which ran from below his left eye to bisect his cheek and finally disappeared under his jaw, further augmented his fearsome appearance, a fact not lost on the attacking Celts if the widening of the man's eyes was any indication. Gunnar knew a moment's regret at the inevitable end to this. The Celt was about to draw his final breath.

A sword hung from the Viking's left hand, and he hefted an axe in his right. Acting on pure instinct, the dark-haired Norseman selected the sword and swung it with a sharp, upward motion. The point penetrated his assailant's unprotected chest and the man's shrieks of fury were instantly silenced. The Celt crumpled to the bare earth beneath him, soon to be swallowed within the bowels of the land he had died to protect.

Gunnar eyed the still twitching corpse at his feet, his gaze dispassionate. The brave fool should have known better. This farmer should have fled along with the rest of his people. Instead, armed with nothing more than a lump of wood, he had faced down a Viking warrior. He should have run away while he still could.

Gunnar tilted his head. He could still hear the anguished, terrified cries of villagers who even now scrambled over the rocks that bordered their tattered homestead, grateful to escape with their lives if not much else. Some would find a safe haven, he supposed. The rest would die, or watch in helpless despair as the Viking horde ransacked their village.

The raid would be swift and decisive. Vikings never remained long, they had no need to. It was their way to attack at speed, to swoop ashore from their swift dragon ships, lay waste to any who might oppose them and take what they would. The raid would be over almost as quickly as it had begun.

Gunnar wiped the point of his sword on the grass at his feet and raised his arm high to rally his men.

"With me," he yelled, "to the village. Follow me." He was off at a run, seeing no need to check that his men were at his heels. They would not dream of doing otherwise.

The Celtic settlement was little more than a few low, turf-roofed dwellings huddled about a central pen. Goats and pigs scuttled back and forth in agitated alarm as the Norsemen thundered past, their war cries designed to terrorise any remaining inhabitants who even now thought to defend what was theirs. A rapid search of the houses yielded no such hardy, yet misguided souls. All had fled, leaving their homes to the mercy of the attackers.

"Take the livestock, and check for anything else of

value." Gunnar issued his command, though he did not expect to find much in the way of wealth here. The abbey, half a day's sailing down the coast, was a different matter entirely. There, he knew, would be gold plate, coin, tapestries—richer pickings indeed. But this fishing village located on the shore had looked tempting enough from the sea and he was never a man to pass up an opportunity. A brief detour had been called for.

Gunnar strode between the buildings to march around the perimeter of the hamlet. A well-trod trail leading inland signalled the likely existence of another village close by and regular traffic between the two, but he had not the time on this occasion to explore more thoroughly. The rest of the local populace could remain unmolested—this time.

He paused, surveyed the deserted settlement, now silent as even the livestock had been herded off by his men. A good hour's work, he concluded. Time to be on their way.

A shrill scream halted his stride, followed by the rumble of derisive laughter. Gunnar cocked his head and listened. The scuffles and grunts he could hear coming from behind the building closest to him betrayed the location of the sport. Doubtless some Celtic wench had been a little too slow to make her escape.

A pity, he supposed. Rape was commonplace among Viking raiders, but Gunnar entertained no personal fondness for it. There were plenty enough willing females back at home, but this act had nothing to do with lust or sexual desire. He had encountered many quite lovely women in his time. He appreciated their appeal and much enjoyed their company but had yet to experience even the slightest impulse to rape any of them. In his view, the raping of defenceless women was about power, conquest, and violence. These villagers were already defeated; it was not necessary to further torment and abuse the weakest of them.

He rounded the building and his eyes narrowed at the sight before him. Three of his men held a Celtic female pinned to the ground. She was spread-eagled, her overtunic ripped and her skirt hiked up about her thighs. One Viking warrior secured her hands, another her feet. The third knelt between her splayed legs and was already unfastening his woollen breeches.

The man holding the woman's feet laughed as the female struggled to free herself, her efforts futile in the face of superior numbers and strength. "Be quick, Sven. We'll all be wanting a turn on her afore we go."

"Aye," agreed the man who pinned her arms. "An' you can see how eager she is for some Viking cock inside her. Let's not be disappointing the slut, eh?"

Another terrified scream pierced the air, though Gunnar doubted their victim understood the Nordic tongue. Still, the intent of the three who assaulted her was clear enough. He knew full well that his men expected him to leave them to their sport, let them enjoy a juicy piece of Celtic pussy to relieve the tension of battle. Many a Viking felt that was little enough to expect on a raid, but Gunnar disagreed. These men would have their share of the spoils, they would just have to settle for that.

"Let the wench be. Back to the longships. Now."

"Eh?" The man who crouched between their victim's thighs, his heavy cock now exposed and swaying before him, turned to scowl at his leader. "We'll be no more than a minute, *Jarl.*"

"Now," repeated Gunnar, stepping forward. "Or you can stay here to face the rest of her kin when they venture back. The boats leave the moment I return to the beach and any man not aboard will be swimming home."

"But—" The man at her feet stood up, ready to argue the point.

"Am I not making myself clear, Olaf Ingrssen? Or do you fancy getting your feet wet, is that it?" Gunnar lifted his sword to rest it across his broad chest, the threat implied rather than explicit, but there nonetheless.

The three shuffled awkwardly, backing away, their grumpy muttering a signal of their discontent. Gunnar was unmoved. He was *Jarl* here, his word was law. He tossed his head in the direction of the beach. "Get on your way, I'll be right behind you."

He knew they didn't believe him. They would fully expect him to take the trembling wench for himself. From the look of her as she cowered before him, that was what she expected also. She spoke to him, brief, desperate words in her Gaelic tongue. He could not understand her, but knew she pleaded for her life if not her virtue. She would be permitted to keep both as far as he was concerned, though she was not to know that.

Gunnar extended his hand, offering to help her to her feet. She stared back at him, disbelief and confusion flitting across her delicate features. Now he came to look at her properly he would own this Celtic peasant was not so much pretty as stunning. Eyes of a vivid green gazed up at him. Her hair was a flaming shade of dark red, the locks tumbling from her hood, which had become dislodged in the struggle. She shoved her rough wool skirt back down to cover her lower limbs but not before he could appreciate the sight of long, slender legs, creamy thighs, and exquisitely sculpted ankles. Her tunic hung from her shoulders, exposing the upper curve of her breast. He was treated to the sight of more flesh, the rich hue of buttermilk, before she managed to right her clothing. Only then did she accept his outstretched hand and allow him to draw her to her feet.

The wench was tall, though he still towered a full head over her. And she was not as young as he at first assumed, perhaps twenty summers. She eyed him warily, clearly uncertain what he intended to do to her but fearing the worst still.

Using just a lifting of his eyebrows toward the trees behind her, Gunnar signalled to her to go, to make her escape while she still could. She took no further encouragement, just turned and ran. In moments, she had disappeared into the forest, just the swaying of a pine branch betraying the path she took.

Gunner sheathed his sword, slung his battle axe across his shoulders, and sauntered back to his dragon ship. The wealth of Lindisfarne Abbey awaited him.

CHAPTER ONE

Ten months later

"Not much to be had here by the looks of it. You say there's a second village, located close by?" Ulfric Freysson shielded his eyes against the glare reflected from the waves as he surveyed the Scottish shoreline from the prow of his dragon ship. He had to shout to make himself heard over the brisk offshore breeze.

"Aye, I reckon so." Gunnar Freysson answered his half-brother from his own vantage point on the dragon ship under his command, less than a hundred feet from Ulfric's vessel. Two more such longships brought up the rear of their raiding party. "I raided this place less than a year ago and I noticed a well-trodden track leading from that village you see there, close to the beach. It had to lead somewhere."

Ulfric nodded, his features set. "We land then, overrun the first settlement fast then head straight inland for the next one. Let us hope there are a fine crop of able-bodied Celts that we can round up and take with us. My granary and harbour will not build themselves."

"I daresay," agreed Gunnar, already bristling in anticipation of the fight to come. Gunnar raised his arm to signal the start of the attack. They had agreed that he would lead the first rush rather than his brother, the Jarl, since unlike Ulfric he had prior knowledge of the terrain. At his command the four dragon ships altered course as one and all skimmed across the surface to swoop upon the undefended little cove. Already people on the beach were running for their lives as the monstrous dragon ships bore down on them, their cries of alarm carrying across the rippling waves. It would do them no good. This time the villagers would not be allowed to flee—the Vikings had come back not for plunder, but for slaves.

Gunnar scanned the dozen or so small figures fleeing before them. He told himself he was not looking for anyone in particular, but even so he scoured the scene for a flash of bright red hair. He did not see her, but that did not mean she was not here.

He had allowed her to go free last time, but not again.

Ulfric wanted slaves to build his granary; Gunnar just wanted *her*.

The scrape of sand under the hull of the dragon ship was the signal for the Viking raiders to leap over the side into the shallow waters. They drew their weapons as they splashed up onto the beach, their war cries deafening even to Gunnar's seasoned ears. How terrified the defenceless Celts must be!

He grinned as he led the charge. That was the intention—shock, terror, absolute surrender.

The hamlet he had attacked on his previous foray some ten months previously was deserted. Fires still burned, skinny dogs prowled the outskirts of the buildings, their tails tucked between their hind legs. An upturned cooking pot lay in a pool of still-steaming broth, evidence of the haste with which the inhabitants had fled just minutes ago. Gunnar paused to right the pot, and he gazed about him. *Which of these meagre hovels was hers?*

"Jarl, should we fire the houses?" One of his men halted at his side, the man clearly ready to lay waste to all around them. Bloodlust was a powerful motivator, mused Gunnar, but it rarely yielded worthwhile results.

"No, we go on, to the next village. This way." He took off at a long stride, rounding the low shed closest to him in search of the concealed track. He found it easily enough, the path freshly beaten from the pounding of feet as the villagers had sought to make their hurried escape.

"Here, to me…" Gunnar yelled, his sword held high above his head. He tore along the rough track, and was soon rewarded by the sound of frantic voices from up ahead. The Vikings were gaining on the fleeing Celts fast. This would be swift and conclusive.

Now, all Gunnar had to do was locate *her*.

He could not have explained what the fascination was with this particular Celtic wench. She was pretty, though that was not uncommon. In Gunnar's view most females were attractive but that was no reason to lose his senses over one, and certainly no cause to lead a Viking raiding party across the North Sea to claim a woman who would recoil in horror from him. His size, his fearsome appearance, the darkness that seared his soul—she would fear and loathe him for those alone, even if not for the vicious scar that marred his features. His quarry would run screaming for the hills if he were to allow her to escape. Which he would not.

Her flaming hair was unusual, granted, but he had never cared that much for such details. Her eyes, too, were memorable. They reminded him of the colour of the seas that lapped the cliffs beneath his home in the Norselands. But she was still merely a woman, a female to be bedded. It did not even matter whether she was willing or not, though this was a detail he preferred not to consider too closely. It had never been Gunnar's way to force himself on a wench. His brother neither—their father had taken a dim view of such matters and impressed upon them both the rewards to be enjoyed with a warm, willing woman.

That was it, Gunnar supposed. He imagined the Celt to be warm, without doubt—how could she not be with that hair? And willing? That remained to be seen but he intended to find out. He preferred not to dwell on how he would respond if she were not. He had lived alone for too long; he yearned for the lively family he had enjoyed as a boy growing up in his father's longhouse, his half-brother beside him and their pretty little sister dogging their heels.

He could have installed many a Nordic female in his household, but had yet to meet one he could envisage sharing his home. In his mind's eye, though, he had instantly seen the Celtic wench ensconced at his hearth and once that image took root he had been unable to dislodge it. He wanted *her*, and no other would do.

So, he had returned to the land of the Celts and this time, one way or another, he would have his little fiery-haired wench.

He rounded a slight bend and the stragglers among the escaping Celts came into view. An elderly man, two old women, a lad on crutches, three women dragging small children with them, one with a baby in her arms. The villagers hastened their steps as the Norsemen bore down on them but in seconds they were surrounded by Vikings, all armed to the teeth and shrieking their battle cries.

Gunnar's voice rose above the rest. "There are none here of interest to us. Leave them. Onward, now." He was aware of the women pulling their little ones off the path and into the shadows of the trees, but he ignored them. Children and women could not build granaries, nor could they row a longboat. It would be a waste of good food and shelter to take these useless peasants, and slaying them would serve no useful purpose since they represented no threat. He left them on the track and sprinted on in the direction of the village, his brother beside him and his men at his heels.

Gunnar could smell the wood smoke now, hear the frantic babble of terrified voices.

"We are close," he murmured.

"Aye," his brother concurred. Ulfric turned to command their men. "Kill none unless absolutely necessary. I want strong backs, not broken ones."

The Vikings burst from the trees and were immediately upon the village that lay in a clearing. A busier place than the hamlet on the shore, and more prosperous perhaps if the larger dwellings were anything to go by, the place was swarming with people frantically trying to flee from their fearsome attackers. The Celts seemed surprised and confused, disoriented, as though they had not supposed the marauders would pursue them here.

Fools. They would pay dearly for their innocence.

Ulfric took charge now that they had located their quarry, barking out brisk commands. "Search every dwelling, assemble all here in the middle of the village, men and women alike. You, Sigmund, take the right. Gunnar, you will search the left-hand side. Kill any who resist, and the rest will present no problems. Olaf, you will guard the prisoners as we take them. None shall escape."

The Norsemen set off at a sprint to carry out their orders. Gunnar strode to the closest dwelling to his left and booted open the door. Inside he found three women cowering beneath a rough table, though none sported the hair he sought. He gestured to them to leave, and was gratified that they offered no resistance. As they scuttled out into the daylight he shoved them into the keeping of two of his men to be taken and held with the rest. Already the clearing in the centre of the hamlet was teeming with captives. The women wept, children clung, white-faced, to their mothers' skirts. Several men offered some semblance of a struggle but that foolishness was quickly quelled by the application of a sword hilt to the head of one, a dagger to the throat of another.

Gunnar had no knowledge of the Gaelic tongue, but his brother did. Ulfric's voice bellowed above the din of battle and Gunnar supposed he was telling the prisoners to accept their fate and they would not be harmed. Some quieted, others appeared not to believe the word of a Viking. Gunnar could not blame them.

He continued his search, discovering an elderly couple, a young man, and a child of about five summers in the next dwelling. The man would make a fine slave, he thought. Ulfric would be pleased. Soon this bunch joined the rest.

A shout behind him caused Gunnar to spin on his heel, his axe at the ready. The manor house that dominated the village lay to his rear, and a man of perhaps twenty summers was charging from the front door, a shovel in his hands. Behind him an older male called out, wringing his hands as he sought to dissuade the young hothead from his obvious folly.

A pity he did not succeed. Gunnar readied himself to parry the attack. The lad would perish, and it would be a waste. Ulfric would not be pleased at the loss of a decent thrall, but there was nothing else for it. Gunnar circled the youth, allowed him ample opportunity to think better of this idiocy and surrender. The old man caught up and he tried to plead with the younger one, but to no avail. The fool swung his shovel at Gunnar who sidestepped it easily. The lad came forward, prodding, swinging his makeshift weapon wildly. There was a madness in his eyes, a crazed glitter, which Gunnar had seen before in those unaccustomed to battle but suddenly exposed to the full horror of it.

There was no point reasoning with this one. The skirmish would end just one way.

Gunnar was quick, and he was merciful. He doubted the lad even saw the blow coming and death was swift. The would-be warrior went down in a crumpled heap, dead before he even hit the earth beneath him. The old man sank to his knees beside the lad, his son, Gunnar assumed. Gunnar bent to remove the shovel, just in case the old man might yet be consumed by a sudden thirst for vengeance. The old one was of no interest to them, he could not work. There was little point in dragging the grieving father away to join the other prisoners. Gunnar left him beside the body of his son. He had work still to do.

He heard her before he saw her. The scream, the

pleading tone, all reawakened his vivid recollection of that day several months before. The sounds came from the bowels of a small hovel, and a commotion from inside suggested yet more futile resistance. He lowered his head and entered the tiny dwelling.

His quarry was there, confronting two Norse men who apparently sought to drag a male of middling years from his bed. The man's sickly pallor, his rapid breathing, all suggested this invalid would be better left where he was. The last thing Ulfric's settlement in their homeland needed was some epidemic brought from across the seas from the land of the Celts. Some virulent contagion could wipe out his brother's slaves in a matter of days, and probably half the Viking community too.

"Leave him," Gunnar commanded. "He is sick, probably infectious." He stepped aside to allow his warriors to leave the cottage, then paused to regard the girl he had not been able to forget and his heart lurched, painful in his chest. Now this—this he had never imagined.

She was pregnant. Heavily pregnant, probably ready to give birth at any time from the look of her swollen, distended abdomen. He thought back to the incident he had disturbed. Had he not been in time? Was this the result of rape?

No, he was certain he had prevented that. She was married, then. Her husband might even be the man sweating and moaning in the bed and giving every impression that this day might be his last. If not, the husband was probably already swelling the ranks of Ulfric's latest batch of slaves.

Did this change things? He rapidly reconsidered, assessing this latest unexpected turn of events, and quickly concluded that it did not. The husband was of no consequence. He wanted her, *still* wanted her. If anything, this unassailable evidence of her fertility heightened his desire for her even more. She was perfect. It was that simple.

"You, you will join the others," he commanded. "Outside."

She shook her head, her expression perplexed. The woman did not understand him, and he could not speak her tongue. For want of a better option he seized her arm and tugged her bodily from the dwelling. She struggled, as he had expected, but he tightened his grip. Gunnar was determined not to harm her, keenly aware of the delicacy of her condition. The less she fought him now, the better.

He towed her across the village and deposited her among the peasants assembled in the centre. "Watch her," he commanded the Viking closest to him.

"Aye, Jarl." The man grinned at him, his toothless smile betraying his glee at their impending victory, the unqualified success of their mission. "She'll be going nowhere—"

The Norseman's words were cut off abruptly when he was hit on the side of the head by a rock. He dropped like the stone that had felled him.

"What the—?" Gunnar whirled but could not pick out the source of this unexpected attack. Even as he scanned the surrounding trees another stone whistled past him to bring a second of their men to his knees. This time he could pinpoint the direction and without thinking stepped between the unknown threat and his captive as he peered into the woods.

Seconds later his brother emerged from the trees, a young Celtic wench slung unceremoniously over his shoulder. Her hands were bound behind her back and, frantic, she struggled in her captor's grasp, though at a few words in Gaelic from his stern-faced brother that futile effort ceased. Gunnar wondered what Ulfric had said to subdue the wench but had no time to ponder that.

Soon the girl was bundled into the growing throng of captives, his brother towering over her menacingly. He had a slingshot dangling from his hand, which explained the brutal effect of the missiles. Gunnar was impressed despite himself. The lass was obviously an excellent shot. More brief words were exchanged, then Ulfric stalked off.

Curious and amused in equal measure, Gunnar eyed the

diminutive Celtic female with interest. She was dark-haired, slender, and younger, he thought, than his own flame-haired beauty who had now melted into the growing crowd of captured Celts. No matter, he would ensure she was selected to accompany them, when the time came to choose the females. Ulfric particularly required male thralls for his building projects, but experience had shown that a handful of women would prove beneficial too. Females had a calming effect on healthy male slaves, as well as which they could cook, weave, sew, and usually didn't eat too much.

He assessed the girl dispassionately. This one was pretty enough to catch Ulfric's eye, without doubt. Another of the Celts, a tall, tawny-haired male, was immediately at her side. As Gunnar watched, the male attempted to release her from her bonds. A sharp shout from his brother put a stop to that endeavour. The man abandoned his efforts but remained close and the two conversed quietly. The man would be coming with them as a slave, Gunnar was certain of that. The girl smiled up at her companion and he wrapped his arms around her. Gunnar wondered what the Celt was to this wench and if this relationship between the two of them spelt trouble for later.

As he pondered this question he watched as the first man felled by one of the Celtic girl's missiles staggered unsteadily to his feet. The injured Viking pressed his huge paw against his temple and let out a low, menacing growl as he shook his head as though to clear his addled wits. His gaze fell upon the wench who had wielded the slingshot and his lip curled. He lumbered toward her.

Ulfric would not wish this. Gunnar moved to intervene at the same time as the Celt male at her side hastily shoved the girl behind him. However, neither was called upon to offer protection as the man's intended retribution was curtailed by a loud yell from their chief. The command to stop caused the man to halt in his tracks, though he did not appear unduly deterred as Ulfric strode toward the group in the middle of the village. Words were exchanged, the Viking warrior appeared sullen, ready to argue his right to exact revenge upon the small female.

There could be but one outcome. Ulfric's word would be law, none would disobey him. Sure enough, the man slunk away, leaving Ulfric to confront the wench and her would-be protector. Although Gunnar was fully aware his brother did not require his aid or support, this was sport he would not miss. He approached and stationed himself behind his chief. Intrigued, he stuck the point of his sword into the ground and leaned forward on the handle, his posture utterly relaxed as he settled in to enjoy the entertainment.

The conversation was in Gaelic so Gunnar could not follow their words. However the belligerent expression on the Celtic male's face told its own story. The girl herself appeared more fearful, more respectful of the power the Viking warlord wielded over all her people now.

Ulfric was aware of Gunnar's presence and turned to him, his expression stony. "Brother, will you see to boarding the prisoners? Take all the males who are able to hoist a rock or handle an oar, and make certain that this wench is taken to the ship intended for the women. You shall select such other females as you think needful. It is time we were on our way."

"Of course," agreed Gunnar, his gaze already scanning the group of Celts for his redhead. "I shall see your new slave safely secured."

"She will remain bound until I say otherwise." Ulfric's features were impassive, but Gunnar knew that look. This little Celt would end up in his brother's bed before long, whatever her handsome yet powerless Celtic protector might have to say on the matter. He knew a moment's sympathy for the man—he could not start to imagine the furious impotence of being unable to protect those dear to him. Still, he was a Viking so the matter would not arise.

Ulfric bestowed one final, stern glare on the unfortunate wench who had crossed him and he strode away.

Left to his duty, Gunnar wasted no time in having the men herded off toward the beach where they could be set to work at once rowing the dragon ships back across the sea. That settled, he scanned the remaining captives and immediately dismissed the elderly and the children. Those released scuttled away, seemingly unable to comprehend their good fortune. Of the remaining women, he kept his brother's choice close to his side while he pointed to just a half dozen or so others who looked to him to be likely candidates—fit, seemingly healthy, not unattractive. His redhead was the first to be selected.

CHAPTER TWO

She knew him.

The moment the huge warrior entered her brother-in-law's dwelling Mairead recognised the dark and fearsome Viking who had saved her all those months ago. His appearance on that day had been terrifying, his raven-black hair loose to his shoulders, his ebony-hued leather tunic and breeches stretched taut across his muscular body, his wolf skin cloak of the darkest grey caressing his wide shoulders and descending almost to his knees. The beast from whom he had acquired the pelt must have been a monster, but this man looked as though he might have been spawned by the devil himself.

He had held a sword on that occasion, the point turned upward as though ready to disembowel any who crossed his path. Yet his actions that day had not been cruel. He had allowed her to go free, unharmed, and she had not the slightest notion why he had been merciful. He had no need to be—she was powerless, helpless, yet he had spared her.

But now, he was back. He had returned, and by his impassive visage as he regarded the scene in the tiny cottage, she expected no such merciful end to this second encounter.

He was similarly attired this time, though he sheathed his

sword as he perused the one-room hovel, no doubt perceiving that the occupants of the cottage offered no threat to him. The dark Viking was no less awesome a presence now and Mairead wished she might shrivel into a ball and disappear. She backed away, words of pleading rising to her lips though they remained unspoken.

At a few curt words in their guttural Nordic tongue, the other Viking raiders slipped from the dwelling. Their chief, if that was his status, cast a dispassionate eye over Ferghus as he huddled beneath his thin blanket. Her brother-in-law had succumbed to a fever just two days earlier and Mairead feared he might not survive it. The Viking appeared disinterested in the fate of the sick man and turned his attention fully to her, just as Mairead's unborn babe chose that moment to deliver a sharp kick to her abdomen wall. She gasped but offered up silent thanks that, thus far at least, her child was unharmed. She must do what she could to ensure that remained the case.

He spoke to her, strange, alien words that she could not comprehend. Mairead shook her head, hoped he would realise she did not understand. It seemed he did, as he offered no further conversation. Instead he seized her arm and marched, pulling her behind him. Acting on instinct she tried to tug her arm free, but he tightened his grip on her wrist. Mairead blinked as they emerged into the afternoon sunshine, then blanched at the scene that surrounded her.

The village of Pennglas was laid to waste, several of the turf-roofed cottages already ablaze. Dughall, the lord of this hamlet, knelt weeping beside the body of his son, Adair. The lad had been a fool and something of a wastrel in Mairead's opinion, but he was the heir and now he was gone. What would become of them?

Her captor barely broke stride as he towed her past the scene of Lord Dughall's grief. A crowd of villagers had been assembled in the middle of the settlement, surrounded by fearsome warriors brandishing an array of weaponry who threatened any who attempted to make a break for it. They were mostly males, she noted, though some women were among the prisoners.

Mairead was not a resident of Pennglas. Her own home was a one-room cottage in Aikrig, the fishing hamlet situated on the coast perhaps a mile from here. She had been visiting her late husband's brother, had brought him some broth to ease his hunger in his illness, when the raiders struck. She had had no chance to flee; indeed, few of the villagers had by the looks of it. And she could not have got far in her condition in any case.

She could but hope that this Viking's dubious mercy might save her a second time.

He uttered a command to one of the guards. The man eyed her with interest, then offered his chieftain a brief nod. He started to speak, but was struck on the temple by a rock. He toppled to the ground, blood seeping from a wound on his head.

Mairead could not tell from where this ill-fated attempt at retaliation might have come, though she heartily wished whoever had unleashed the missile had not done so. The Celts were already defeated and resistance would only bring more misery, more violence down upon their unprotected heads. Even as she arrived at this conclusion a second stone hurtled past to bring down another of their attackers.

"Oh, sweet Jesus," murmured Mairead. She clutched at her abdomen in an age-old gesture of maternal protection, fearing that the Norsemen might at any moment set upon the prisoners in a burst of murderous vengeance. However before they could muster sufficient wit to do so, the trees at the edge of the hamlet parted and another huge Norseman strode forth, the struggling, wriggling body of a girl slung unceremoniously across his shoulder. Mairead recognised the woman at once. It was Fiona, daughter of Dughall. Her slingshot dangled from her captor's hand.

Fiona was a fine shot, the best in the village, probably. Mairead should have known there was but one who could have found her mark with such unerring accuracy not once but twice. Although she did not know the girl as the lord's daughter was somewhat above her own lowly station, Mairead felt sorry for the lady now as she would surely pay for her actions with her life.

But seemingly not, or at least, not yet. The Viking deposited his captive among the other prisoners and left her there. Mairead heaved a sigh of relief. There had been more than enough bloodshed this day.

Her own dark Viking captor also appeared to have lost interest in her, thank the dear Lord. Mairead shuffled back to conceal herself among the other prisoners. She peered about, anxiety warring with relief as she failed to spot the other she sought. Her other child, Donald, a lad of just seven summers, had been left with neighbours in Aikrig whilst she tended to Ferghus. The villagers on the coast would have seen the raiders coming, and would have had those precious few minutes in which to flee. She had to hope and pray that Donald had managed to escape.

"Have you seen my boy?" She made the fretful enquiry of those closest to her. "He is small, just seven years old. His hair is red, like mine…"

Most did not answer, concerned solely for their own welfare, their own kin. Those who did shook their heads, shrugged, expressed their conviction that he would be safe.

How could they know? None of us are safe. Mairead fought back tears as she moved through the frightened peasants, scanning each face, seeking the neighbour to whom she had entrusted her son but failing to find the woman.

Her fears grew as the Vikings began to separate the men from the women. *Sweet Saviour, what do they intend to do now?* The men were herded out of Pennglas onto the track leading back to Aikrig and the coast. She recognised the chief of their own village among them. Taranc was betrothed to Fiona of Pennglas, and his usually benign features were contorted in fury as he and the rest were led away at sword point.

The men gone, the group remaining was depleted to just

a couple of dozen or so. The dark Viking strode around their huddled throng, selecting the older prisoners and one woman who had two small children with her. These people were released. Their faces betrayed their startled, grateful astonishment when they were allowed to rush away and hide in the surrounding trees.

The fierce Norseman paused beside Mairead and she held her breath. Surely he would release her too. Once again this unlikely protector would free her from the horror of Viking brutality. He had to. She prayed in silence, awaiting the command to flee.

Perhaps her prayers might have been heeded had her unborn babe not chosen that precise moment to deliver an almighty kick. Mairead gasped and lurched forward, to be caught in the firm grip of the Viking. His hands on her elbows, he steadied her and murmured something incomprehensible but not ungentle either. Mairead opened her mouth to thank him, but the infant was not to be ignored. Another solid thump from within her swollen abdomen caused her to flinch and she was certain the movement was discernible by those around her should anyone care to observe.

The Viking observed. One dark brow lifted in surprise, then in understanding as he realised what had caused her to stumble. He lowered his gaze to her distended middle and watched the intimate display of lumps and bumps as the child again made his presence felt.

Mairead was mortified. She was embarrassed, humiliated, and above all terrified of the consequences of drawing the fascination of this ferocious warrior. And fascinated he was. His lip quirked in a grin of genuine amusement when her belly lurched again. He met her gaze and he smiled at her.

The smile transformed his appearance. She had known this fearsome man was handsome, in a rugged and savage sort of manner, his jaw strong, his eyes almost black and exuding a cruel authority that both attracted and repelled her. Now, he was simply breath-taking.

"*Gorvel?*" He spoke softly, the intonation suggesting a question though she did not understand his words.

"I am sorry…"

"*Gorvel?*" he repeated, this time extending the flat of his hand toward her belly. He raised his brows and waited. It was as though he sought permission, though of course that was impossible.

Except—he wanted to touch her. Mairead could only assume her captor wished to feel for himself the insistent wriggling and kicking from within. He could have simply laid his hands on her body and there would have been nothing she might do to prevent it, but instead he sought her consent.

Baffled, Mairead nodded.

The Viking placed his palm on her belly, then grinned widely as the babe executed what felt to Mairead to be a fair rendition of a Scottish jig. He adjusted his stance, looking from her face to her belly and back again as the child shifted in her womb. He said something else to her but she could not understand him. She did, however, know that the baby had altered position and much movement was now taking place lower down. He would miss it if she did not…

Mairead took hold of the Viking's leather-clad wrist and shifted his hand down her belly to the spot where he would find more activity. No longer afraid, she waited, motionless, as he pressed his large palm against her.

The babble that surrounded them, the chaos and confusion, the terror and despair melted into a vague and distant fog for Mairead as she and the dark Viking stood together in silence, united in their shared experience of the baby's kicking. Long moments passed, until at last the child went still once more, clearly exhausted. With a wry smile the Viking offered her what might have passed for a polite bow, and he strode away.

Mairead glanced about her. Just a handful of women remained, all fairly young and none but her with children.

Was she to be taken after all? Did it not count that her babe was as yet unborn?

She found herself next to Fiona, who remained bound. The lady's face was ashen and despite her own concerns Mairead sought to offer comfort.

"We will survive, I know it. We must remain calm, do as we are told…"

"My brother is dead. They killed him." The other woman's voice was little more than a shocked whisper. Mairead's heart went out to her despite her own terrors.

"I know, I saw. But he died swiftly, I am certain of it."

"My father…?"

"I saw him, earlier. He was alive then."

"Oh! Are you certain? He was not among those captured and taken."

"I saw him, it was definitely Dughall." Mairead saw no reason to mention that when she last saw Lord Dughall he had been weeping at the side of his dead son. The fact that he had not been among those brought to the middle of the village did not bode well, but neither woman wanted to voice that.

The dark Viking spoke again, raising his voice to gain their attention. His words were unknown, but his meaning clear as he gestured with his sword and the few remaining warriors shoved the women in the direction of the route to Aikrig. They were to follow the men to the beach.

Fiona struggled to keep her footing as they were bundled along the rough track, but Mairead took her elbow. Another woman, Quinn, a weaver also from Aikrig stationed herself at the other side and between them they aided the bound girl. Mairead dismissed Fiona's whispered thanks. They must all help each other at a time like this.

Apart from Quinn and her daughter, Briana, Mairead did not know the other two women with them but names seemed unimportant. None of the women captured with her had seen Donald. Mairead began to hope, believe, that her son might have made it to safety. His father dead these four years, and his stepfather lost at sea just three months ago, Donald would be alone. Would the kindly neighbour take care of him? Surely she might for he was a fine boy and the middle-aged widow had no young children of her own now.

The beach came into view and already three of the dragon ships were bobbing on the waves several hundred yards out to sea. Just a rough cargo vessel and one dragon ship remained. The women were directed to the cargo boat, a slower craft but powered by a sail rather than brute force. Mairead was relieved; she had dreaded being forced to row.

One by one the women were lifted bodily and carried through the shallow waves to be bundled into the small craft. There they huddled together in the bottom of the boat, damp, cold, and utterly terrified. The vessel put to sea, the crew of just four rough Norsemen handling the rigging with practised ease. For the most part they ignored the shivering captives, although one did think to toss them a blanket as night fell.

Neither the dark Viking nor the other one, the man who had captured Fiona and who also appeared to be a chief of some sort, came with them. Mairead assumed they were aboard the other dragon ship and would be off to mount further raids on unsuspecting communities along the Scottish coast.

She hated them, Mairead decided. She hated every last one of them for separating her from her son and for endangering her unborn child. Despite the gentle concern of the Norseman who had appeared so fascinated, he had not seen fit to leave her safe in her home, among those she knew. Surely her baby would struggle to survive its first few precarious months of life as a slave to the cruel Nordic raiders. What had they done to deserve such a fate, any of them? Least of all the unborn innocent she carried. She hated the Vikings for their uncaring cruelty, their greed, their arrogance that they considered all before them fair game. They stole, they murdered, they raped, and they ruined lives. They tore communities apart, wrecked families, left children as orphans, and all for their own selfish ends.

May their ships flounder, their wells sour, and their crops rot in the soil. Mairead despised them all, and she loathed the dark Viking the most for wrecking her naïve fantasy that he might be a kind and merciful warrior, a man of honour. She had learnt this day that he was no better than the rest, a barbarian, a killer, a vicious savage.

The voyage took three days and three excruciating nights. Despite the blanket and huddling together for warmth, the women were freezing cold, damp, hungry, and aching with fatigue by the time land was sighted. Yes, she was right to hate these Vikings; they were cruel, unfeeling, quite without mercy.

The crew became excited as they neared their destination, waving and calling to those on the shore. Mairead ventured a peep over the rail of the boat and could make out a shoreline not that dissimilar to the Scottish coast. Tall pines swayed in the breeze, sandy coves were dotted at intervals, and towering cliffs dropped into the churning waves. This was a land of some beauty, she had to admit as she raised her gaze to take in the snow-capped mountains in the further distance. The landscape was harsh but majestic, a vibrant kaleidoscope of colour and shade.

And it was cold, much colder than her native Scotland though it was still not yet quite the end of summer. She shivered and hugged her arms across her swollen abdomen and wondered what it would feel like to be warm and dry again. Would she ever know?

The boat docked at a bustling harbour, a busier place than any Mairead had seen before. Men called out, laughed, jeered and women yelled back in the strange Nordic language that was starting to sound familiar after three days of listening to the crew of their small boat. Children scampered between the boats lined up in the port, and animals mingled freely among the human occupants.

There were buildings, many more than in Pennglas and

Aikrig combined, most with thatched roofs. They were built of wood for the most part, with stone walls at the base. Mairead picked out one structure, larger and more imposing than the rest and with a many layered roof constructed of wood. She assumed this to be a place of greater significance, perhaps intended for worship or trade, but she could not ask as no one here would understand her Gaelic tongue.

The men who had sailed the craft back now barked orders at their confused captives.

"They mean us to climb up the side and onto the dock," guessed Quinn. "Come, Briana and I shall help you."

Mairead was glad of their assistance as she clambered clumsily up the planking to grab the rail at the top. A hand under each of her feet propelled her up still further and at last she was able to scramble onto the wooden decking that made up the quayside. She offered her hand to Quinn to aid her up, but the other woman refused with a tired smile.

"No, lass, you can't be lifting my weight. You save your strength, you never know when you might need it."

Quinn scaled the side of the boat more easily that Mairead expected, and Briana was even more nimble. Her hands were stiff from the cold and Fiona had not the slightest chance of making the climb, a fact not lost even on the rough sailors. One of them grabbed her about the waist and hefted her over his shoulder, then climbed the side of the craft until other Viking males could grab her from the dock. She tumbled down beside them, gasping for breath.

Both Mairead and Briana stepped forward to assist her but were grabbed before they could offer aid. Rough hands shoved all the women along the dock and behind a low building into a small enclosure. Here Mairead was both startled and relieved to spot the Celtic males they had last seen three days previously in Pennglas, along with other men she had not met before. All appeared to be either Celts or Saxons. It would appear the slave-harvesting mission had encompassed other villages also.

She spotted Taranc at once, and he made a beeline for

them.

"Is Fiona with you? Did they harm her? Are you well?"

"We are fine," confirmed Quinn, "considering. And Fiona too. She is still on the quayside."

"Bastards," muttered Taranc under his breath. Mairead had to concur.

"Women, make a line," commanded a small, pugnacious individual. He managed a form of broken Gaelic, sufficient to make himself understood. Should his words fail to make his point, Mairead supposed the vicious-looking switch he carried in his hand and was happy to swipe in every direction would assist him.

Resigned to the inevitable they shuffled obediently into a ragged queue, only to recoil in horror when, as one, they realised what was intended. The enclosure bordered a small forge, where a smith was busily engaged in securing a shackle around the left ankle of each captive. On closer inspection Mairead realised that the men had already been shackled, and they were chained together in rows three deep. Presumably the women were to be similarly hobbled.

It was all she could do not to sob when her turn came and the heavy iron band was wrapped around her ankle, then secured with a metal pin that the smith drove into place with a huge mallet. The vibrations of the hammer blows rattled her very bones and she cried out as the bruising strokes fell. The anklet was a dragging weight when she tried to walk, rubbing painfully against her skin above her leather sandal. It was even worse when she was pushed into her position in the line, chained between Quinn and another woman who she had learnt was called Fingula. Each looked as miserable as she felt.

Mairead started when she glanced across the enclosure and caught sight of the dark Viking once more. In contrast to the dejected prisoners he looked clean, rested, well fed. Fiona walked by his side. Mairead shrank into her place, unwilling to attract the Viking's attention, but she could not miss the flash of angry resentment in Fiona's expression as she, too, was shackled and forced to join their wretched group. The Viking chief paused to peruse the assembled captives, his dark gaze falling at last on Mairead. His lip lifted in the start of a smile as their eyes met, and she thought for a moment that he intended to speak to her.

She scowled at him, heedless of the consequences for once. Resentment, bitterness, and rage churned within Mairead, emotions she could barely recognise. Normally mild-tempered and placid, compliance had been bred into her and nurtured her entire life. Servitude was a way of life to her, obedience deeply ingrained. But slavery was not and she boiled with unaccustomed anger. Most of all she feared for her innocent, defenceless child who had been thrown at the mercy of these brutes, savages who would put her people in chains like animals.

Let that Viking bastard even try to speak with her… she would spit in his dark, cruel eye. She met his hooded gaze again and this time made no attempt to conceal her fury. He saw, he understood. His brow furrowed and the hint of a smile evaporated. Something twisted in the pit of Mairead's stomach. She did not think, this time, that her baby could be blamed.

As her tormentor turned and marched off, the switch-wielding Viking took over command.

"You, listen all," he began. "You walk now, two days. No slow down, no stop. All must work, all will walk, yes." Was she mistaken or did the vile little man allow his gaze to fall on her distended abdomen, as though challenging her to request some sort of special treatment? Mairead resolved not to, though the prospect of a two-day forced march, in chains and dragging the weight of her shackle, reduced her almost to tears. But she would manage, she had no choice.

"Mairead, look," Quinn murmured in her ear, and pointed to a group of men closer to the front of the line. "Is that your boy?"

"What? No, surely it cannot be…" Mairead strained her neck to see, and her heart sank. There, chained between two men she did not even recognise, was the diminutive form of her little boy. Donald was dwarfed by the men on either side, his narrow shoulders slumped and his sandy-haired head bowed. Already he looked exhausted and her heart wept for him. He should not be here, he was of no use to these Viking brutes.

"Donald! Donald, it is me. Donald…" she called out, anxious to let him know that she was there, that she was close even if she couldn't reach him yet. Perhaps if they were taken to the same place, the same village, the same Viking master, they would be reunited. As long as they were together, they would survive, she knew it. She had to believe that.

The boy turned, his pinched face betraying his fatigue. His eyes lit up though when he saw her. He reached across the yards separating them as though to take her hand. Mairead extended her hand to him, and smiled her encouragement, the best she could offer him at this point.

"Take care, do as you are told, and we will be all right." It was a foolish promise to make, but she could do no other. Her boy had to have hope; it was all that remained.

CHAPTER THREE

The sound was the worst. The clanking, clattering grind of metal on metal, the rattle of links scraping against each other as the weary, dejected party made their way north. The prisoners tramped along the rough trail in the direction of the settlement that was apparently their final destination and lay some two days hence, the home of their Viking captor who had seized them for his own use. Mairead dragged her weary limbs onward, her huge abdomen weighing heavier with every step she took. She wrapped her arms beneath the swell in the hope she might support the weight of her pregnancy, but it made little difference.

As her weary steps faltered, the bad-tempered little slave master appeared alongside her. "You. You walk fast. No stop, not slow others."

Mairead picked up her pace and stumbled on.

Quinn threaded her arm through Mairead's. "Come, I shall help you. We can make it, together."

She estimated they had been on the road for perhaps two hours, and in another hour or so it would be dark. Surely the march would have to stop then, surely they must be allowed to rest for a few hours. She could manage until nightfall. She had no choice. Already the hateful little Viking had returned several times to stride alongside her, always shouting, always threatening. Once he actually struck her with the switch he always carried, the harsh blow falling across her shoulders and causing her to almost fall to her knees. But she didn't. Somehow, she kept her footing and continued the relentless march.

Mairead was glad of Quinn's quiet encouragement and support during her ordeal and wondered that they had not really been friends before this. Perhaps they might have been, had Alred been different. Her husband had never cared for socialising much and had not permitted his wife to mix with the other women of the village. He considered them a disturbing influence, flighty even, and they would distract her from her duty, which was to care for him and his home. And to bear his children, naturally. He had been a stern man, uncompromising and joyless. She had tried hard to gain his approval but had failed utterly.

She should have been more grief-stricken than she was when the sea claimed him. They had been wed just six months when Alred died. Barely a bride, she was already a widow, and for the second time. Her first husband, Donald's father, had died of a fever when the boy was just four years old. Niall had been a good man, and a kind one. She missed him still, but a dead man cannot put food on the table nor logs on the fire. With a son to provide for she had felt she had no option but to remarry so had succumbed to her family's urging and had left her home on the outskirts of Dundee to move to Aikrig where Alred had offered for her. He was an acquaintance of her mother's brother, and she had understood him to be a man of wealth and standing. He was neither as it turned out and her marriage had proved a bitter disappointment in every respect.

It was surely better than this miserable existence though, she reflected as she trudged on in the gathering gloom.

The monotonous clanging of chains was drowned out by the beat of hooves. Several Vikings cantered past on horseback, and Mairead glanced up in time to recognise her dark Viking captor among them. He met her gaze again, though his face did not bear a smile this time. He scowled at her and she wondered how she might have contrived to anger him. It would not do to attract unwelcome censure. She well knew these Vikings would not hesitate to deliver a whipping for any transgression. She had endured enough such treatment at her husband's hands; she certainly had no wish to be subjected to Viking discipline.

The men on horseback had barely disappeared from view when a fierce scream rent the air and one of the captives shackled in the row behind her stumbled and hit Mairead hard in the middle of her back. Mairead staggered forward and would have fallen but for Quinn's steadying arm. The pair turned.

Fiona lay writhing and sobbing on the ground. She grasped awkwardly at her ankle, the one not sealed within the merciless grip of the iron shackle, and rolled onto her side. Willing hands, including Mairead's, reached to assist her to her feet but Fiona was unable to right her manacled ankle, and the free one was clearly injured and unable to take her weight. She screamed again as she attempted to put her foot to the ground.

The women who had clustered about the injured girl scattered as the slave master hurled himself among them, his vicious switch striking all who did not shift quickly enough.

"What happens? Why stop? Why all this din?" He reached Fiona and took one look, then let out a torrent of Norse abuse that none of them understood. The general gist was clear enough—he did not appreciate this interruption to their progress and he clearly held Fiona responsible.

He crouched and loosened the links in the chain that tethered the slaves together, then opened it to slip Fiona's shackle free of the rest. He turned to issue a curt command to another guard who had appeared at his rear, leaving the man to secure the prisoners again whilst he dragged the casualty clear of the rest.

Mairead winced as Fiona screamed again. The Viking was without mercy as he tossed the injured woman onto the grassy verge beside the track and stood over her to assess the damage. He reached his conclusion in mere moments, and his features were set as he drew his dagger.

Mairead was stunned, speechless. Surely he did not intend to—

He did. The slave master bent to grasp the front of Fiona's woollen smock. The girl was ashen as she shrieked again, but was helpless to protect herself.

A sharp shout, then hoof beats interrupted the macabre scene. The Viking chieftain who had passed them but moments earlier cantered back into view, the dark Viking with him. Both dismounted. The chief spoke to the slave master, the exchange quick and angry. The Viking crouched to better peruse his damaged property, then said something else to the man under his command. The slave master started to argue then seemingly thought better of it. He shrugged, his pudgy features sullen as he relinquished the sobbing prisoner to the mercy of his chief. He started back toward the prisoners, breaking into a run as unrest surged among the men who had watched the scene unfold.

Taranc's voice rose above the general shouting and babble. "Let her be, you animals. I shall carry her. I will—"

The odious slave master laid into the Celt, wielding his ever-present switch with determined enthusiasm but that merely served to incite the angry and now mutinous captives into yet more raucous defiance. Voices raised, men fought to be free of their chains. The mood was angry, but Mairead feared this would only end in tragedy as the Viking guards closed in, clearly ready to apply whatever force might be required to quell this uprising.

The blond Viking chieftain strode across to the protesting slaves and at first Mairead believed he, too, intended to join in the melee. Instead he gestured his guards to back off, whilst he confronted the furious Taranc alone. The men stood nose to nose, the one all powerful, the other snarling his rage at his captor. From where she stood Mairead was unable to hear their low-voiced conversation, but she was struck by the expression on the Viking's handsome features. He was utterly calm, his self-assured confidence absolute. He did not posture or threaten, but his words gave Taranc pause. The Celt answered, and whatever he said seemed to satisfy the Viking. Their exchange at an end, the Norseman turned on his heel and marched back to where Fiona still lay on the ground.

The dark Viking with the scarred face had watched all of this with apparent amusement. His stern features split in a wide grin as the blond man strode back to where he stood beside Fiona and something twisted low in Mairead's belly. Despite the scar, or maybe because of it, the man was beautiful when he smiled. Utterly terrifying, of course, but still quite beautiful.

The blond crouched beside Fiona. His dark companion offered some remark or other. His chief seemed irritated but the dark one grinned yet more. He was clearly enjoying all of this, a fact that should have angered Mairead but instead she found herself fascinated. The blond seemed to be their leader, but the dark warrior was not in the least subservient to him. Surely Fiona was in no danger now. These men had prevented the slave master from murdering her at the roadside. But what exactly were their intentions?

She had little opportunity to ponder that. Already the slave master was shouting at the prisoners to get back into their lines and move off. He sought out Mairead in particular to prod her with his switch.

"You, you will walk faster. Not slow others."

She nodded, determined not to draw further unwelcome attention, then clutched her belly as her baby chose that precise moment to deliver another sharp kick.

"Oh, ouch!" Mairead gasped and lurched forward, but not before the slave master spotted her distress.

"Halt. Wait," he barked. In moments he had loosed the chain once more and this time removed Mairead's shackle from the rest. He straightened and grabbed her arm. "Too slow, too heavy. No use." He dragged her out of the group, his grip brutal as he jerked her forward.

"No, oh, no, please…" Mairead pleaded. She staggered in his grasp, then, overcome by exhaustion and sheer terror she sank to her knees.

The slave master raised his switch and in an age-old gesture of maternal protection Mairead sought to curl her body around her huge belly. The switch fell across her shoulders and she screamed.

There was another voice too, not hers. A shout, angry, authoritative. She glanced up and out of the corner of her eye caught sight of the brute again reaching for his dagger. Mairead let out an agonised moan. Cheated of his first victim, it seemed her tormentor had seized upon her as his consolation. He would cut her throat for the crime of being pregnant and not quick enough.

The dark Viking was suddenly beside her, his furious gaze turned on the vile beast who seemed intent upon murder. He thought better of his plan when confronted by the scarred face of her protector, even backing away as the Viking glared at him and unleashed a torrent of Nordic abuse on his head. Mairead could not understand the words spoken, but his meaning was clear. The slave master was left in little doubt either, and hurried back to the remaining Celts. Moments later the procession was on its way again.

Donald!

Mairead watched in helpless agony as the group of men surrounding her son started to move off. He was being taken away, she knew not where. She had been so close to him, and now she might never see him again. She could not bear it.

Anguished, she attempted to scramble to her feet. The Viking at her side offered her his hand and, unthinking, she took it. She tried to follow the departing prisoners, determined even now to appeal to the vicious thug in charge. She had to remain with her son; she couldn't lose him now.

The Viking grabbed her arm, not roughly as the slave master had but his grip was relentless even so. Mairead struggled, fighting to be free of his hold, pleading with him.

"My son! My boy! He needs me. He is but a baby. Please, let me go! I have to remain with him. I can manage…"

The dark Viking knew no Gaelic. He stared at her, clearly unable to make sense of her reluctance to remain with him rather than continue her journey in the slave master's cruel care. Mairead's struggles became more frantic as the group of captives trudged further away.

The blond chief called out to him and the dark Viking's expression transformed from puzzled to incredulous. A rapid exchange ensued between him and the chieftain, culminating in the dark-haired man seizing a purse of jingling coins from his belt and hurling it at the blond Viking.

The chief laughed out loud and called an order to the slave master. Moments later Mairead was astonished when Donald was shoved unceremoniously from among the Celtic males. The small boy stood, uncertain, scared, looking about him at the assembled Vikings. They presented a fearsome sight indeed and Mairead's only instinct now was to get to her son and comfort him.

This time when she pulled away the dark Viking released her. She made her ungainly way toward where Donald hovered, clearly unsure what he should do now or what was to happen to him. The boy caught sight of his mother, the one familiar face, the one who represented safety and warmth in a world gone mad. He rushed to meet her and flung himself into her arms.

Again, Mairead sank to her knees and this time Donald went with her. She heard the shambling footsteps of the prisoners as they trudged off, but she clung to Donald as though she would never let him be parted from her again.

She glared back at the dark Viking as though daring him to so much as attempt to separate them, but his attention was no longer on her. Instead he watched the interaction between Fiona and the blond chieftain.

It appeared that the Viking intended to examine her injured ankle, but Fiona was clearly of another mind. Perhaps she misunderstood his intentions, because before Mairead's horrified eyes the younger woman swung a rock that she had concealed within her hand. The blow caught the Viking on the side of his head and he collapsed over her.

The dark Viking swore and sprinted to where the other man lay prone in the dirt. Fiona scrambled from beneath his body and attempted to crawl away. Her efforts were doomed; she could barely drag herself a few feet across the inhospitable terrain let alone make her escape.

Two guards set off in pursuit but halted at a word from the dark Viking who now bent over the blond male. Already the downed man was showing signs of recovery. He pushed himself up onto his knees and started to look around him. The other man patted his shoulder and ambled off after Fiona.

He did not hurry, had no need to. Mairead's heart sank; she had liked the other woman but could not imagine Fiona of Pennglas would survive this day after all. She had attacked her new master, actually injured him. She would be killed now, without doubt.

Even knowing it was hopeless Mairead opened her mouth to plead for mercy for Fiona. The dark Viking was not a vicious man, or had not seemed so in his limited dealings with her. The Vikings had even allowed her son to remain with her so perhaps they were not entirely without mercy.

"Please," she began. "It was a misunderstanding. You cannot…"

The dark Viking reached where Fiona now lay in the damp grass. He bent to grasp her shoulder then rolled her onto her back. Fiona curled into a ball as though to defend herself even now, the gesture futile but instinctive.

Long moments passed as the dark Norseman gazed

down at the terrified, injured woman at his feet. Mairead held her breath, then let out a sharp cry when the Viking bent to deliver the death blow.

But he did not. Instead, he scooped Fiona up in his arms and carried her back to where the blond man now knelt in the dust, his expression thunderous. The man in black leather deposited the girl beside his chief and the two conversed again in their Nordic tongue. The dark Viking offered a brief nod and strolled over to where his mount still waited patiently. He spoke briefly to another Viking, a young man of no more than eighteen or nineteen summers by Mairead's estimation and one of the guards who had started off in pursuit of Fiona. He tilted his chin in the direction of Mairead and Donald. The youth replied and started to move toward them. Meanwhile the dark Viking took a length of leather and a roll of linen from his saddlebag and returned to the pair on the ground.

Mairead stiffened as the young warrior approached.

"You ride with the Jarl. The boy with me." His Gaelic was slow but comprehensible.

Mairead tightened her grip on her son. "No, we must stay together. You have to—"

"Together, yes. We go to Gunnarsholm. All of us."

She narrowed her eyes, not quite daring to believe. "Gunnarsholm? Where…?"

"Two days riding. Further north. Come, I will help…" The young man assisted Mairead to her feet, then ambled off to retrieve his mount. He returned towing a grey horse in his wake and another stallion of coal black. He beckoned to Donald, who stepped forward uncertainly. The Viking grinned at him then grabbed the boy and slung him up onto the saddle. He proceeded to mount up behind the startled lad then turned to regard the approach of his chief.

The dark Viking said nothing as he towered before Mairead, merely beckoned her to him. She saw no alternative but to obey. Standing beside the huge horse he bent and linked his hands to form a step. Mairead placed her foot in his palms and was hoisted up into the saddle. The dark Viking mounted behind her and signalled to his men to follow. Moments later he, the youth with Donald, and four more of the Viking guards cantered away along the track into the gathering gloom.

Confused, scared, bewildered, Mairead leaned back against the solid man at her rear. He wrapped his arms around her to manage the reins and they rode in silence for several minutes. At last Mairead could bear it no longer. She twisted in the saddle to look up into the stern features of the man behind her.

"Mairead," she announced, her hand splayed against her chest. "Mairead of Aikrig." She pointed to her son. "Donald."

He regarded her for several more moments, his handsome features stern and unreadable. Then, just as she was about to admit defeat for now and face the front again, his dark eyes appeared to soften, to warm slightly. His mouth curled in the semblance of a smile and he made a brief nod of greeting.

"Gunnar Freysson," he replied.

CHAPTER FOUR

What had he been thinking? A heavily pregnant woman could never manage the gruelling march all the way from the port at Hafrsfjord where the women had been bundled ashore, to his brother's homestead at Skarthveit. Nor did she have to, for Skarthveit had never been her destination. The flame-haired beauty would be traveling with him to his own homestead, Gunnarsholm and he had no intention of forcing her to walk there.

He should have intervened earlier, insisted that his captive ride with him and his brother. It was only when Gunnar passed the convoy of slaves on the road that he realised how much his little Celt was struggling. He had been on the point of announcing to Ulfric that he intended to claim one of the prisoners as his own when the commotion started. He might have known their females would be at the heart of it.

Fucking Dagr. His brother's slave master might be adept at managing thralls and Gunnar knew how much Ulfric valued the man's services, but the bastard was pitiless in his pursuit of results. And wasteful. Even if it were not for the more personal circumstances that came into play, it was sheer madness to slaughter a perfectly decent fuck-slave.

The idiot had been quite prepared to dispatch two, and one of them his. Dagr was fortunate to retain his fucking arm after this day's work since Gunnar had been ready to hack it off when the slave master laid into his flame-haired captive with that bloody switch.

Gunnar was not above applying a spot of well-deserved discipline, a skill both he and his brother had learnt at their father's knee. Women responded well to such an approach, he had observed. But he was never needlessly cruel, he hoped, and certainly not a bully.

The woman nestling in his arms shifted against him and his cock hardened. He ground his teeth and willed his unruly erection into submission since it was clearly impossible to so much as contemplate seeking gratification for the time being. He was uncertain quite why the prospect of injuring her or her baby filled him with such revulsion, but it did, so she would remain untouched until after she had given birth. Even then, he did not imagine she would share his bed willingly, but he would work on that.

He glanced over at the slight figure of her son. The boy had been a surprise and he racked his brains to try to work out how the lad came to be among those taken. He had deliberately not selected women with little ones, and certainly no unaccompanied children. Where would be the sense in that? His brother wanted able-bodied slaves, not more helpless, dependent mouths to feed.

Had he been so preoccupied with securing his alluring captive that he failed to pay due regard to the rest of his duties? He would need to watch that if he intended to remain alive. A careless Viking would soon enough find himself greeting his ancestors and the gods in Valhalla, an experience Gunnar harboured no immediate urge to sample.

He signalled to the man mounted behind the boy. His karl brought his mount close.

"Steinn, you speak the tongue of the Celts?"

"A little, Jarl. My mother taught it to me."

Gunnar nodded. His own mother had been a Celt also, seized in one of his father's numerous raids on the lands across the sea but she had died when he was very young. He had been raised since babyhood in his father's longhouse, speaking only the Nordic language. It often struck him as ironic that his half-brother, a full-blooded Viking, could speak the Celtic language with such fluency whereas he knew barely more than a few words. In truth, Gunnar had had no use for such a skill before now.

"You will speak with the boy, seek to ascertain how he came to be among the male slaves for I have no recollection of taking him."

Steinn nodded, and steered his mount away again.

The day was fading fast. Gunnar had hoped to make better progress before stopping for the night, but the events back along the road had conspired to hinder their journey. There was no help for it, it would be unsafe to continue after dark. He spotted a grassy clearing a few yards ahead and raised his arm to signal that they were to halt here.

"Make camp," he instructed. "We continue at first light."

The men dismounted and hurried to do his bidding. All knew their tasks and before long a small fire burnt. Furs and blankets had been slung on the ground close to the flames, and a structure fashioned of twigs balanced over the blaze. A rabbit, skinned and spitted, was soon dangling over the fire and the men settled in to await their supper.

Gunnar glanced over at Mairead and the boy who huddled together on the opposite side of the fire. He rose and went to his mount where he kept spare furs and a blanket. He offered these to the pair, and was pleased at the grateful smile his largesse elicited from the Celtic woman. Her earlier resentment appeared to have abated somewhat, perhaps as a result of her brush with the harsh realities of slavery and his intervention to alleviate those. Gunnar resumed his seat across from her, the better to scrutinise his latest acquisition.

Mairead. A pretty enough name, he supposed, though

not one familiar to him. She would be complicated, he had known that when he took her. By the determined and defiant manner in which she hugged her small son it was clear he had underestimated the extent of the challenge. His longhouse would be full to overflowing with her offspring.

There was a husband, that much was obvious, but where was the man? Perhaps back in her homeland, or worse, among the thralls now in his brother's possession? Gunnar beckoned to Steinn.

"What is the word for husband in their language?"

The man grinned and told him what he needed to know.

"And how do I ask where the man is?"

More grinning, and the karl provided the appropriate phrase. Gunnar repeated it with care, then made to rise.

"Jarl, will you understand her answer?"

Gunnar paused. "Good point. You will assist."

"Aye, Jarl." Steinn fell into step at his side.

Mairead looked exhausted, and the boy visibly cowered when the two huge Vikings approached. Neither reaction pleased Gunnar overmuch but he crouched beside the pair and managed to dredge up something akin to a smile.

"I have questions for you..." he began.

At her wary frown Steinn quickly translated his words. Mairead nodded and pulled her son closer to her.

Gunnar tried out his new phrase, stumbling over the unfamiliar sounds but it would seem he managed to make himself understood because she replied at once. Unfortunately, he had not the slightest idea what she said.

"Her husband is dead," offered Steinn. "He drowned at sea some months ago."

Gunnar heaved a sigh, his relief a surprise to him. So, one less complication, two if he also counted the fact that the man had not perished in the raid on their village. Even so, he offered his condolences.

Mairead gave him a wan smile, and might have said more had the silence between them not been rent by the growling of a hungry stomach. The boy blanched and shrank even further into his mother's embrace. She looked up at Gunnar and spoke quietly to him.

"The boy has not eaten since yesterday," Steinn put in. "She asks that he be permitted some of the meat we have on the spit."

Shit. Gunnar called to another of his men, and the karl approached their little group.

"How many rabbits do we have?"

"Three, Jarl. I can but roast them one at a time though."

"The first is for the prisoners as they have not eaten this day. Bring me bread now, and cheese if you have it."

The man nodded and went to do his chief's bidding. He returned moments later with a hunk of rather stale, flat bread. "We have no cheese, Jarl, but these are good. And sweet." He held out a metal dish containing a dozen or so gooseberries.

It did not escape Gunnar's notice that the boy's eyes widened at sight of the fare. He thanked the karl and took the food, then held it out to the lad. The boy hesitated, but Mairead did not. She took the proffered dish and placed it in her son's hands. The boy took no further persuading and the berries were gone in moments.

"Thank you," murmured Mairead. Gunnar was glad this was one of the few phrases he did understand of her tongue. He found himself smiling again.

"You shall have meat also, when it is ready. You will not go hungry, either of you." He rose to his feet. "Eat, then sleep. We leave at first light."

Gunnar strode away as Steinn repeated his words in the Gaelic tongue. It was enough, for now.

• • • • • • •

He woke to the sound of panting and a shrill squeal of distress.

What the fuck? Gunnar sprang to his feet and reached for his sword. In the hazy pre-dawn light he could just make out the shapes of his men, still sleeping. Across the camp, on the other side of the dying embers of their fire, his captive rolled heavily from side to side. She was the one making the peculiar noises.

Gunnar moved around to investigate. Was she ill? Seeking to escape?

The lad lay stiffly at her side, his eyes wide and frightened. He peered up at Gunnar anxiously, but did not cower from him this time. It was amazing the effect a full belly would have on a small boy, the warrior reflected as he bent to better scrutinise his prisoner.

As he peeled back the blanket that covered her, Mairead let out a sudden shriek. It was enough to alert the entire camp. Suddenly his men were awake and demanding to know what was amiss. Gunnar had an unhappy feeling he knew the answer to that.

"The baby is coming." Steinn had appeared behind him and gave voice to Gunnar's fears.

"Is it time?" Gunnar looked up at his karl. "Ask her when the child is due."

There followed a brief exchange between the karl and his writhing captive.

"The child was due in three weeks' time, Jarl. It is early, but not especially so. The stress…"

"Yes, yes." Gunnar dismissed the explanation irritably. This was all he needed, and it was entirely his own fault. That march yesterday…

Fuck. Fuck. *Fuck!*

"We will need blankets. And mead. Steinn, you will assist as you can speak her tongue."

"Aye, Jarl. We shall not be breaking camp then?"

"What do you think," growled his chief, already cradling the stricken woman in his arms. "Find someone to keep an eye on the boy. He cannot remain here."

Mairead mumbled something, clinging to his arm in seeming desperation. She appeared even more distressed than her current condition would account for. Gunnar looked to Steinn for some sort of explanation.

The man frowned. "She is begging you not to leave her here, Jarl. She asks that you not abandon her and her children."

Odin's balls, what had he caused? What sort of a monster did she believe him to be?

Gunnar took Mairead's hand in his and squeezed it tight. He cupped her chin in his hand and brought her face around so she had to meet his eyes. "We will take care of you," he promised. "We will take care of all of you." His words were in Norse and Steinn did not translate, but Gunnar believed she had grasped his meaning because her delicate features relaxed. At least they did until the next contraction gripped her.

The next few hours passed in a blur. Mairead screamed, moaned, panted, and grasped at his hand with the brute strength of a mountain bear. All the while Gunnar remained by her side as his men hovered nearby. Childbirth was not their natural environment; this was women's work and best left to the mysterious skills of the midwives. The hardened Viking warriors looked on with a curious blend of horror and fascination as events unfolded.

The only relevant experience Gunnar could draw upon had been gained among horseflesh, but how much different could this be? It was merely a matter of assisting nature surely, and of tending to the babe when it slithered into the daylight. Gunnar refused to dwell on the terrifying mortality rate among women in childbirth. His own stepmother had died that way just five years earlier, struggling to bring their stillborn sister into the world. Mairead would not perish the same way, he would not allow it. He had only just found her; he was determined not to lose her so soon.

"It will soon be time," he muttered, though on what he based that assertion Gunnar was not entirely sure. Certainly, though, matters seemed to be reaching a crescendo if Mairead's ear-splitting howls were anything to go by. Her contractions were just seconds apart now, and she was straining to expel the little life buried within her contorting abdomen.

Gunnar lifted the blanket that covered her and peered between her widespread knees. *Was that…? Yes, it was. It most definitely was.* He could see the head, the little mop of dampened red-gold hair quite unmistakable.

"Almost there," he called to Mairead. "When the next contraction comes you will push. Yes?"

Steinn translated, though Gunnar was no longer sure this was needed. He and his Celtic captive were in perfect accord on this. Pain seized her again and this time he reached for the little being struggling to join him in his world. The head was fully out and he was able to gently turn the tiny form so the child was facing upwards. The eyes were closed, the nose and mouth covered in birthing fluids. Gunnar wiped the baby's puckered face, just as another, final contraction caused Mairead to shriek in agonised triumph as the rest of the tiny infant slipped into his waiting hands.

It was a girl. And she was perfect. Something twisted deep within Gunnar as he peered into the peaceful, reddened little features. She was still attached by the cord, and even as he gazed in wonder at the minute scrap of humanity Mairead heaved again and the rest of the afterbirth slipped onto the blanket beneath her.

Should she be crying? Babies always cried as soon as they were birthed, he was convinced he had heard that. This one was silent. And still. Too silent, too still.

Mairead reached for the child, her distress showing in her ravaged features. She knew. She, too, waited for the tell-tale wailing that would announce the new life safely delivered. Instead, there was only silence.

The child must breathe. That was vital. Gunnar poked the tip of his finger between her tiny lips to check there was no blockage. He found nothing, though in truth he did not know what he sought.

Mairead muttered something, her words incomprehensible. Gunnar looked to Steinn.

"She says you must hold the child by the ankles and slap her bottom. She will breathe then."

An unlikely tale, in Gunnar's view, but he had no better plan to offer. He gripped the skinny ankles in his fist and upended the infant, then dropped a light slap on her rump. It made no difference.

Acting on instinct alone, Gunnar cupped the tiny baby in his palms and raised her to his face. He pursed his lips and blew softly into her tiny rosebud mouth. For a few seconds she lay still, then a shudder rippled through the fragile little body.

The minuscule mouth yawned wide, the child took in a long, ragged breath, then let out the most strident screech Gunnar thought he had ever heard. And the most beautiful. Even his battle-hardened warriors cheered and thumped their shields at the sound.

The baby was wriggling now, and exercising her lungs to good effect in making her general displeasure known. Gunnar passed the noisy infant to her mother while he busied himself in tying off the cord and slicing through it, exactly as he would with a newborn foal or lamb. By the time he looked again she was already rooting within Mairead's smock for the nipple that would be her new lifeline.

Gunnar got to his feet, straightened, tried to work the kinks from his shoulders. It had been an easy birthing, he decided, all things considered. And both mother and child had survived the ordeal thus far.

They had much to thank the gods for. As soon as he returned to his settlement, Gunnarsholm, he would offer the sacrifice of nine newborn lambs to Frey, the goddess who protected his family, in gratitude for her generosity and kindness in bringing this about. Meanwhile, he was ravenous and he supposed Mairead would be too after her labours this day. The aroma of roasting meat filled his nostrils and he smiled at the sight of a roasting haunch of meat dripping its juices into the fire. His men had not been idle whilst he was otherwise occupied, and the rest of the young boar they had hunted lay close by, ready to be transported back to their village.

Gunnar drew his dagger and carved a generous portion. He dumped the succulent pork onto a metal dish and took it to Mairead. She accepted with her free hand, the other arm tucked around her baby who suckled hungrily at her breast. The sight of the tiny cheeks hollowing rhythmically cheered Gunnar. A babe with such a healthy appetite would fare well enough.

"Donald…?" Mairead peered about for her other child. The lad was nowhere to be seen, no doubt unnerved by the peculiar goings-on around the campfire.

Gunnar had no doubt the boy would be hungry too. He would need to check if the lad had been fed today.

No one could say. The lad had been around, hovering, quiet and fearful as ever. He had watched his mother from a distance, several men had seen him earlier, but none recently. The last time anyone was certain he had been present was over two hours ago. Gunnar swore under his breath. Had he not ordered that someone keep an eye on the boy? He commanded his men to search the camp and the immediate area.

They found nothing. The lad was gone.

"Perhaps he hid, and decided to sneak away while everyone was distracted. He did that before, back in his village."

Gunner scowled at Steinn's comments. "What do you mean? What happened back at the village?"

"You asked me to speak with him, to find out how he came to be taken with the rest."

"Yes. And?"

"He followed his mother to the second village. She had gone there to offer aid to his uncle. I understand the mother is skilled in the use of herbs for healing. Anyway, the lad remained outside the cottage. He heard our approach and fled moments before we stormed the settlement. He

50

concealed himself in the trees close by and watched as the villagers were rounded up. He saw you bring his mother from his uncle's cottage and put her with the rest. He listened too, and heard your brother tell the Celts that they were to be taken as slaves. He remained hidden as the men were led away, but when he saw his mother among the women to be taken also, he was terrified of being left alone. So he ran down to the beach in time to hide among the men who were already being loaded into the longships."

"Did no one see him? How could he manage to conceal himself from everyone?"

"He didn't. The other Celts knew he was there, but not that he was not supposed to be."

Gunnar nodded. It made some sort of sense, he acknowledged. Not particularly accustomed to putting himself in the position of those they attacked, it did not take an enormous leap of imagination to comprehend their point of view. As far as the Celts were concerned none of them were supposed to be forced at sword point onto a Viking dragon ship and taken into slavery. One small boy cowering among the captives would not have seemed particularly out of place.

"But why run off again now?"

Steinn shrugged. "Perhaps he believed his mother to be ill, dying. I was with you, and no one else would be able to explain to him what was happening, even had he asked."

Gunnar was at a loss, but one on point he was quite certain. The boy must be found. Mairead would never forgive him if he lost her child. And he had paid an exorbitant price for the lad. His brother had used the opportunity to make Gunnar return the purse of fine silver he had won from him at dice the previous night. Ulfric was ever a poor loser.

"Erik, Sven, you will remain here and guard our camp, and the woman. The rest of you, with me. We will scour the area. The boy was not trying to conceal his tracks, I doubt he even knows how. We will pick up his trail easily enough and find him. He can't be that far away if he was seen close to the horses just two hours ago."

His men were quick to obey, and within minutes the shout went up from one who had discovered a set of small footprints heading out of their makeshift camp and in the direction of the coast.

Surely the lad does not think to swim home? Gunnar had a bad feeling suddenly, and broke into a sprint.

The trail was distinct enough, and soon the Vikings following emerged onto a narrow cliff path. They followed it for a few yards until the path petered out and they came to a halt.

"He must have doubled back," suggested one of the men.

"Or fallen," offered another, peering dubiously down the cliff face.

Gunnar shook his head. The tracks definitely led along the path as far as the point where they now stood, then the trail just disappeared. There had been no prints heading back the other way, and if the lad had fallen, his battered remains would be plain to see on the rocks below. It was low tide, the body would still be visible if there had been one.

He cupped his mouth in his hands and called out, "Donald. *Donald!*" If the lad was hiding then of course he would not answer, but Gunnar had to try.

They stood in silence to listen, but the only sounds were the calls of seabirds, the whistle of the wind, and the crash of the waves a hundred feet below them.

"Donald, where are you?" Gunnar called out again, louder this time. He signalled his men to join in. If the lad was within earshot they would make sure he heard them.

"Where are you, lad? Show yourself, you will not be harmed," Steinn called out in Gaelic. "Your mother is worried, she wants to see you. You have a new sister."

Gunnar nodded his approval. This news might bring the lad to his senses.

The Vikings went silent again, listening for any sound that might betray the boy's whereabouts. Gunnar was about to start shouting again when they heard it. A small, tentative voice, and coming from somewhere below them.

"What was that? Did you hear?"

Steinn nodded, already dropping to his knees to lay on the edge of the cliff and gaze down the sheer face.

"There! Look, down there."

Gunnar dropped to the ground and lay beside Steinn, his chin over the edge of the precipice. He directed his gaze to where Steinn pointed. Donald's tear-streaked features peered back up at him.

"By Thor's fucking hammer, how did he get there?" breathed Gunnar. More to the point, how were they to get him back? The boy perched on a narrow ledge perhaps twenty feet below them.

"I think he was probably trying to climb down and got stuck." Steinn pointed to several rocky lumps protruding from the flat cliff wall. "There are places to cling on, but he must have run out of hand-holds and taken refuge on the ledge. One of us could probably get down there, but there's no way anyone could climb back up with the boy."

Gunnar got to his feet. "Yngvarr, go back to the camp and bring rope, and a couple of horses." The man took off at a sprint.

Grim-faced, Gunnar quickly shed his sword and cloak. "I'll climb down. You talk to him, tell him to remain still."

"But Jarl…"

"We can't take the risk of him falling, not now." Gunnar eased himself over the edge of the cliff, feeling with his booted feet for any outcrop sturdy enough to take his weight. He found what he sought and inched lower. His fingers burned from the effort of clinging to the unforgiving rock, but he was determined to reach the boy. Little by little he worked his way down the cliff face, jabbing his fingers into the tiniest crannies, balancing his feet where he could. Dust and small stones became dislodged and tumbled down onto the rocks below. Gunnar prayed to Frey and to any other gods he could call to mind for their aid in seeing him safe through this. His fervent entreaties were answered when his toe at last encountered the solid sanctuary of the ledge where Donald huddled.

Gunnar eased himself onto the narrow space. It was perhaps two feet wide, just enough room for him to turn around and face the cowering child.

With no words to offer that would make sense to the boy Gunnar settled for the more direct approach. He crouched, held out his hands to the boy, smiled at him, and beckoned with the fingers of both hands.

Donald eyed him warily. The lad was fighting not to cry, but his pale grey eyes glittered with tears. His hands shook, his lip trembled, he was on the point of giving in. Gunnar recognised abject fear when he saw it, and crushing despair.

"Come to me, Donald," he crooned, even knowing the boy would not comprehend his words. Perhaps though he would recognise the tone of his voice, draw courage from that. "I can help you. I can keep you safe."

Slowly, uncertainly, Donald moved forward. One foot, then another, he closed the gap between them. When the boy came within touching distance Gunnar moved forward too, just as the boy launched himself into his arms. Gunnar clasped the lad to his chest and rolled back, pinning the pair of them against the cliff face.

"Okay, lad, I have you."

• • • • • • •

Back on the springy grass at the top of the cliff Gunnar loosened the rope he had tied about his waist. Yngvarr led away the two horses who had dragged the pair of them up the cliff as Gunnar worked to release the boy who remained clamped to his side. He had tied a rope about the boy's waist too and secured the pair of them to the rope attached to the horses' harnesses. From that point they were in no real danger, but the boy had not known that and had clung to Gunnar the entire time they were inching their way back up the rock. He seemed disinclined to ever let go, but Steinn produced a hunk of bread and some of the roast pork, and this seemed to offer sufficient temptation. As the boy gobbled down the food Gunnar decided he really did need to have a proper word with Donald about the dubious merits of running away and hiding whenever he felt threatened, but now was not the time. And in any case, would he have perhaps done the same had he experienced such an ordeal?

No, he reflected, as they made their way back to the camp. No, he and Ulfric had been brought up as Viking warriors, trained from childhood to meet an enemy head on and to never back down. Their father had expected no less, and neither boy would have wished to disappoint Osvald Freysson. Perhaps Donald had had no such influences to shape his young life, but that had changed now.

A Viking took his responsibilities seriously. Gunnar would be no exception. So he flinched, but did not comment or pull away when the small boy inserted his hand into Gunnar's as they paced along side by side. He did, however, glower with unconcealed menace at the warrior behind them who actually chuckled. The man was seized by a sudden fit of coughing.

Serves him right. Gunnar bent to swing the lad up onto his shoulders and picked up the pace. He was keen to restore the boy to his mother, and to see her radiant smile when he did so.

CHAPTER FIVE

Her son was sleeping now, his pale features untroubled in a manner she had not seen in months, maybe years. The boy had endured much in his short life and this day should have numbered among his worst nightmares. Yet he slept peacefully and for this she had Gunnar Freysson to thank. Mairead was never one to shirk her duty. Extricating herself with care from among the furs that covered her and the tiny baby nestling in her arms, Mairead got to her feet. She hugged the infant to her as she made her way gingerly across the small encampment. Her body still ached from her recent ordeal, but not as much as she had expected. Childbirth clearly became easier with each pregnancy and she was fast regaining her strength.

Gunnar stood a few yards away, his back turned to her. He wore no cloak, and his ebony hair hung loose to his shoulders, lifting slightly in the gentle breeze. The black leather of his tunic caressed the hard contours of his shoulders, masking the power sheathed within. His heavy sword hung from his belt and the hilt of a dagger protruded from his boot. The man was never other than armed to the teeth, yet she could not bring herself to consider him dangerous. Not any more.

He spoke with two of his men, Steinn and another who she believed was called Yngvarr. Their tones were low, as though they did not wish to disturb those who they believed to be sleeping. Mairead could pick out one or two words which were becoming familiar to her—*thrall, boy, woman*. They were discussing her and her child, but she did not feel threatened by this knowledge as she would have even a few short hours ago.

"Thank you, for Donald." Mairead spoke softly and laid her hand on the black leather sleeve of the scarred but strangely beautiful Viking.

He turned to face her, his expression one of concerned surprise. His response was to gesture back to her little nest of furs.

Mairead shook her head. "I am fine, really. I just wanted to... talk to you."

He frowned and turned to Steinn, who quickly translated.

"What?" The single word, spoken in Gaelic, did not suggest any great desire on his part to chat, but Mairead was undeterred.

"You saved my son's life. He told me what happened, what you did..."

He shrugged and murmured something that sounded nonchalant and dismissive, which at least suggested he had understood her words. Mairead was not fully convinced that he grasped the magnitude of today's events, at least to her. Donald had told her of his misadventure, and that the dark Viking had climbed down the cliff to save him. Her child would in all likelihood be dead now, but for the courage of this enigmatic man.

He attacked defenceless villages, killed without mercy, enslaved, robbed, yet he would deliver a baby without flinching and risk his own life to save the child of a thrall. He made no sense to her at all, yet she was drawn to him. She had been both terrified and fascinated by him from the outset, right from that first meeting when he rescued her from certain rape or possibly worse.

She might not understand him still, but she knew she no longer feared him.

The baby shifted in her arms and started to snuffle, seeking out her nipple once more. Mairead began to arrange the infant within her clothing but paused and again lifted her face to regard her unlikely champion.

"What is your mother's name?"

His puzzled frown was answer enough, but again Steinn intervened.

"The Jarl's mother is dead," Stein explained after a brief exchange with his chief.

"I see. Then, would you ask him if he might object if I were to name my baby after her?" Mairead enquired.

Gunnar's expression was one of utter incredulity when his karl conveyed the request. He held out his hands and, unhesitating, Mairead placed the infant in them. Gunnar lifted the tiny form to his face and scowled at her. The child turned her unfocused gaze on him and pursed her mouth in a toothless parody of a smile.

The corner of the dark Viking's lip curled. He said something to Steinn, who grinned and nodded. Then Gunnar fixed his attention on Mairead.

"Tyra. Name is Tyra." He handed the baby back and turned on his heel to march away.

Mairead watched him go, clearly intent on performing some sudden and urgent errand concerning the horses. She smiled at his retreating back and hugged the baby to her, then kissed the soft reddish-gold curls on her head.

"Hello, Tyra," she whispered. "I believe we have both made a friend this day."

• • • • • • •

Mairead awoke to the quietly efficient activity of the men breaking up their small encampment. Dust had been kicked into the fire and already the embers were cooling. All the beds but the one in which she and Tyra nestled had been packed in saddlebags, cooking and eating vessels were stowed away. The men were milling about, fussing with their horses and clearly ready to depart. Her eyes instinctively sought out her son, and she found Donald scurrying about among the Viking warriors. He was fetching and carrying as directed and clearly enjoying his involvement. The men gave him lighter loads to bear, and joked about his puny limbs though the ribbing was good-natured and not unkind. Throughout it all Donald beamed from ear to ear.

Seeing she was awake, Steinn approached her. "We must leave this morning. Our journey is a long one…"

"Of course. Yes, I understand. I shall make haste. Someone should have woken me…"

"The Jarl forbade it. You should eat first." He offered her a hunk of bread not yet stale. Mairead took it and realised she was ravenous. She chewed quickly.

"There is more if you wish. Or if you need a few moments to… to, er…"

"Thank you." She put the youth out of his misery. "I do not require any more food right now but I would like a minute or two of privacy. I wonder, could you hold Tyra for me?"

The young warrior accepted his charge with all the enthusiasm of one ordered to comfort a wounded boar. He held the child as though she might spontaneously burst into flames. Mairead grinned to herself as she tripped away into the undergrowth to do what was necessary.

When she returned a few minutes later it was to see that her bed had been removed and packed away. Steinn was busily engaged in saddling his mount, assisted by a chattering Donald. She glanced about and found Gunnar now holding the baby, and he appeared somewhat more at ease with the burden than had his karl. The Viking chief had seated himself on a fallen log, the infant laid out on his thighs. Gunnar appeared fascinated by the minute fingers and toes, which had escaped the confines of the sheepskin wrap provided by him the previous evening to keep the child warm. He prodded the tiny hands and feet with his fingertips. The baby seemed equally entranced, gazing up into the stern, dark features of the man who smiled down at her.

"Shall I take her?" Mairead stepped forward to stand beside him and held out her arms.

Gunnar nodded and passed the baby to her, then rose to tower over his latest acquisition. He again wore his huge cloak of dark grey wolf skin, and his mount pawed the solid earth behind him. He glanced over his shoulder, then gestured to Mairead to follow him. Beside the stallion he again took the baby, then offered her his free hand to use as a mounting step. In moments Mairead was in the saddle, her baby once more tucked within her clothing. Gunnar leapt up behind her, raised his arm to signal their departure, and they were off.

How long would this journey take? Mairead vaguely recalled that Steinn had told her their destination, Gunnarsholm, lay two days riding away to the north. Two days would not be overly arduous, she told herself. She was not expected to make the trip on foot, she was comfortable after a fashion, and she had eaten. Her son was beside her, and they were safe.

She leaned back, taking comfort from the solid presence behind her. Gunnar said nothing, but drew his heavy cloak around her and Tyra to encompass them all in his warmth. Soon, Mairead drifted off to sleep.

When she awoke Tyra was no longer in her arms. She knew a moment's panic, then relaxed as she caught sight of the tiny red-gold head poking out from within the black leather of the Viking's tunic. The baby was sleeping, Mairead saw no cause to disturb her and soon fell asleep again.

They made slow progress, and Mairead was convinced the Vikings were setting a much steadier pace than they otherwise would in deference to herself and the children.

Again, she was surprised, had not expected to be treated with such consideration. They stopped twice each day to eat and the fare was good, usually game that the men hunted on the way—rabbits, wild duck, a small doe. There were berries too, and nuts. Meals were taken together around a small fire, and Mairead was cheered to see Donald clearly at ease among these huge warriors who treated him with gruff kindness. It became her habit to tuck Tyra within her own clothing to feed the baby, and at a curt command from Gunnar the men discreetly pretended nothing was happening. All in all, despite the length of the journey, Mairead was content.

She listened all the time to the Norse language as the men chatted around her. Steinn continued to translate when asked, but Mairead could pick out a handful of words for herself now. Donald, too, was rapidly learning the unfamiliar tongue, occasionally replying to one or other of the warriors in their own language.

On the third morning, as they prepared to depart, Stein told her that they would reach Gunnarsholm that afternoon.

"What is it like?" asked Mairead. "Is it a large settlement? Are there many thralls there? Celts such as Donald and I?"

"Not large, no. Perhaps thirty or forty people. Most of the men are here with us, those left behind are women, children, the old. There are slaves, there are always slaves. And yes, some Celts. They work in the fields mostly."

"You are farmers?"

"Yes, and we trade. That is why we raid, to gain goods to sell. Or slaves, since they are also valuable."

Mairead recalled the scene of a few days earlier when Gunnar had bought her son and a cold shiver played along the length of her spine. Despite her growing sense of security, despite Donald's blooming confidence, it would be so easy for their fortunes to change. All depended on the whims and favour of one man. She resolved to speak with Gunnar, ask him exactly what he intended to do with her, with her children. She no longer really believed he meant her harm, but the uncertainty was stifling her. However, this was not a conversation she was prepared to conduct through an intermediary. She rifled through her growing Norse vocabulary and found it still woefully lacking. Mairead sighed and resolved to learn enough of this new tongue to be able to manage for herself—and quickly.

• • • • • • •

They crested a hill soon after their midday meal and Gunnar pulled his stallion to a halt. Below them, perhaps two miles distant, lay a small collection of low buildings. The rocky drop to the sea bordered one side and inland the hamlet was ringed by fields of crops.

"Gunnarsholm," announced the dark Viking.

Mairead surveyed the scene in the valley. The place had its own beauty, though the landscape was both stark and rugged. The backdrop of mountains, already capped by snow, hinted at a harsh climate and a hard life if she and her little family were to survive here, but she could not find it in her to dislike her first sight of this new home. They could be content, surely…

"It is beautiful," she murmured, and she meant it.

"Yes," concurred Gunnar, in her tongue. "Yes, beautiful." He nudged his mount back into motion and they started the long descent into Gunnarsholm.

As the warriors approached the village people came running to greet them. Women, children, dogs, and even several chickens seemed delighted at the return of the raiders. Their arrival was met with much din, shouts of greeting, tears and laughter in equal measure. Donald remained on the horse as the young Viking he had shared with dismounted and led the animal forward. He exchanged an affectionate hug with a girl of perhaps fifteen summers, his sister, he informed Mairead with a wide grin. The other Norsemen seemed equally delighted to be reunited with the women who had kept their longhouses clean and warm for them in their absence.

Mairead realised she was dreading the moment one of these Viking women claimed Gunnar as her own returning hero. She held herself stiffen in the saddle, glancing from one side to the other and eying each female she saw with anxious suspicion.

In all, she counted about ten longhouses, all windowless and constructed of wooden planks with stone footings. The roofs were thatched, and the doors stood open, she assumed to let in light. One of the structures was clearly a smithy, another served as a tannery. The rest, Mairead supposed, would be the dwellings and these must serve both human and animal occupants since there appeared to be no separate sheds to house the varied livestock roaming freely among the longhouses. Apart from the dogs and poultry there were goats, cattle, a few sheep, and pigs. Clearly the occupants of Gunnarsholm appreciated a varied diet.

Most of the dwellings were perhaps twenty feet in width and thirty or so in length, though the structure in the centre of the settlement was at least twice as long as the rest. Gunnar brought his stallion to a stop before the entrance to the largest longhouse, just as two figures emerged. A man and a woman, both of middle years and wearing the rough wool clothing that denoted them as thralls. They both appeared pleased to greet their chief, their features beaming. Their expressions became more puzzled as they regarded the woman and baby with him.

Gunnar spoke to them in rapid Norse. He tossed the reins to the man and dismounted, then held up his arms in invitation for Mairead to pass the infant to him. She did so, and he handed Tyra to the woman, then turned to reach up for Mairead herself. She slipped down into his embrace, staggering a little as she sought to regain her feet after so long in the saddle. Gunnar chuckled and held her until she was steady, then gestured to the woman to hand the baby back.

Donald had appeared at her side. The boy moved in

close, clearly nervous now. So was Mairead, though she refused to allow that to show.

She wondered which of the dwellings would be theirs. Would she and Donald be allowed to live together? It might not matter, this place was small, all the inhabitants lived in close proximity. There appeared to be no separate slave quarters, though she could not really tell.

"Where...?" She paused, searching for the correct words.

Gunnar used his thumb to indicate the entrance to the larger of the houses. Swallowing hard, Mairead followed his direction and stepped inside.

The longhouse was dark, as she had expected, though not gloomy. The door offered some illumination, and the rest of the available light came from the fire pit running down the centre. Two rows of stout wooden posts were arranged the entire length of the building to create a central aisle and separate areas nestled beneath the eaves. The central aisle provided access to the rest, and the portions under the eaves were split into several rooms. These were marked by curtains or rough boarding to offer a degree of privacy. The furnishings were sparse but sufficient: a long table at one end, benches, raised platforms with blankets, clearly intended for use as beds. As she had thought, the livestock did share the accommodations, though they were restricted to one area and the rest was kept clean and well aired.

The woman who had come to greet them outside bustled up. Her face still bore an expression of bemused curiosity, but she appeared friendly enough as she smiled at Mairead.

"You must be tired, lass. I shall show ye where to put your things."

"Oh! You are a Scot." Mairead had not anticipated meeting others from her land here, so far from their home.

"Aye, me and Weylin both. I am Aigneis." The woman offered her hand and Mairead took it.

"You live here?" Mairead was trying to make sense of this household and failing so far.

"We do. Me an' my man have the room at the end, there, ye see? An' this'll be yours, for ye and the bairns." The woman gestured to an area about midway along the hall, close to the fire pit.

"We are to live here too? In the main house?"

"Ye're here to serve the Jarl, are ye not? Where else would ye live?"

Where else indeed? Mairead peered into the space apparently designated to be her new home. It was fine enough, she supposed, certainly as good as her cold, cheerless little one-roomed cottage back in Aikrig. And a whole lot warmer. Already the heat from the fire offered a heady sense of both comfort and security.

"I shall have to find ye some blankets, an' maybe a chair for ye tae be nursing the bairn…"

"That is very kind. Thank you."

"Not at all, not at all. Now you be takin' a seat while I just see to everything. The Jarl will be wanting food, I expect…"

Mairead had no notion what the Jarl might be wanting, but supposed Aigneis would have as good an idea as any since she seemed to keep his house for him. Was Mairead to be an assistant to Aigneis? The woman appeared competent enough. And Donald? What would be his role here? Mairead's head swirled with questions as she sank onto the bench beside the table.

"May I go outside?" Donald had apparently overcome his initial nervousness and was eager to explore. There had been children as they rode into the village, several of them. But they were Vikings, not captive Celts. Not playmates for her son.

Mairead tugged him down to sit beside her. "No, not yet. We must remain here until we know what is required of us, what is permitted…"

"But, I want to find Steinn."

"Steinn is with his family. They will have missed him. It is better to stay here."

"But—"

"No." Her reply may have been sharper than she intended. Donald was not the only one battling his fears, though he appeared to be winning. And now, she realised, she had a rather more urgent need of her own to worry about. "Aigneis," she called. "I wonder, could you direct me to the privy. I find I need…"

"Ah, yes, yes, of course. And this fine lad can take care of the little mite while ye're gone, I daresay."

Mairead passed Tyra to Donald, with strict instructions not to move from the bench until she returned, then she followed Aigneis from the house.

The privy was a small, fenced stockade at the rear of the longhouse. Aigneis showed her the place, then left her to complete her ablutions in privacy.

Mairead was just rounding the corner of the longhouse on her way back inside when she heard a sound that made her flesh quiver. Surely she was mistaken. That was not—

The whistle of leather slicing the air, followed by a shrill, agonised scream dispelled any lingering illusions. Some hapless soul was being flogged close by. Despite her trepidation Mairead could not help it, she had to look. She had to know.

She crept back the way she had come, past the privy and into a cleared area on the edge of the settlement. There, a couple of dozen villagers had gathered to witness the proceedings.

In the centre of the group a stout pole had been erected, and to this was tied a young man. He was naked to the waist, and his shoulders already bore the vicious marks of the whip. Beside him, Gunnar poised to strike again. The Viking was also stripped to the waist, his torso glistening in the late afternoon sun. It would have been a truly glorious sight but for the long whip that hung from his right hand, the lash snaking about his booted feet. As she watched, her fist pressed against her mouth to stifle her own breath, Gunnar flexed and swung the whip again. The lash landed on the unfortunate victim's shoulders and he let out another cry.

The Viking flicked his wrist to ready the whip for another stroke and Mairead could bear it no longer. "No!" she shrieked, dashing forward to grab at Gunnar's arm.

He halted and glowered at the sobbing woman at his side. "Nei," he snapped and shook his arm to loosen her grip.

"Please, you must not do this. He is just a young man, you will kill him…" She did not know why she pleaded for a stranger, but she did so anyway. "This is brutal, barbaric—"

Gunnar cut off her entreaties with a torrent of rapid Norse. She did not need to understand his words to grasp his fury and she backed off in alarm. What had she done? He would not mitigate his behaviour just because she asked him to, and now he would probably punish her too for her insolence.

As she retreated Gunnar pursued her. Mairead considered turning and running from him, but her feet were rooted to the spot. He caught up and stood before her, towering over her, the loathsome whip still in his hand.

His features might have been hewn from granite. His dark eyes were like flints, harsh, unforgiving. He had never appeared more terrifying to her. Mairead opened her mouth to apologise, to beg him not to hurt her.

He reached for her and cupped her chin in his free hand. His grip was not rough or painful but she could not move as he forced her to meet and hold his gaze. When he spoke next his tone was low and even, his expression cold. She could not comprehend his words, but even so his meaning was clear.

Do not interfere. Do not gainsay me. I am master here and you will accept and obey.

She nodded, and he released her. With a sharp tilt of his head she was dismissed, commanded to leave him. With a sob she whirled on her feet and fled.

Once around the corner of the longhouse and out of sight of the proceedings in the clearing she leaned against the outer wall and fought not to be sick. Bile rose in her throat but she willed her stomach to settle. For reasons she could not start to fathom she felt compelled to witness whatever might happen. She made her way cautiously back to the edge of the dwelling and peered around the corner again.

Gunnar had returned to the man who now gripped the pole with his fists. Their heads were close together; the Viking was speaking to the bound slave. As she watched Gunnar paused, shook his head as though in disgust, then proceeded to deliver two more punishing strokes. The man jerked in his bonds, kicked his feet, and wailed piteously. The watching crowd seemed as unmoved as Gunnar by the man's plight. They observed, impassive, as the punishment was doled out. It seemed to take an eternity but in reality it must have been just a minute or so, but eventually Gunnar lowered the whip and issued a curt command to Weylin, who hovered close by. The slave rushed to release the other man from the post. Two more thralls rushed forward to assist, and together the trio helped Ferris from the clearing.

Gunnar narrowed his eyes as he watched them go, then bent to retrieve his tunic, which he had laid on the ground while he delivered the whipping. As he shrugged back into it he glanced up, right at Mairead.

Their eyes met, his the colour of midnight and every bit as terrifying. The dark irises seemed to glint at her as though issuing a stark warning.

I can be gentle when I choose to be, but do not cross me.

With a strangled sob Mairead whirled again and this time fled back to the dubious sanctuary of the longhouse. There, she grabbed her baby from her startled son and hugged both her children to her.

Whatever it took, whatever she had to do, she would protect those she loved from these barbaric Vikings. She must learn never to trust the darkly handsome one with the scar and eyes that conjured up her wildest fantasies and evoked her deepest fears.

CHAPTER SIX

Gunnar groaned. This he did not need.

It was bad enough that he had returned home after weeks away to be greeted with the news that one of his thralls, Ferris, had taken advantage of his master's absence to resume his old habits. Gunnar had hoped several previous visits to the stocks might have cured the man of his propensity to help himself to food that had been stored in readiness for the coming winter. Seemingly not. Worse, the idle thrall had also decided to indulge in a little doze when he should have been keeping watch over their livestock. As a result, raiders had made off with several of Gunnar's fine ewes, many of them due to drop lambs in a couple of months' time. The food wasn't a massive issue, they had plenty, but there was an important principle at stake here. An example needed to be made or all his slaves would be taking the same liberties.

Gunnar might have been more sympathetic if the slave had been short of food, but Ferris certainly hadn't been going hungry. No one wanted for food at Gunnarsholm. The man's behaviour was the result of greed and complacency. Ferris had thought it safe to steal from his master, and from the village, because he believed he wouldn't get caught. Unfortunately for him, the slave had underestimated Weylin's watchful eye and devotion to duty.

The ewes though, that was more serious. Not only were the animals valuable, though that was in itself sufficient consideration to warrant punishment, but Gunnar's reputation was now at stake. If word got around to the many hordes of cutthroats and bandits who inhabited the surrounding mountains that his settlement at Gunnarsholm was poorly guarded, a village ripe for the picking, he would be fighting off raiders every night. He had no choice but to deal severely with Ferris now in order to ensure no other sentry opted to snooze the night away rather than do his bloody duty. Then he would have to hunt down the thieves and take back his ewes.

Shit!

Never one to put off an unpleasant task, as soon as Weylin reported the matter to him Gunnar determined what must be done. He waited until Mairead and her little brood disappeared inside his longhouse then he ordered that Ferris be brought from the back of the smithy where he had been secured in the stocks for the last two days awaiting his master's return. Discipline was merited and it was to be swift and severe, but he preferred it not to be witnessed by the newcomers so early after their arrival in his home. The boy, in particular, would not comprehend why this apparent brutality was necessary.

Gunnar's expression was grim as the offending thrall was brought to the whipping post in the middle of the village, stripped to the waist and tied to it. The post was not in frequent use, but Gunnar believed its presence here served a purpose, reminding those who answered to him who was master at Gunnarsholm and the consequences of failing in their obligations. It was a deterrent.

The man had wailed and pleaded and tried to deny his crimes. Gunnar listened, questioned Weylin, and others who could bear witness to what had transpired. He had entertained little doubt to start with, but others, karls and

71

thralls alike, corroborated Weylin's account. The proper punishment would be twenty lashes.

He sighed and resigned himself to what must be done. Gunnar shed his leather tunic and accepted the long whip from Weylin, one reserved for just this purpose. Gunnar knew that it hurt like a bitch, and Ferris would long remember this day. Whether in the future the man would remember to keep his hands off that which did not belong to him remained to be seen, though a decent flogging tended to have a salutary effect on the memory, Gunnar found. It also markedly improved a slave's diligence, obedience, and general attitude, changes badly needed as far as this man was concerned.

Gunnar positioned himself behind the sobbing thrall and delivered the first couple of strokes. The lash left narrow streaks of vivid red across the man's shoulders as the skin reacted to each stroke. Gunnar kept them relatively light. He could make his point without reducing the man to a blood-soaked mess.

As he raised his hand to deliver the next stroke he was interrupted by a piercing shriek from behind him and suddenly his newest slave was there, clinging to his arm and babbling at him. Tears streaked her face, her distress and terror evident as she attempted to stop the whipping.

Did she think to wrestle the whip from his hand? The woman was in for a rude awakening if she thought he would tolerate such insubordination, especially not in front of half the population of Gunnarsholm.

"What the fuck do you think you are doing, wench? Take your hands off me or I shall…" His angry rebuke died in his throat as her slender courage crumbled before him. She released his arm and backed off, her lovely green eyes wide as she regarded him.

Fuck. He regretted having scared her so, but she needed to learn who was master here. He strode after her, and was relieved that she did not attempt to run from him. For that, at least, he could be grateful.

Steinn was nowhere to be seen so he could not have his words translated for her, but hopefully she would take his meaning anyway. Equally important, his people would hear what he said and his authority would be reinforced.

"Slaves obey. I am master here, I make the laws and I enforce them. If a whipping is required, I will ensure it is delivered. You will learn to accept my authority, as all do, or you will pay the consequences for it."

He paused, and was gratified by her small nod. It was enough. He gestured to her to make herself scarce, and was pleased that she did, now, flee.

So far so good. Now he had just to complete his business with Ferris.

The next four strokes reduced the slave to incoherent groaning as he hung from the post. He muttered something, the words lost as he ground his face against the timber.

Gunnar lowered the whip and moved in closer. "What did you say?"

"Please, Master…"

"You said something. What was it?" demanded Gunnar.

"I am sorry. I said I was sorry and will not steal any more."

"I am pleased to hear that. It would be a pity if you and I were to have cause to meet here again."

"We will not, I swear it, Jarl."

"Good. Is there more you have to say to me?"

"I will watch the sheep every night. I swear I will not fall asleep again."

"Excellent, but you need not keep watch every night. Your night-time shepherding duties are to be doubled however."

"Yes, Jarl. Th-thank you."

"You may thank me when your punishment is over." Gunnar resumed his position and raised the whip again. The man before him trembled but offered no further protest. Gunnar was satisfied, his work was almost done here. He had determined that the man receive twenty lashes, but saw no valuable purpose in pursuing this ordeal right through to the end now that he had achieved the desired result. He had delivered nine strokes so far, and decided that a dozen would suffice.

The whip whistled through the air again, and the lash landed across Ferris' shoulders. Gunnar shook his head to clear it, then proceeded to finish this day's unpleasant business. The final two strokes were swift and harsh, and each elicited an agonised shriek from the recalcitrant and now sufficiently contrite thrall.

Gunnar was glad to be done with the matter, and he suspected Ferris to be even more so. He lowered the whip and instructed Weylin to release the man. As he shrugged back into his tunic a slight movement to his left caught his attention. He turned, and found himself gazing into the startled, terrified eyes of his flame-haired Celt. Mairead gaped at the spectacle before her, beautiful green eyes the colour of autumn moss as they darkened in horror. Then, stifling a scream, she turned on her heel and this time she really did flee.

Odin's fucking ballocks. He could have done without this complication at such a delicate stage in their relationship. He was still exploring the possibilities in his own mind, uncertain just what the status of his recent acquisition might be. His options were narrowing by the moment if the look of fear and revulsion displayed across her beautiful features was anything to go by.

"Fuck," he muttered to himself as he fastened his tunic. It was not as though he could catch her up and talk to her and better explain the necessity for the scene she just witnessed. *Where was Steinn when his translation skills were needed?*

Gunnar took his time in following Mairead back to his longhouse, fast coming to the conclusion that explanations would have to wait. Aigneis spoke the Gaelic tongue but he was reluctant to converse with Mairead through another slave. In any case, the sooner he set off in pursuit of the raiders who had seized his sheep, the better the chance of regaining his valuable property. The bandits had a two-day start on him already; he could not delay his departure.

He entered the longhouse to find a white-faced Mairead seated on a bench by the table, her baby in her arms. Donald leapt up as soon as Gunnar entered and started jabbering something at him. Gunnar looked to Aigneis for some sort of explanation.

"The boy wishes to explore. His mother said he could not leave the longhouse without your permission."

Ah, right. Such caution was a good sign. The woman did at least comprehend her precarious position in his settlement even if he did not.

Gunnar nodded and gestured Donald to the door. "He can go. Make sure he knows he is not to leave the village in any circumstances."

Aigneis conveyed that stipulation and the lad nodded with enthusiasm as he dashed for the exit. The three adults left within the longhouse regarded one another warily as the boy's running footsteps receded.

This is my fucking house. Gunnar repeated that truth to himself as he took his seat at the table opposite Mairead and refused to back down under her accusing stare. He turned to Aigneis.

"I shall be requiring food and fresh clothing. We leave within the hour."

"So soon, Jarl? You have but this moment walked in the house…"

"We need to be after the robbers, while there are still tracks to follow. I intend to retrieve our livestock, and teach those brigands the folly of attacking us here."

Aigneis set a bowl of broth before him, and a hunk of bread at his right hand. "I understand, Jarl, but—"

"You will take Mairead and Donald to Sindri at the forge, and bid him remove their shackles."

"Yes, Jarl." She did not question his command, and he did not expect her to. Indeed, it would have been strange if she had since none of Gunnar's thralls bore the shackles favoured by his brother.

"Mairead is to sleep in my bed, the baby with her. The boy shall be found a space elsewhere in the longhouse. Somewhere warm though."

"Of course. There is room close to Weylin and me. She is to be your bed-slave, then? The Celtic woman?"

Gunnar fixed his servant with a glower. It was not her place to question him in this manner, though she and all others would draw the inevitable conclusion when it became known the red-haired female shared his bed. Or would share it, as soon as he found himself at leisure long enough to stretch out on his own mattress again. Gunnar glared at Aigneis, then at Mairead who regarded him with undisguised apprehension as she sought to hush the fretting baby. No doubt she had recognised her own name on his lips and feared what that might mean.

"The child is hungry," observed Gunnar.

Aigneis translated his words and Mairead gave a short nod. She proceeded to enclose the squirming, complaining infant within her loose clothing, and soon all was silent but for the soft sounds of suckling. Would that all issues might be so readily solved.

Gunnar ate his meal without further conversation. Aigneis bustled about the longhouse gathering supplies for his coming journey, as well as the fresh clothing he required. By the time he pushed the bowl away, all was in readiness. Throughout, Mairead had uttered not a word. No questions, no comments, not so much as a hint of censure at what she had seen. Words were not necessary, her expressive features spoke for her.

She feared him, and she loathed him.

Gunnar rose to his feet and strode to the door. He addressed his final words to Aigneis. "We shall be gone at least a sennight, maybe longer. I shall send word when we are on our way back."

He encountered Weylin in the doorway and quickly

apprised him of his intentions. The man offered no comment, just assisted Aigneis in carrying the supplies out to Gunnar's waiting stallion. Gunnar had called for a fresh horse, and already several of his men were leaping into their newly saddled mounts. It required but a few minutes for him to instruct them as to their new mission, and issue the signal that they were off. The party formed up behind their chief and they cantered from the village. Gunnar did not look back.

· · · · · · ·

"So, he has taken ye as a fuck-slave then."

Aigneis offered the bald, crude statement as she showed Mairead around the longhouse. The servant had already answered Mairead's questions regarding their master's hasty departure and offered her a tour of the homestead. The female thrall had explained where various foodstuffs were stored, shown Mairead the boxes where blankets were kept dry and free from vermin, and the smaller chest that housed the few medicinal supplies they possessed. Mairead was particularly interested in this since her own bags of herbs and healing potions had been left behind, abandoned in her brother-in-law's house in Pennglas when she was taken. She found the Vikings' range of remedies woefully lacking and was just compiling a mental list of plants to seek out, leaves and roots that she might collect and dry in preparation for future ailments among her new community, when Aigneis made her stunning comment.

"No! Of course not. Why would you think that?" She gaped at Aigneis, open-mouthed.

"He said it. Ye're tae sleep in his bed. That can mean but one thing."

"You are mistaken," insisted Mairead. Why, the very notion was ridiculous. A man such as this dark Viking, this powerful, cruel Nordic chieftain who exuded masculine beauty and could have any female he chose, would not spare a second glance for one such as she. She went on to explain. "I am not young. I have borne two children, one of them just two days ago. My body is… not one which he would find in the least attractive."

"Ye will be sleeping in his bed." For Aigneis this was all the evidence required.

"Perhaps he offered it as his bed is the most comfortable. He has been most kind, most considerate since Tyra was born. And as he will not be here…"

"He will be back, in a week or two."

"Yes, and when he returns he will doubtless require me to move to another part of the longhouse."

Aigneis merely shook her head so Mairead opted to change the subject, raising the matter that had so shaken her.

"Earlier, when I went to the privy, I heard noises and went to investigate. There was a man, tied to a post and… and…"

"Ah, I wondered if ye saw that." Aigneis shrugged, her features hardening. "Ferris had it coming. The man is lazy, and a thief. All here know that."

"A thief? But…"

"It is the law. All must obey. Ferris knew what would happen if he stole from the village, from the Jarl. Gunnar had no choice but to deal with him severely."

"Will he… Will the man be all right?"

"In a few days, I daresay. Let us hope he has learnt his lesson." Dismissing the matter of the hapless thrall, Aigneis dusted down her hands on the front of her woollen skirt. "Come, we must find your boy and go to the forge."

"The forge? Why?" Mairead closed the lid on the medicine chest she already thought of as hers.

"Those need to come off." Aigneis pointed to the heavy shackle that had bruised Mairead's slender ankle during the few days she had worn it. "The Jarl ordered it. No one here wears chains."

"They do not?" Mairead was surprised, especially given

the whipping she had stumbled across. Gunnarsholm had not struck her as a settlement sympathetic to the plight of slaves.

"No need. We are too remote here, no one would be foolish enough to attempt to escape just to be devoured by wolves or murdered by cutthroats. The shackles serve no purpose and just get in the way of the work. 'Tis best they be gone. Come, while there is daylight still."

Aigneis led, and they rounded up Donald on the way. He had been sitting on the ground with two other boys and the three of them played a game that involved tossing sticks into a circle etched in the dust. He was reluctant to leave his new friends, but Mairead insisted and the trio trooped across to the smith's forge.

Donald flinched as the smith clouted the metal pin out of the shackle on his ankle, but it was the work of moments and suddenly he was free. Mairead allowed him to scamper back to his game and passed Tyra to Aigneis as she extended her own foot for similar treatment. The vibrations rattled up her leg as the smith swung his mallet once, twice, and a third time before the pin flew from her shackle in a shower of sparks. The smith stamped on the smouldering sawdust that covered the rough dirt floor, and once he was satisfied that there was no imminent danger of his forge going up in flames he offered the women a toothless grin and returned to his workbench.

"Come." Aigneis was already striding back toward Gunnar's longhouse, Tyra still in her arms. "You will no doubt be wanting a bath, then you can get some sleep. Tomorrow we have much to do. You will help me with the washing, then we shall collect berries. I want to check if the turnips we planted are ready to be harvested yet, and there is flour to grind. If we have time I would like to… "

Mairead followed in the woman's wake, her ears still ringing from the din of the forge. Yes, a bath would be welcome, and she was more fatigued than she could recall in a long time. Even if her Viking captor did demand his sleeping chamber back on his return, and he surely would, for now it was hers and she was ready for it.

• • • • • • •

The next few days passed peacefully enough. Despite the dizzying list of tasks that she had reeled off, Aigneis insisted that Mairead rest and concentrate on caring for Tyra. The Viking's bed assigned to her was large, comfortable, and above all warm as the sleeping chamber was served by its own small fire. Mairead usually curled up within the furs soon after dusk fell, and did not venture out until daylight poked through the gaps in the eaves above her head.

She assisted Aigneis in her work and found life at Gunnarsholm not especially onerous. There was always work to be done, but plenty of willing hands to share the labour. Donald preferred to spend his days with the other boys who seemed to accept him readily enough within their midst. He enjoyed herding geese and milking goats but was particularly keen to assist in the stables.

With the natural ability of a child, Donald picked up more of the Nordic tongue with each hour that passed. Mairead also found that she was starting to understand more and more of the conversation around the settlement. She could exchange greetings and conduct a simple exchange with the other women when they all gathered at the river to wash clothes. Her new life was neither harsh nor unpleasant and the work not especially arduous. The community was cheerful enough, and welcoming. She began to think that perhaps, despite the inauspicious beginning, she and her little family could be content here.

"May I go out of the settlement this morning, to collect plants? Herbs, for cooking or for treating ailments? I am not sure what is permitted…" Mairead had observed that everyone, thralls and karls alike, came and went at will.

"Of course, but you should not be alone. Go with others. There are wolves, bears, wild boar, not to mention the dangers presented by the robbers who roam these lands."

"I see. Then, who…?"

"We shall both go, and Weylin too. He can trap a few rabbits for the pot…"

"I have no wish to inconvenience anyone. I just thought… this is something I could do, to help…"

"We have no healer, no one who understands herbs and such like. All will be glad of your skills so it is no inconvenience to aid you in assembling whatever ingredients might be needful. Come, we shall go at once. What plants exactly are you seeking?"

"Burdock if I can find it, perhaps poppies, a little ground ivy or St. John's wort. These are all useful. Do you have wild garlic hereabouts? That would add flavour to the pot, as would marjoram or sorrel. There are plants good for use in dyes too, such as woad, madder, and tansy."

"You can recognise all of these?" Aigneis looked uncertain.

"Of course. Shall I teach you about them?"

"Nay, I am too old to be learning such new tricks, but I shall enjoy the excursion, as will Weylin though he will doubtless complain the entire time we are out. He will be glad enough of the flavouring in his food though, and so will the Jarl when he returns."

"Has there been word? Do you know when Gunnar might be back?"

"No, lass. He will be at least another week though." Aigneis rose from the table where they had been sharing the *dagmal*, the morning meal that the entire household took about an hour after rising from their beds. Donald and Weylin had already left to be about the day's chores leaving the women to clear up. "Will your boy come too?"

"I shall ask him." Mairead disengaged a sleeping Tyra from her nipple, rearranged her clothing, and left the longhouse in search of her son.

She almost failed to recognise Ferris when she passed

him close to the forge. It had been over a week since the other slave's ordeal at the hands of Gunnar, and though he walked with a certain stiffness in his gait he appeared recovered. Nevertheless, Mairead felt compelled to offer aid.

"I can make you an ointment if you require it, a salve to aid healing..." She made her offer as he slunk past her. Ferris paused and turned to regard her, his expression considering and not especially pleasant.

"You are his fuck-slave."

"No." The comment might yet turn out to be true, and in any case the entire question was not in her control, but Mairead was affronted by his insolent manner. She shook her head. "I am to work in the Jarl's longhouse, that is all. And, I am a healer, so if you would like my help I would be happy to—"

"I need no help unless you are offering to slip a dagger between that bastard's ribs as he sleeps. That would be a service to all of us."

Mairead was shocked. "I did not... I would never..."

"No?" The other thrall shrugged, his expression spiteful. "Pity."

Mairead watched, unease crawling over her body as Ferris sauntered away.

· · · · · · ·

Two more weeks passed without word of Gunnar. Mairead now considered herself fully recovered from the trials of Tyra's birth and the journey from her home in Scotland to this remote Nordic settlement. She was surprised to find she took genuine pleasure in her new life, and had amassed a fine array of herbal preparations in readiness for all manner of ills. The population of Gunnarsholm thus far had presented nothing but rude good health so she devoted her attention to augmenting Aigneis' culinary efforts and had started to brew a range of blue and red dyes since many of the Viking women were skilled at weaving. Donald assisted her when she could drag him away from the other children, but most of his time was spent outdoors. He appeared happier than he had in a long time. Tyra was growing fast, too. Her children thrived, so Mairead had no cause for complaint.

"Mairead, would you come, please?"

She lifted her gaze from the myriad drying leaves spread before her on the table. "What is it, Aigneis? Is there a problem?"

The other woman flattened her lips, a sign of her displeasure. "Perhaps. This way."

Mairead rose to follow Aigneis down the central aisle in the longhouse to the sleeping quarters at the far end. Here was where Weylin and Aigneis had their beds. Donald's, too was tucked away in an alcove but the lad himself was nowhere to be seen.

Weylin stood beside the small pallet where Donald slept, and as the women approached he bent to lift the blankets. Beneath the bedding Mairead saw a baffling collection of articles, none of which seemed to her to have any place in a small boy's bed. A carved bone comb, several clothing brooches, a small dagger, a hairpin made of bleached bone, a horn mug, and a small silver amulet blinked up at her. Mairead recognised the hairpin; she had seen Aigneis wear it on a number of occasions. She also thought the dagger belonged to Weylin. The other items she had not seen before.

"What is this? What are these things doing here?" Mairead looked from one serious face to the other.

"Quite." Weylin folded his arms and leaned against the outer wall of the longhouse. "We hoped you might have some notion."

"Me? How should I know? Where is Donald? He will know, I daresay. We must ask him." Mairead turned to go in search of her son.

Weylin caught her elbow. "I have sent a lad to find him."

"Oh." Mairead sank to perch on the edge of her son's small bed. "I see. Then we shall wait."

Donald offered no reasonable explanation, though his guilt in the matter was beyond question. His cheerful face crumpled at the sight of the treasures laid out on his pallet and he clung to his mother uttering words of apology and contrition. Despite her urging, Mairead could extract nothing in the way of a reason for the theft of the items. They learnt that the comb had come from the longhouse of Steinn's family and was the property of the young Viking's mother. The horn mug had been stolen from another cottage, and the amulet rightly belonged to Gunnar himself. Donald had found it in the sleeping quarters occupied by his mother and had liked the gleaming sheen of it.

"You must return everything, and tell those you have wronged that you are sorry. We cannot take things which belong to others, and we have no need to. And you must promise me never to do such a thing again."

Donald nodded, his tearstained features testimony to his remorse. "I will. I am sorry, truly."

Mairead turned to face the other servants who had watched the scene in stern silence. "I am sorry this has happened but I swear it will not occur again. Donald is a good boy, but these recent months have been hard for him…"

"The Jarl will deal with the matter. You have no need to apologise to us." Weylin's gaze was stony.

"Please…" Mairead's heart lurched, then sank. "Please, there is no need to involve Gunnar. Donald has apologised, there will be no further problems, I swear it."

Weylin shrugged. "It is for the Jarl to decide what must be done. That is the way here."

Mairead knew exactly where that way would lead. Vivid recollections of a man tied to a post and whipped by the harsh Viking chief still haunted Mairead's unguarded moments. The thought that the next thrall to suffer such treatment might be her own little boy was beyond unbearable. She reached for Weylin, ready to plead, prepared to do anything, to offer anything if he would just agree to let this matter drop. Her pleas fell on deaf ears. The man merely shook his head, turned and marched away.

"What can I do?" Mairead appealed to Aigneis next, her friend and companion. The woman's features were more sympathetic, but she echoed Weylin's statement.

"It is a matter for the Jarl. He will be back in a few days probably. You must speak with him, seek to explain and convince him to be merciful. He will listen…"

Gunnar would not listen. She knew it. She knew exactly what would happen to Donald as soon as Gunnar returned.

• • • • • • •

Two days passed, days during which Mairead thought of little else but the impending return of the Viking chief. She dreaded seeing Gunnar ride back into the settlement, knowing that Weylin would waste no time in imparting the news of Donald's misdeeds. She had given up seeking to reason with the other slave; he was implacable on the matter.

Mairead sighed as she set down the pail of water she carried from the river that skirted the edge of the settlement. The brook ran clear and cold, providing ample good drinking water for the settlement. It had become her task to keep the longhouse supplied and she made regular trips, Tyra huddled against her chest, carried in a sling that Aigneis had fashioned for her. She stretched, rolled her shoulders, then picked up the bucket again and set off, taking care to spill as little as possible.

She started as she rounded the corner of the first dwelling she reached, when Ferris stepped from the shadow of the building. Precious water sloshed across the ground to seep into the earth.

"You startled me," she complained. "Now I shall have to make another trip."

Ferris shrugged, unconcerned at having added to her labours. She wondered if he might make amends by offering to help carry the bucket, or even refill it for her.

It was not to be. The other thrall merely leaned on the cottage wall at his back and smirked at her. Unease became fear. Ferris made her flesh crawl, though she could not exactly say why. She should pity the man, he had suffered at the dark Viking's hand, but any such sympathy had evaporated now as she picked up her pail again and made to pass him.

"Did you think about what I said?" He moved forward, barring her path.

"Excuse me." Mairead stepped to the side.

He moved again, still obstructing her way, though now it was clear he did so deliberately.

"Let me pass," demanded Mairead. She glanced about her but saw no one. Should she scream for aid?

"I asked you a question." He lowered his tone, leaned in to whisper in her ear. "Did you think about my words?"

"I have no wish to talk to you. Please, get out of my way or I shall tell Gunnar what you said and you will be flogged again."

"Ah, so you do remember. Have you considered my suggestion, then?"

"What suggestion?" She knew full well what Ferris referred to but was hedging for time, for some way to extricate herself from this confrontation.

He stepped back, his smile cold. Ferris placed both hands under his cheek and inclined his head to the side mimicking sleep, then he made a stabbing motion with his right hand. His mime was clear enough and Mairead backed away, terrified now.

"You are mad, quite deluded. He will kill you…"

"Only if you tell him, but you won't do that, will you? You know where your loyalties lie, and who knows what may happen to your precious little family if you betray your people. We are Celts, slaves, all of us. These Vikings are our enemies and they deserve all they get. You know that to be true."

Mairead knew no such thing. She could not name just what the Viking was to her, but she was certain that Gunnar was not her enemy. He had delivered her baby and rescued her son, and she could no more plot to murder him than she could sprout wings and fly home to Scotland.

She shook her head. "I will not help you. I want no part of this."

Ferris shrugged. "As you like, but everyone knows what your brat did, and what will happen when the Jarl returns. If you want to protect him, protect all of us, you will do as I say."

"I will not." The very idea was laughable. Even if she was minded to sneak up on him while he slept, Gunnar would be more than a match for her. She was a healer, not a killer, and she would not repay the kindness the Viking had shown her by seeking to murder him in his bed. "Now step aside or I shall scream fit to raise the dead."

If anything, Ferris' smile broadened. "No, you will not. You will keep your pretty mouth shut, or you will pay the consequences. Do I make myself clear?"

He reached for her and stroked her cheek before she could move to stop him. Mairead recoiled but he followed her and now she found herself backed against the wall of the building. Ferris laid his palm across her mouth, sealing in the scream that bubbled in her throat.

"Quiet. You will say nothing of this, of me. Ever. Do you understand?"

Mairead nodded and clutched Tyra to her chest. She would say anything, promise anything, if only he would let her and her baby go unharmed.

Ferris leaned in, the sour heat of his breath filling Mairead's nostrils as he placed his mouth beside her ear. "The Jarl will tire of you soon enough. Perhaps I would enjoy sampling what is left…"

No! She squirmed in his grasp, desperate now to escape.

Had she been alone she would be fighting in earnest, but with her baby she dared not—

"Mairead. Mairead, where are you?"

The sound of Aigneis' voice was never more welcome. Ferris hissed in annoyance and turned toward the interruption. Aigneis' footsteps could now be heard, in moments she would appear.

"Another time," murmured her assailant. He released her and slunk away around the opposite end of the cottage just as Aigneis came into view.

"Ah, there you are. What about that water…?" The older woman paused, peered at Mairead. "Are ye all right, lass? Ye're as white as snow."

"Yes. Yes, I am fine. I was just… just a little fatigued." She stumbled forward to pick up her bucket, now barely half full. "I must have spilt the water. I shall go back to the river and—"

"Ye will do no such thing. Ye need tae rest, 'tis but a fortnight since you gave birth. Go back to the longhouse, I shall bring the water."

Mairead was grateful to hurry away, her thoughts swirling.

Should she tell Aigneis what Ferris had said, what he had done? Should she tell Gunnar?

No, she decided. She was too new here, she did not know the ways of this place, or who she could trust. She would not participate in any of Ferris' malicious scheming, and he was quite wrong if he believed there would be 'another time.' She would make certain to avoid him from now on. He would have no help from her and he would be unable to perpetrate his scheme without it so Gunnar could sleep easy in his bed. Neither would she make enemies if she could help it so she would remain silent.

And whatever the vile thrall might like to suggest, she would find another way to protect her son from the wrath of the Viking chief.

CHAPTER SEVEN

"Gone? What do you mean, gone? Where the fuck has she gone? And why? What happened here?"

Gunnar glared at Weylin and wondered, not for the first time, why he should not merely throttle the man now. The Celt's devotion to duty was not in doubt, but did he have to look quite so fucking pleased with himself?

"The boy is a thief, Master. We discovered his wrongdoing and his guilt was beyond doubt. Rather than allow you to address the matter in a way which you might deem appropriate, the mother believed she knew better. She left, took the boy with her, and the baby."

"Thor's fucking hammer." Gunnar actually growled as he tunnelled his fingers through his hair. He strode across the central aisle of his hall and entered his sleeping chamber. The evidence of recent occupation was obvious in the dishevelled pelts strewn across the raised dais he slept on, and the now greying embers in the small fire pit. He knelt beside the cinders and held his hand above them. The meagre hint of warmth still rising from the doused fire told him what he needed to know—his flame-haired captive was not long gone.

Gunnar left the longhouse at a sprint, yelling for Steinn

as he charged across the settlement toward the crude
outbuilding that served as a stable.

"My horse, now. We leave at once."

Men came running, their brief homecoming at an end
but none questioned their chief.

"Jarl, what has happened? Where are we going?" Steinn
threw a bridle over his horse's head and tightened the buckle
as he spoke.

"Mairead has fled. We will track her, bring her back."

"Fled, Jarl? Why would she do that?"

Why indeed? A child's mischief was no cause for such a
desperate act. There had to be more to this and he intended
to know what that was. Provided he got to his Celt before
the wolves did.

"Where is Ormarr? His tracking skills will be needed."
Gunnar swung into his own saddle as Weylin fussed about
him.

"Jarl, she is but a thrall, there is no purpose in such haste.
Eat, rest, I shall—"

"You shall shut your fucking mouth unless it is to tell me
exactly when she left and what direction she took."

The servant fell silent under his master's withering
glower. It was Aigneis who stepped forward to offer the
information he required.

"She left soon after *dagmal*, Jarl. Your man arrived and
told us that you would be returning this day, with the stolen
sheep. I ordered food to be prepared in readiness and
Mairead said she would take Donald to harvest fresh turnips
for the broth. I did not think to seek her out until much
later, when she did not return for the noon meal."

The woman wrung her hands, her concern etched across
her kindly features. Gunnar softened his tone. "Did she take
anything with her?"

"I do not think so, Jarl. She has few possessions and
there is nothing gone from the larders. And no horse is
missing either."

"Fuck," he muttered again, under his breath. She was out

there, alone, in danger, with no food, no protection, and two small children, one of them a babe barely a month old. *Had the woman not the sense she was born with?*

"Jarl, there is more." Aigneis dropped her gaze, her next words barely audible. "Mairead saw Ferris."

He narrowed his eyes. He was aware that his new thrall had witnessed the punishment. Had Mairead spoken with the man since then?

"Ferris? What has he to do with this?"

"It is my fault. Mairead was... upset by the whipping. It frightened her and she asked me about it. I told her Ferris was a thief and that he had earned his punishment. I said that all must obey the law. When Donald was discovered to have stolen from others here, perhaps she thought... I mean, might she have expected that you would... would...?"

"She believed I would have her child whipped? Or even do it myself? By Odin, why would she imagine that?"

The woman did not reply, but her glance toward Weylin said all that was required. Gunnar leaned down from his saddle and beckoned the man to him.

"Look at me, Weylin and mark me well. If harm comes to Mairead, or to either of her children, you will answer to me for it."

"But—"

"You had better hope I find her in time." He straightened and lifted his arm to gain his men's attention. "The woman is on foot and carrying a baby. She will not have got far. Ormarr, you will go ahead and find her trail."

"Jarl?" It was Aigneis again, close to tears now.

"There is more?"

The woman nodded. "Two days ago, Mairead asked me the distance to the closest town or village. I thought nothing of it then, merely that she might be wondering about a market, a place to purchase medicines..."

Medicines? Questions clamoured for answers but Gunnar was focused on one goal right now. "What did you tell her?"

"I told her that you usually go to Drafnsund to trade, about twenty miles north of here. I am sorry, I never imagined—"

"I know. It is not your fault. Ormarr, you will start with the route to Drafnsund, check if she headed north."

The man set off at a canter as Gunnar leaned down to speak again with Aigneis. "Why did she have need of medicine? Is one of the children ill?"

"No, Jarl, nothing like that. Mairead is a healer; she wished to build a stock of herbs and the like, in order to be able to help us here. We collected some plants, things which grow hereabouts, but there were others she wished to acquire. I believe she meant to suggest that you purchase the items…"

He nodded. It made sense. When he took her from Pennglas he had found Mairead in the house of a man who was sick. Perhaps she had been there as a healer. There was much he needed to understand about his newest thrall, but first he must get her back and teach her the folly of her actions.

A shout from Ormarr caught his attention. The man was waving from the far end of the settlement, beckoning his chief to follow.

"We have a trail. Come." Gunnar kicked his mount into a gallop and they were off.

● ● ● ● ● ● ●

"These tracks are fresh, Jarl. They passed this way less than two hours ago. One small adult, and a child." Ormarr settled on his haunches beside the track, his gaze on some pattern in the dust that the karl could discern and Gunnar could not. Ormarr had led them to his missing sheep; he saw no cause to doubt the man's skills now.

"It has to be them," breathed Gunnar. "Only two hours? We will overtake them soon." He waited until Ormarr remounted, then the Vikings fell in behind the tracker.

"There! See, Jarl, see there." Ormarr pointed at the sloping meadow perhaps two miles ahead of them. Squinting against the sun, which was now low in the sky, Gunnar peered in the direction indicated by his warrior. He could make out the two small figures struggling up the incline, the larger of the pair stopping frequently to wait for the smaller one.

"They are tiring, moving slowly," offered Steinn.

"Yes. You are with me," Gunnar ordered. "The rest of you, follow at this distance. Keep us in sight."

Gunnar set off at an easy canter, Steinn in his wake. It was not long before the sound of their hoof beats reached their quarry. Mairead turned, grabbed at Donald, and tried to drag him along faster. Her renewed haste made little difference, and in just a few minutes the men on horseback closed the gap. Mairead sank to her knees as Gunnar rode up alongside her. She clutched her baby in her arms, and a white-faced Donald flung his arms about her neck.

Gunnar hauled on the reins to halt his stallion. "Steinn, you will tell Mairead that—"

"Let us go. Please, please do not hurt him. Please…"

Gunnar gaped at her. "You speak our tongue very well, Mairead. I am impressed."

"I have been learning. I thought to please you, but…"

She *did* please him, but now was not the time to dwell upon that. "But instead you decide to take off alone. Do you not realise the penalty for absconding? You are my property, all of you." His stern gaze encompassed the children too. "You had no right to leave Gunnarsholm without my permission. Do you care to explain to me why you chose to do so?"

"I… I… please, I will make this right, I swear. He is but a child, too small to… to… Donald meant no harm."

She was stammering, almost incoherent in her fear and grief. This had to stop. Now.

Gunnar dismounted. "Donald, you will go with Steinn, back to Gunnarsholm."

The boy would have obeyed him, but Mairead grabbed at her son's arm and held him fast. "No, you cannot do this. Please, I beg you."

"He will not be harmed, but the boy needs to return home now. He is tired and hungry."

"My children must remain with me. I will not let you take him."

The reality of her situation was stark. There was not a thing this female slave could do to prevent him taking her son and they both knew that, but Gunnar preferred to persuade rather than force the issue.

"My quarrel at this time is with you, not your boy. I know of his stealing, and will address that issue in due course, though I suspect not in the manner you clearly expect. You should have trusted me to know the difference between a lazy, dishonest servant who has been warned countless times and a frightened, confused child. Viking justice can be harsh, but it is also fair. Your boy will not be harmed, you have my word."

Mairead stared at him, hope flaring in her stormy gaze. "Do you...? I mean, will you not...? I saw what you did, to that other slave."

"I know what you saw and I am sorry you witnessed that. I should have spoken to you, made sure you understood why it was needful. I bear responsibility for that oversight, but it does not excuse your actions today. Had we not been able to track you and find you swiftly, it is likely that none of you would have survived the night. Have you any notion of the dangers you face out here alone?"

"I... I had no choice. I know of the bandits, and the wolves, but I thought—"

"You thought me more dangerous?"

She nodded, tears now streaming down her cheeks.

"Well, you were wrong and you shall pay the penalty for your error, Mairead."

Her grip on her son had slackened and Gunnar drew the boy slowly away. He beckoned Steinn to come closer, and at Gunnar's nod the man leaned down to haul the child up before him in the saddle. Gunnar returned his attention to the weeping woman who knelt before him and kept his tone low, for her ears alone.

"Mairead, you are to be punished for what you have done today. You endangered yourself and your children, my property all of you, and I will not tolerate that. You are to be spanked, my belt to your bare bottom, but I see no merit in having your son witness your punishment. He will return, now, to Gunnarsholm and you will see him there soon enough. It is better, also, that Tyra go with him."

"No! No, my baby needs me. You cannot take her." Mairead backed off, pressing her baby against her body and glaring her tearful defiance.

Gunnar crouched beside her and laid a gentle hand on her shoulder. "I will not take your baby from you against your will. If you wish her to remain with you while you are punished, I will permit that. But if you will agree to feed her, tend to her needs, then allow her to be taken home with her brother, I promise you she will be kept safe for you until you return."

Long moments passed. Mairead did not speak, but her lips were working as she considered his words. She glanced up at Donald, now seated on Steinn's mount and no longer so ashen-faced. She turned to meet Gunnar's gaze once more. "I may feed her, you say?"

He inclined his head. "Of course. Take as long as you need to satisfy yourself that she is well. You will not be separated for long, I promise."

"She will be with Steinn?"

"Yes. You know you can trust him. He will hand her to Aigneis when they get back to Gunnarsholm."

"You promise?"

"I do. You can trust me to ensure your children come to no harm."

She said nothing more, but her nod was sufficient. Gunnar rose and moved away to allow her some privacy to feed her baby. He waited by his horse until she started to get to her feet then he returned to offer her his hand. She made no protest as he took Tyra from her then passed the little one up to Stein.

"The babe is to be cared for by Aigneis until we return. Take half the men back with you, the rest are to await us where they are. No one is to approach unless I summon them."

"Aye, Jarl." The warrior wheeled his horse about and set off back the way they had come. Gunnar watched as Steinn rode up to his men, then a few moments later the youth continued on, accompanied by four of the eight Vikings who had accompanied him on his quest. The rest remained where they were.

Satisfied his instructions were to be carried out, Gunnar turned his stern gaze on the woman who stood white-faced at his side. "Do you understand why you are to be punished?"

She nodded, and lowered her gaze to examine her leather-shod feet.

"Look at me, Mairead, and tell me why you deserve to feel my belt across your buttocks."

Her features reddened at his explicit description, but she met his gaze. "Because I tried to escape. I left Gunnarsholm without permission."

"Not good enough. Try again." He deliberately hardened his tone.

Her lovely eyes widened. "Because I put myself in danger."

"Yes, that is better. But there is more."

"I endangered my children too. I did not trust you, I allowed myself to believe that you would hurt my son."

Gunnar moved in close, so close that she had to bend her head back to maintain the eye contact he insisted upon. "What should you have done instead?"

"I am not certain, Jarl."

"No? Then what might you suggest? I will tell you if you

are wrong."

She gnawed on her lower lip, and Gunnar noted that not once had she asked for leniency for herself. She was ready to plead with him on her son's behalf, but not her own.

"I should have waited. I should have trusted you to be fair, and to understand why Donald stole those items."

"Oh? And do you understand why he did that?"

"No," she murmured.

"Nor do I, but I will, by the time this is done. Your answer is satisfactory. So, tell me now, Mairead, have you been spanked before? Your husband, perhaps?"

She gave a sharp little nod. "He was often angry, his temper was easily roused."

"Do you believe me to be in a temper now, Mairead?"

"No, Jarl, but you are angry."

"Yes, I am, but my temper is quite under control. I am not about to raise my hand to you in anger." He paused. "Is that what your husband did?"

"He would slap me, across my face usually, and call me cruel names. He… he would shout, a lot. At me and at Donald."

"Were you afraid of him?"

Her lip trembled. "A wife should fear her husband. Is that not so?"

He gave a wry laugh. "I can think of many Viking women who do not fear their husbands in the slightest. Respect is not the same as fear. A wife should respect her husband and accept his authority. A slave, also, must submit to her master."

"I know that. I never intended—"

"Will you submit to me, Mairead? Now? Will you remove your clothing, lean against yonder tree, and lift your bottom for my belt? Will you thank me for the lashes I shall give you and swear to me that you will never endanger yourself like this again?"

"Yes. Yes, Jarl, I will do that."

Her voice was little more than a whisper, but he heard

and it was sufficient. "Very well. Follow me."

He strode off into the shadow of the large pines that edged the meadow where they stood. His men would be close enough to hear him if he summoned them, but he would afford Mairead the privacy he believed she deserved. After all, it would not be proper for half the men of Gunnarsholm to be treated to the sight of his future wife's naked bottom.

Later, as he considered this intimate exchange between them, he would seek to identify the precise moment he determined that she was to be his wife. The best he could arrive at was that instant when she consented to allow him to take her baby from her. She had placed her trust in him, handed over the most precious and fragile thing she had in the world in the knowledge that he would keep Tyra safe. Donald too. She had accepted his promise, and he was lost. Now he merely had to convince her that she might marry a Viking, but that would come in due course. First, there was the matter of her proper punishment.

"You will undress, Mairead."

"I could just raise my skirt. It would be—"

"Your clothes, all of them. I want you naked. Now."

She flinched at his harsh tone, then nodded and started to unfasten the loose smock that she wore. She removed it quickly and folded it, then reached behind her to undo the tapes that held her woollen skirt in place. She bent to untie her boots, kicked them off, then stood before him clad in just the linen undershirt or sark that she wore next to her skin.

"That too," he affirmed, though more gently now. He wanted obedience from her, not fear.

She pulled the remaining garment over her head and stood before him, nude, shivering slightly, her face downcast. Her hair was loose and fell in thick waves across her shoulders and breasts, a red mane that he itched to sweep aside in order to properly assess her lush curves. As she began to lift her hands as though to cover her body as best she might he shook his head.

"Do not. I wish to see you."

"I am embarrassed."

"I know. And a little cold perhaps since your nipples are hard and swollen, like the berries of the holly." He allowed himself a sensual curling of his lips as he admired the vision she presented.

"Please, do not—"

"You are beautiful, Mairead. I knew that you would be."

"I am not young," she protested, "and I have borne two children."

"How old are you?"

"Twenty-five summers, Jarl."

He did the calculation. She must have been young when she was first wed. Despite her words, and even knowing she had a son of seven years, he would have guessed her to be not yet twenty, though such details were immaterial to him.

"I repeat, you are beautiful. And you are mine. Do you accept both these truths?"

Her brow furrowed in confusion. "I do not understand. What do you want of me?"

"I want nothing *of* you, just you, yourself."

"It is true then, I am to be your bed-slave."

"You will share my bed, yes."

She lowered her gaze again. "I do not fear this, if that is what you are expecting. I have been wed twice, and widowed. I am no stranger to what transpires between men and women. I can submit to you in this way, if that is what you require."

Something in her resigned acceptance struck him amiss. She seemed unusually acquiescent, and whilst he desired her submission he found he did not much care for this subdued compliance. The flame in her fiery hair was not echoed in her deferential demeanour and he would not have it.

"Look at me." He cupped her chin and held her face still so she could not break his gaze. "I desire you, and I shall have you. We both know that. But not by force. You will be safe with me, and I will take care of you." He searched her deep green eyes for some clue, something he might say to awaken the spark he knew must be there, lurking hidden beneath the maternal cares and female vulnerability. "Despite your marriages and the advancing years you claim, I believe you know very little of what *can* transpire between a man and a woman. I believe you still have much to learn, and it starts here, now." He released her chin. "Go stand by that tree, rest your hands on the trunk, and lean forward."

Now her lovely eyes widened, darkened. She was afraid. *Would she do as he asked?*

Slowly, with obvious reluctance, Mairead moved toward the tree he had selected. It was a pine, tall, the trunk straight, smooth and free of branches to a height well above both their heads. She reached for it and placed her palms on the grey bark, then turned to regard him over her shoulder.

"I am not sure what you wish me to do."

"Lean forward, bend at your waist, and arch your back. I want your bottom high and your shoulders low."

She blushed crimson as she turned to face the front again, but his instructions were clear enough and Gunnar was gratified when she shuffled her feet away from the tree and bent as low as she could. The woman was trying. She wanted to appease him but this was hard for her. He could only guess at the violence she had experienced at the hands of men in the past, and he did not wish to draw this out.

"Six strokes. They will be hard but you can take this, and you will learn from it."

"Yes, Jarl. Please, be quick…"

The timing of her punishment was for him to determine, but he would not take issue with her on this right now. Instead, he unfastened the pin that secured his great wolf skin cloak and dropped the garment to the ground, then he unbuckled his sword belt. Mairead flinched again at the sound of the leather coming free, but she held her position. Her shoulders were stiff, her legs straight. Her pretty, pink quim was just barely visible, the delicate lips of her cunny quivering between her upper thighs. He wondered if he should instruct her to spread her legs and allow him a decent view of what was his.

Perhaps, on another occasion…

Gunnar positioned himself behind her and slightly to her left. His belt, doubled with the buckle contained within his fist, dangled from his right hand. With his left hand he caressed her smooth, creamy buttocks.

"Such a sweet, round bottom, Mairead. You will bear well the marks I shall give you today, and you will remember what it is to trust."

She did not reply. He had not expected her to. Without further preamble he lifted his right arm and swung the belt.

CHAPTER EIGHT

"Aaagh!"

Pain exploded across both her buttocks. Mairead let out a shrill cry and made to stand.

"Do not move." The stern command pinned her in place as surely as if he had bound her to the tree. Mairead dragged in a harsh breath and braced for the next stroke.

Gunnar did not keep her waiting. There was a whooshing sound as the belt swung again, and a streak of fire snaked across her upper thighs. Mairead screamed and her knees almost buckled beneath her.

"Steady yourself, and tell me when you are ready to continue." His voice was low and compelling and utterly in control. It was that air of iron-willed mastery that gave Mairead the courage to continue without pleading for him to stop. He would hurt her, he *was* hurting her, but he had sworn he would not harm her and she believed him.

Alred had never inspired such confidence, quite the reverse. Even Niall, her first husband who was altogether a much gentler soul, could be testy on occasion. Neither of these men had ever stripped her and taken a belt to her bare arse but even so she did not fear injury at this dark Viking's hands.

Mairead recovered her composure, such as it was. "I… I am ready, Jarl."

The next stroke set her right buttock alight but she managed not to scream. Gunnar wasted no time in delivering another, this time landing across her left cheek. How many was that? Mairead attempted to count but had already lost any sense of the number. All she knew was that she hurt, everywhere.

"Arch your back again for these final two." Gunnar paused to allow her time to obey his instruction.

Just two more. She could weather that. She must. Then this Viking would take her home and she would see her children again. Mairead lifted her bottom again in obliging obedience, and gritted her teeth in readiness for the last two strokes.

Whoosh. Her entire bottom took the force of the leather across the fullest part. Her flesh seared under the onslaught and Mairead whimpered in pain, gasping now.

Just one more. Thank the blessed Virgin and all the saints that it was only one or she feared she might lose her resolve and beg him to stop. Instead she dug her fingernails into the bark of the tree and held her breath.

"Aagh! Oh sweet Jesu, please…" The final stroke fell on her upper thighs again, right under the curve of her bottom. Mairead lurched forward to hug the tree and willed her knees not to give out. She would not collapse at his feet, she absolutely refused to do that.

She remained where she was, shaking under the shock of what had just happened to her. Mairead was dimly aware of the sound of leather on leather as he rebuckled his belt, then the clink of iron as he restored his sword to the loop he always hung it from. She turned her face in order to watch out of the corner of her eye as he bent to retrieve his cloak. As he stepped toward her she closed her eyes, uncertain what he might do to her next.

The rough warmth of the pelt covering her shoulders was not what she had anticipated. Neither were the strong arms that encircled her torso and drew her gently up until she stood upright. He turned her in his arms and pulled her to him then held her close against his chest. For want of a better option she clung to him as she had to the pine. He was warmer, somehow more solid than the tree and she wished she might never let him go. It was as it had been the day Tyra was born. This fearsome Viking offered strength, certainty, and safety in a perilous world that seemed to shake under her bare feet.

Could she confide in him about Ferris? Should she?

No. Ferris was odious, but the more she had considered his delusional threats in the days since, the more she had realised the thrall was both powerless and harmless. He could not hurt her, or Gunnar. If she told the Viking what Ferris had said, what he had done, and assuming Gunnar believed her though she knew of no reason to suppose he would not, then another whipping was assured. She could not bear that on her conscience.

The matter was best left as it was, the inane ramblings of a bitter, humiliated slave who found comfort in railing against his master.

"You did well, my flame-haired Celt. I am proud of you." Gunnar murmured the words against her hair, his breath feathering across her cheek as she snuggled closer and dismissed Ferris from her thoughts.

Proud? No one had ever said that to her before. People had occasionally expressed gratitude when her herbal concoctions provided them with ease, and when she was much younger her mother had often praised her diligence and her helpfulness, qualities that had seen her wed at eighteen years of age. But no one had ever before told her she made them proud. She found she rather liked it, and more astonishing still, she actually believed Gunnar.

"Thank you," she murmured.

"My pleasure," came the low reply as he pulled the wolf skin around her and tucked the edges together at the front. With no further words he lifted her in his arms and strode deeper into the wood.

"Where are you taking me? You said we could go home after... after..."

"Soon, I promise. First, there is something I wish to show you. A place I believe you will like."

"Is it far? Tyra..."

"Not far. Your baby is being well cared for."

That was true, she supposed. She stilled in his arms and allowed her eyelids to droop.

• • • • • • •

"Mairead, can you stand?"

"What? Where are we?"

Gunnar had stopped walking but he still held her in his arms. She craned her neck to peer about her.

He lowered her feet to the ground and she gazed in puzzlement at the small pool that glistened several feet in front of them. It was surrounded by flat rocks, and unless she was hallucinating the crystal-clear water appeared to be steaming.

"I do not understand? What manner of place is this?"

"This is a hot spring. The water is warmed by heat from within the earth. It is good for bathing, and I believe it to be especially soothing for recently spanked bottoms."

"You mean I should splash it on my... on my...?"

"No, I mean you should lower your entire body into it and allow the waters to heal whatever ails you. Come, I shall show you." Gunnar stepped from behind her to approach the pool. He went down on his haunches to scoop some of the sparkling water up in his hand then brought it to her nose. "There is an aroma, not unpleasant. The waters tingle against the skin. See, the pool bubbles..."

Before her astonished eyes the little pool did indeed seem to boil as though heated by a fire beneath. Surely such a thing was impossible, not natural.

"I do not think... oh!"

Gunnar had already started to undress. Mairead gaped as he dropped his belt, complete with sword, to the ground, then tugged his black leather tunic over his head. He ignored her startled gasps and his boots were soon unlaced and dumped beside the tunic. He glanced at her as he started to work on his leather trousers. "You will not require the cloak, Mairead."

"But—"

Her words died in her throat when the tall Norseman peeled his trousers down to reveal his cock, erect and proud and jutting at her. Gloriously naked and utterly unashamed, Gunnar grinned wickedly at her.

"I have seen your body, and now you have seen mine. This is fair, I think."

"Fair…?" Mairead's tenuous grasp of the Norse language failed her. "I do not understand…"

Gunnar appeared to have not the slightest interest in what she might or might not understand. He ignored her and strode across the flat rocks that surrounded the pool then lowered himself until he sat on the very edge, his feet dangling in the water.

"Have a care, you might burn yourself." Mairead was confused and anxious. The water he had scooped up did not seem unduly hot, but there might be other parts of the pond that were. Who could possibly know with such a bizarre phenomenon? Her every sense urged caution. "Perhaps we should move further away."

"These hot springs exist all over our land and my people have enjoyed bathing in them for centuries. There is no danger, just pleasure. Join me, Mairead." He extended his hand to her but she was rooted to the spot.

"I would prefer to return to Gunnarsholm, if you do not mind."

"We shall, soon. But first I shall require you to trust me once more. Come, Mairead. Leave the cloak there and come into the water with me." His eyes were soft, dark as midnight and utterly compelling. The command was softly spoken, but obedience was required nevertheless. And he had promised the waters were safe.

Slowly, cautiously, Mairead lowered the wolf's pelt, baring her body to him again. Was she mistaken or did his eyes darken yet more? His hand was still outstretched and she stepped forward to take it. He smiled at her, his even white teeth flashing as he pulled her to him.

"Sit beside me and put your feet in, as I have."

Mairead did as he instructed, and almost laughed out loud at the warm, tingling sensation in her lower limbs. "It tickles," she exclaimed. "It is like… like…"

"Like the caress of a thousand elves, or fairies as you Celts would say."

"There are no such things as fairies, or elves." Still, she kicked her feet and giggled.

"No? I disagree. Anything is possible when you immerse yourself in the magical waters. Like this."

He shoved himself forward and sank into the bubbling pool. As his dark head disappeared under the surface Mairead at once started to panic.

"Gunnar? Jarl? Where are you? Stop this, you are scaring me."

He did not re-emerge and she peered anxiously into the depths. She could see him shimmering beneath. The waters were perfectly clear and he seemed to hover just a couple of feet below the surface. Perhaps if she were to—

Gunnar broke the surface in a shower of glittering, warm bubbles. His grin was infectious, and despite her recent alarm Mairead laughed. He seemed to be standing on a ledge as he remained quite still, the water at chest height. He reached up for her.

"Come in, I will hold you."

Without another thought she leaned forward, dropped into the water and his outstretched arms. At once he wrapped her in his embrace and turned her so her back was to his chest. He looped his arms under hers and she allowed her feet to drift upwards until her toes broke the surface.

"H-how deep is the pond?"

"In the centre? Perhaps twenty feet or so. Do you swim, Mairead?"

"No. I am sorry…"

"Perhaps you will learn, as you have learnt our tongue. For now we shall stay at the edges. There are ledges and rocks to stand on, or to sit if you prefer. Or I could simply hold on to you like this."

"Do not let go. Please."

He chuckled into the shell of her ear. "Do not fear. I have already gone to considerable trouble for you. I have no intention of letting you drown in a hot spring." He leaned back against the side and drew her with him until just her head remained above the surface. "How do you like your bath, my Celt?"

"It is… most pleasant, my Viking."

"The correct term is Jarl, or master, or even Gunnar since we do seem to be on intimate terms, but I find I do not object to being your Viking also."

She half turned, instantly remembering her precarious position with this fearsome man. She should not be fooled by his apparent playfulness. "I apologise, Jarl. I meant no disrespect."

"And I meant no censure. When I am angry, you will know it. Relax, enjoy the waters." He smiled at her again, and Mairead was not entirely certain that the warmth that enveloped her came solely from the bubbling pool. His features were stark, but beautiful. The scar he bore did nothing to mar his stunning good looks, while his smile caused something to curl and quiver deep within Mairead's core.

"May I ask you something, Jarl?"

"If you wish. I may not answer." He nuzzled the hair on the top of her head and, unthinking, Mairead angled her chin to afford him access to her neck. He kissed the delicate spot beneath her ear and she almost forgot her question.

Almost, but not quite. "How did you come by your scar,

Gunnar?"

He paused. "Does it upset you?"

"No, not in the least. You are beautiful and the scar makes you more so."

"Men are not beautiful. We are—"

"Most men are not, this is true. But some are, and you are one such. I... I thought so the very first time I saw you. When you came to Aikrig and rescued me from those other men who would have raped me. Your appearance was terrifying that day, but you were still beautiful."

"And now, do I still terrify you?"

She shook her head. "No, you do not, though I would be wise to be wary of you."

"Indeed you would, Mairead." He paused, then, "I was injured in a raid, on a monastery on the north coast of England. An abbot there was singularly reluctant to give up the church treasures. He put up a good fight, but I was better."

"How long ago was this?"

"I am not certain. Two years, perhaps three. I was fortunate that the blade was clean and the wound did not become infected or I might not have survived. I tend not to underestimate my opponents now."

"I am glad that you survived."

"Are you? Had I died then you might have remained unmolested in your Scottish village."

"My life has changed, but I do not believe I am any worse off here than I was as a widow in Aikrig. My children had no father, I was alone."

"You are not alone now, and I have promised to care for your children."

She turned in his arms again. "No, you did not promise that. You swore not to harm them, that is all."

"It is the same thing, is it not?"

"No, I do not believe it is."

"Then allow me to be clear, and let us avoid any lingering doubt. I will care for your children, the two you have already, which I remind you are my property just as you are, and any more you might bear. They will all be mine."

Property? This arrogant Viking claimed the right of ownership and she supposed that was the truth under Viking law. But she believed the taking of slaves was surely wrong, a sin, and people could never be the property of another. Or could they? She had always owed allegiance to someone, been under the power and control of first her father then each of her husbands. Gunnar's mastery was no more onerous than theirs had been, and his treatment of her children considerably better. She allowed herself to relax in his arms. She could do worse that rely on this dark-haired Norseman.

"Spread your legs for me, Mairead."

"What?" She lurched within the cradle of his arms. "Why?"

"Earlier, you told me that you had much experience of what transpires between men and women. I am minded to test the boundaries of your knowledge."

"You would take me? Here? I am not sure that I am ready, after Tyra…"

"I know, and I will allow you all the time you need to recover from the birth. I can be patient, and I have no wish to harm you. But, there is more to what happens between men and women than just fucking."

"You are very direct, Jarl, yet still I find myself uncertain. What do you mean?"

He chuckled again, the sound warm and rich and very knowing. "I shall show you what I mean, but first I require you to hook your legs over each of mine and allow me to spread your thighs wide. Will you do that or must I insist on having access to explore what is mine?"

Why, when he spoke to her thus, when he half-threatened her, when she should be terrified and cringing in fear, did his soft, sensual command cause her stomach to clench and heat to flare between her legs? Why did everything he suggested to her sound so… enticing?

"Mairead? What are you waiting for?"

What indeed?

"I am sorry, Master." She lifted each leg in turn and draped them across his thighs, the position already opening her to his questing fingers. He kept his left arm across her chest just above her breasts, but he reached down with his right to tease the reddish-golden curls at the apex of her thighs. Mairead stiffened, but did not move.

"Good, you please me very much. So soft, so pretty." He tugged at the curls then proceeded lower still. Mairead expected him to reach down far enough to plunge his fingers inside her since this was the usual prelude to a man's fulfilment. It would be quick, she knew that, and not overly unpleasant.

But Gunnar halted just below the downy curls. His fingers stroked, explored, caressed, as though he sought something else. He widened his own legs, and in so doing pulled her thighs further apart. He bent his knees too, which had the effect of raising her up out of the water, exposing her to his gaze.

She opened her mouth to protest, but swallowed her words as a peculiar sensation overwhelmed her. Something deep and piercing, warm, intense, and delicious unfurled right where he touched her. Mairead let out a startled gasp and tried to close her legs.

"No, remain still. I wish to pleasure you."

"How? I do not understand…"

"Like this." He stroked that sensitive spot again, his movements precise and knowing as she writhed in his arms. "Am I hurting you?"

"No." She shook her head. "But it is strange, I do not believe I like it."

"No? And this?" He altered the angle of his hand to apply pressure to that quivering little button, then he took it between his finger and thumb and she thought that perhaps he squeezed.

"Oh. Oh!" Her inner muscles were clenching,

convulsing in a manner quite beyond her control or comprehension. "What are you doing?"

"I told you, I am pleasuring you. I intend to do this often, in preparation for you taking my cock when you are fully healed and quite ready. Will that be long, do you think?"

"I… I am not sure." Oh sweet Jesus, she hoped not. His busy, clever fingers were teasing her, awakening something she had only half-understood, a dim and elusive awareness suddenly coming into sharp focus as he stroked and tormented her. As she writhed against his thighs he applied more pressure, increasing the intensity until she felt she might burst, or shatter, or simply expire from wanting.

"Do not fight this. Allow it to happen. I have you." His words were murmured against her ear, his breath warm on her neck. His lips were on her sensitive skin, kissing, licking, nipping.

"Have me? What…? Why…? Oh, oh, dear Lord."

"Now, Mairead. Let it happen now."

She required no further urging or explanation. The sensation he had built so quickly seemed to spiral and surge within her until she could bear no more. She thrust her hips forward and her head back and let out a squeal of pure delight as waves of ecstasy washed through her. The tingling that bathed her body on the outside was within her also, coursing right out to her fingers and toes, to the very ends of her hair. She was weak, powerless to resist yet invigorated by the sensual feast he laid before her and that she now savoured.

The storm of sensation soon passed. Mairead's trembling body relaxed. She lay within the Viking's arms, limp and sated in a manner she could not even start to describe. He had satisfied a hunger she had not even known she possessed, but having tasted this joy once she would never wish to be without it again.

Something had been missing before. Some mysterious secret had remained hidden, but no longer. Gunnar had shared the revelation with her and now she knew what she needed

Who she needed.

• • • • • • •

"Are you ready to return now?"

Mairead opened her eyes. Gunnar dropped a soft kiss on her forehead as he held her in his arms. They were still in the water, though now she was cradled in his arms like a baby. His cock, solid and thick, nudged her punished bottom and she wondered if she were to turn just so, perhaps…

"We are three hours' ride from home. Tyra will be hungry by the time we arrive."

"What? Oh?"

"You have been asleep and I was sorry to wake you, but—"

"My baby. I need to get back."

"You do, I fear. We both do." He stood with her in his arms and stepped up out of the pool.

The shock of the cool Nordic climate against her warm skin was sufficient to dispel any lingering sleepiness. Mairead shivered and at once Gunnar grabbed the discarded wolf's pelt from the ground and wrapped her in it.

"Your clothes are back there, by the tree where you presented your lovely bottom for spanking. You may use my cloak for now."

She hugged the fur close and breathed in the heady scent of the Viking that permeated the cloak. It smelled of woods and leather, and something elusively masculine that was him alone. Gunnar dressed swiftly, belted his sword back on, and turned to pick her up.

"I can walk," she protested.

"Not without your shoes." He allowed no further debate and she snuggled against him as he strode back through the forest. Neither spoke. They had an understanding, she thought, and it would do for now.

CHAPTER NINE

It was dusk when the small group cantered into Gunnarsholm. As they neared the largest longhouse, which was his own home, the grumpy, grizzling cries of a hungry baby reached their ears. Gunnar turned his mount toward the house and halted before the door. He took Mairead's arm and lowered her to the ground.

"Go," he commanded. "She wants you. I will see to the horse and I shall be in soon."

He watched as she scampered across the hard-packed earth to disappear inside his home and wondered what he must do to ensure she remained there. Nothing, perhaps. She was his property after all, where else might she be? He found that conclusion strangely unsatisfactory.

Weylin followed him into the stable. "Do you require help with your horse, Jarl? I can see to him. There is food prepared… you must be hungry."

Gunnar turned from unbuckling the saddle to regard the man behind him. He *was* hungry, but that was not the matter uppermost in his thoughts. "No, I will do it. I would be obliged, though, if you would bring me the items stolen by the boy. I trust you still have them."

"Of course, Jarl." The man bowed his head and

withdrew.

A few minutes later Gunnar entered his longhouse, the stolen items in a small bag. Aigneis crouched beside the fire, stirring the cauldron that always hung there but otherwise the central hall was empty. He set the haul on the table and seated himself. At once Aigneis placed a dish of steaming broth before him.

"Thank you." He managed a smile for her. She was a good and willing servant. "Where is Mairead?"

"In your sleeping chamber, Jarl, tending to the little one. The boy is with her."

He nodded and reached for the hunk of bread she now offered him.

"Jarl, about the lad…"

The kindly face was etched with concern—yet another female slave who feared his brutal justice. *Was he truly such a monster?*

"Not now, Aigneis." He was at once weary, and acutely conscious of the fact that he had spent the past month pursuing robbers, sleeping under the stars, living off the land, then chasing down runaway thralls. He wanted his food and his bed, but there was a matter he must address this night if any of them were to have the peace they needed. "I will eat first, then deal with him."

Aigneis nodded and returned to her pot.

He could have returned to Gunnarsholm sooner, he knew that and so did his men. The pursuit of the robbers had been relatively swift, and it had taken him a little over a sennight to regain his stolen sheep. He could have driven the flock straight back, but instead opted to rest them and allow the animals to benefit from a few days of good grazing on the inland pastures. When he finally did tell his men to prepare for the journey home, their pace had been leisurely. He had offered the excuse that he wished to spare the horses, but this was not really the true reason.

The truth was, he had been avoiding his latest female thrall. If he had to look upon her, share a bed with her, he was not convinced he would be able to stop himself from having her. He would need to fuck her, to bury his cock within her and pound her until she screamed his name. He had but to observe Mairead, only to cast an eye over the gentle sway of her hips, the bright sheen of her hair, the mossy green of her eyes, and his cock swelled. He was permanently hard in her presence and out of it, and it was her fault.

He groaned and promised himself the ordeal would soon be over. It had now been a month since the birth of her baby and she seemed well enough. She had been responsive when he took her to the hot spring, had enjoyed his touch and been relaxed in his company once the whipping was out of the way. He knew many men would not have waited even as long as he had, but despite his desire for Mairead, Gunnar had no appetite for forced lovemaking. His slave would accept him, when she was ready. He might press her, and he would without doubt do what he could to entice and seduce her, but ultimately, he would wait.

The broth was good. He accepted a second bowl and more bread, followed by apples stewed in honey, and all washed down with a mug of fine mead. Replete, he could put off his final task no longer, though he remained uncertain just how he intended to resolve the matter. Perhaps it would be clearer when he had heard the lad's side of it. He rose from the table and approached the curtain that screened off his private chamber.

He paused to listen to the soft voices from within, Mairead's gentle tone and Donald's slightly higher one. She was telling her son a tale, recounting some legend from their Celtic folklore. Gunnar listened for a few moments to the story of a selkie stranded on a beach, lamenting his lost home in the deep. He presumed this to be a sea creature since the being had emerged from the waves to become trapped when the tide turned. The boy seemed dissatisfied with his mother's account of events, demanding to know why the selkie did not simply magic himself back into the water because surely he possessed such powers. Selkies could do anything they chose, just like Vikings.

Ah. He gritted his teeth and pulled the curtain back.

"Donald, come with me." The words were softly spoken, but a command.

At once the boy scrambled from the bed where he had been sitting with his mother and baby sister. Mairead made to follow him.

"No, you stay here. Just the boy."

"But—"

"Stay here. Please." He added the final word as an afterthought, his attempt at reassurance. She appeared to understand because she settled back against the furs, though her eyes never left the small figure of her boy as he followed Gunnar from the room. The Viking paused to drop the curtain again, then led the way back to the table where the stolen items still waited, concealed within the small sack.

Gunnar dismissed Aigneis with a gesture. He wanted to speak with Donald alone. When the servant bustled out of the hall on some errand that took her to another of the cottages, he sat down and beckoned the boy to come closer and stand before him.

Donald chewed on his lip, a nervous gesture Gunnar had seen before, on Mairead's pretty face. He supposed the lad had reason to be anxious, though he did not seem unduly frightened. Gunnar was pleased; he took no pleasure in scaring children, or helpless women for that matter.

Gunnar reached for the sack and tipped the contents out onto the table. "You know what these items are?"

Donald nodded.

"Tell me about them."

"I... I..."

"Did you steal them, Donald?"

The boy nodded now, his eyes glistening a little despite his best efforts not to cry.

"Can you tell me what it is to steal?"

"It is when you take things which belong to another."

118

"Thank you. And is it wrong to steal?"

"I… I think so. I am not sure."

"Weylin tells me these items were concealed within your bed. If you are not sure that it is wrong to steal, why did you hide them?"

"I… I thought everyone would be angry. And that they would take my things back."

"Your things? They are not yours. They belong to those you stole them from." Gunnar selected the amulet from among the pile. "I recognise this. It belongs to me."

The lad shifted from one foot to the other, clearly uncomfortable. His features hardened, as though he now considered himself to be the victim of some dire injustice. His mouth worked, and Gunnar knew there was something the boy was bursting to say but he feared retribution.

"Donald, tell me what you are thinking. I will listen, I promise you."

He shook his tawny head. "I cannot."

"You can. Tell me, because I want to understand why you took these things, why you stole my property."

There was a long pause, during which Donald screwed up his small face and stared at the floor before him. Suddenly he lifted his gaze to meet Gunnar's eyes and blurted out, "Because you stole it first. You stole it, and it became yours. I took it, so now it is mine."

"I stole it? No, I didn't—"

"You did. I saw this before, or one like it, in the manor house at Pennglas. You stole it from someone when you raided their village. You must have."

Had he? Gunnar thought back, tried to recall when and where he had acquired the amulet and had to acknowledge that the lad was probably right. Not Pennglas. The only time he ever went there the Viking attackers had taken only slaves, but he had likely seized the piece on some other raid. It was a Celtic design so the boy might well have seen similar items in his homeland.

"So, you believe it is permitted to steal, because that is

what Vikings do?"

"No, not really."

Gunnar took a long, deep breath and tried to make sense of what he was hearing. There was some logic to the lad's account, and Gunnar could start to grasp the dilemma here but he felt it was more complex still.

"Why do you say that? Why is stealing not permitted?" He deliberately gentled his voice, sensing that he was close.

"Because people get hurt. They lose things they love, or are killed trying to defend them. It is wrong, but it happens and those who steal are strong. They are safe because they have wealth."

"Wealth that they stole from others?"

"Perhaps. Yes, sometimes. It does not matter where they got their riches from."

"You wanted to be wealthy? Is that why you took these things?"

The boy flattened his lips and nodded. "If we have money, enough to buy food, my mother will not need to be married. I do not want her to marry again."

Gunnar could envision no circumstances whatsoever in which he would permit Mairead to take another husband but he did not say that. Instead he picked up on the boy's last remark. "Why do you not want that?"

"I do not want another stepfather. They are mean. They make me scared and my mother cries."

"Not all men would do that." Even as he uttered the words he knew the boy would not be convinced. Why would he be? The weak and powerless took what was handed to them.

"I do not want it. If we have enough money…"

"You have a home here, and plenty of food. There will be no new husband, no stepfather."

"But, you will sell us again. When you get tired of us, or need more money, you will sell us. Then what will happen?"

Gunnar was incredulous. This he had never expected. "I will not sell you. Why would I wish to do that?"

The lad shrugged. "It is what happens, that is all. You are kind, my mother says so, but you are a Viking and…" The boy stopped, his lip quivering as though he knew he had said too much.

Gunnar leaned forward, his elbows on his knees as he peered down into the small, scared features. "I am a Viking, this is true. And I take what I want, because I can. You are right about that also, and you are right that I am strong. I will protect what is mine. *You* are mine, so are your mother and your sister. I will protect all of you."

"Yes, but—"

Gunnar picked up the amulet. "You were also right about this, about where I got it from. I make no apology for my way of life, but I do understand your resentment and your confusion. The best I can find to say to you is that it is wrong to steal from your friends, your family, your master, and those who live about you. We take care of each other and find safety that way. Does this make sense? Any sense at all?"

"I… I suppose so. Will you beat me now?"

"I will not. I promised your mother that I would not harm you. I will punish you though, because it is against our laws to steal from one another and you must atone for what you have done."

The boy hung his head, silent.

"Weylin has told me you have spent a lot of time in the stables while you have been here. You enjoy working with horses?"

"Yes, Jarl."

"That is good, but for the coming sennight you will confine yourself to the longhouse and do chores in here. You will help Aigneis. I expect to see you sweeping, preparing vegetables, helping with the washing. You will do just as Aigneis says. Is that clear?"

"A whole week?"

"A week, yes. And that is not all. You will return each of these items to the person you took it from and apologise to them."

The boy grimaced, but managed a small nod. Gunnar scrutinised the amulet he still held in his hand. "I will demonstrate." He held out the piece to the boy. "I took this from your people. I apologise. Please accept it back."

The lad stepped away from him, perplexed.

"It is rightly yours," Gunnar continued. "Please take it."

"Mine? How is it mine?"

"By your own explanation. This is a valuable piece, easily valuable enough to purchase your own freedom and that of your family, should the need arise. If I do ever decide to sell you, you can buy yourself."

"You are giving this to me? To keep?"

"I am giving it *back* to you. Yes, it is yours, to keep and to use as you will. You now have the wealth you sought, and therefore no further need to steal from those around you. Are we quite clear on this matter?"

"Yes, Jarl." Despite his words the boy still did not take the amulet from him so Gunnar leaned forward and slipped it around his neck. The thick leather thong hung almost to his waist.

"Take good care of what is yours, Donald, as I do."

• • • • • • •

Gunnar sank onto his bed, exhausted. Mairead was in the shared hall, he could hear her voice and that of Aigneis as they banked the fire pit and prepared the longhouse for the night. Donald was already asleep, his prized possession still dangling around his neck. Gunnar knew from her bewildered expression that Mairead had no idea why he had awarded the boy such a gift, but Gunnar did not care. The lad got it, he understood the significance of the amulet and that was sufficient. They had arrived at an understanding, he and Donald, and Gunnar was pleased.

Should he have made more of an example of the lad? Perhaps, but it was for him to decide and the matter was now closed.

He closed his eyes, pulled the furs up around his body, and allowed fatigue to overcome him. In moments he was asleep.

• • • • • • •

Gunnar awoke to silence. The longhouse was sleeping now, and he was surrounded by the deep, pitch darkness of the night. He turned to his side, expecting to encounter the warm body of his bed-slave, and found nothing. He was alone.

What the fuck? If she has run again…

He got out of bed and fumbled in the dark for the lamp he always kept to hand. He lit it with a taper from the smouldering fire pit and used the torch to light his way as he shoved the curtain aside and strode into his deserted hall. He scanned the space, but knew it was empty. The gentle snoring and snuffling sounds from the far end of the longhouse confirmed that his servants were in their beds, but what of Mairead and her little brood?

He moved silently down the hall to the spot where he knew Donald's bed lay. The lad was there, wrapped in blankets, his fingers grasping the amulet even in sleep. Gunnar heaved a sigh of relief. She was here, then. She would not have left without her son.

He moved on, and quickly found what he sought. Mairead had made her own bed on the floor a few feet from Donald's. She slept on her back, Tyra sprawled on top of her. She had collected a few furs but the arrangement did not appear especially warm or comfortable to Gunnar. More to the point, it was not what he had instructed for her.

He sank onto his haunches and reached for her shoulder. "Mairead, wake up."

Her eyes popped open, the sea-green of her eyes dark in the lamplight. "Gunnar? What is it?"

"You disobeyed me. I find I am very displeased with

you."

"I did not. What are you—?"

"Why are you here?" He interrupted her, gesturing to the makeshift bed she had fashioned. "I distinctly recall leaving instructions that you were to sleep in my bed."

"I know that, but…"

"But? If you wish to make excuses, thrall, you may do so in the morning. After I have spanked you for your insubordination. For now, I will require you to go to the place I selected for you. You will put our baby into the cradle beside our bed, and we can all get some sleep." He stood and offered her his hand to help her to rise.

Mairead accepted his assistance and followed him back up the hall to his sleeping chamber. She was barefoot, but wore a long undershirt or sark, made of linen. He noticed that his little thrall shivered in the cool night air but he did not throw extra wood into the fire pit. It was warm in his bed and she would soon enough learn not to leave it. Her bottom would be smarting by the time he was done with her.

Wordlessly she tucked Tyra into her tiny cradle and covered her with the soft blanket provided by Aigneis. The baby never stirred. Mairead scrambled into the still-warm bed and settled among the furs.

Satisfied, Gunnar stretched alongside her. "Come here," he commanded.

She scooted across to him. He turned her so her back was snuggled up hard against his chest and he wrapped his arms around her. "You are cold."

"Not now, Jarl. Now I am warm."

"Good. Then sleep. Tomorrow, we talk."

"Talk? Not spank?"

"Spank, *then* talk," he amended, and laid his palm on the curve of her bottom to better emphasise his intent.

She did not respond, but the gentle sound of her breathing, low and even, told him she slept. He closed his eyes and did likewise.

• • • • • •

"Jarl. Jarl, Tyra is crying."

Gunnar awoke to a none-too-gentle prod to his shoulder. He growled his displeasure.

"Please, she is hungry." Mairead nudged him again.

He buried his nose in the pelt beneath his head. "Are you suggesting I should feed her?"

"Of course not. I must go to her."

"Then why are you pestering me with this news?"

"You said I must not leave the bed without permission. You threatened to spank me if I did."

"I did not threaten, I promised."

"Well—"

"Feed the baby. You have my permission to feed your baby whenever you need to. Do it quietly though."

The bed dipped as she scrambled out. He listened to the low crooning as Mairead plucked the infant from her tiny cot and settled back into his bed with the little one, then near silence when the baby started to feed. Further sleep eluded him and he rolled onto this back to regard the homey sight.

"Is it dawn yet?"

"No, Jarl. But soon, I should think."

"Does she often wake in the middle of the night?"

"Always. I am sorry…"

"Is this why you chose to sleep elsewhere?"

"In part. I did not wish to disturb you. Also, I assumed you would want your bed back, once you returned."

"I have my bed back. What I want is you in it."

"Yes. I know this. I am your bed-slave."

Why did the sound of this on her lips irritate him so? It was, after all, the truth.

"You object to your role here?"

"No, not really. Especially if you will do… that thing again."

"That thing?" He knew exactly what she meant but would hear it from her anyway.

"That thing when you touched me and… it felt very pleasant."

"You mean that thing when I required you to spread your legs for me and I stroked your delightful clitty until you screamed in my ear and spent like a harlot?"

"I am not a harlot." She glared at him, indignation writ across her face. "I could not help what happened yesterday. You—"

He cut off her protest. "Not usually, I grant you that, but I will expect you to play the harlot in my bed, for me. Will you do so, Mairead?"

She hesitated, then, "I expect I shall. If that is how it feels."

"It will be just like that, perhaps better. There is much I have to show you, my slave, and much you will love to learn."

She glanced down at him over the baby's downy head. "Will we return to the pool? I enjoyed our visit there."

"Maybe, if you wish. There is another hot spring however, much closer to Gunnarsholm. We might not find the privacy we desire there, though, since it is a favourite spot for most of my people."

"Oh." She appeared disappointed. He was pleased to see it.

"I could, I suppose, instruct them to leave us to ourselves, though as often as not bathing in the springs is a very public affair for us. Very social. My karls might enjoy watching me fuck you."

She turned her startled gaze on him now. "You would not do that. Please, Gunnar…"

He grinned at her. "No, I would not do that so you may calm yourself. I will not force you to do anything you do not wish to do."

"Except spank me."

"Except spank you, though I am not convinced you truly

do not want that."

It was still too dark for him to see the flush stealing up from her throat, but he was sure she was blushing.

"You should not speak of these things, not in front of Tyra."

"I do not think our baby will object to my words, not for a little while, at least."

He heard the slight hitch in her breath, then silence.

"Mairead? Have I upset you?"

"No, Jarl. But, that is the second time you referred to her thus."

"Referred to who?"

"You called Tyra 'our baby.' You said it last night, also."

He had, it was true. The words had rolled naturally from his tongue. "I helped bring her into the world, I believe that gives me the right…"

"And you own her, as you own all of us."

"I did not mean it in that way. I think of Tyra as…"

"As what, Jarl?"

"Never mind." Gunnar rolled onto his back and closed his eyes again. He longed for sleep, but the moment had passed. After a few minutes he gave up the effort and rose from the bed.

"Where are you going?"

Gunnar reignited the lamp he had used in his earlier search for his missing thrall. Mairead's features now flickered in the guttering light as she regarded him anxiously. The baby still suckled contentedly at her breast. *His* baby, he reminded himself, though he could not quite name the reason he felt that. It was sufficient that he did, and he would not be questioned on it.

"I have work to attend to. You finish feeding Tyra, then get some more sleep. You will remain here until I return. It will be light soon, but do not rise with the rest of the household. And do not dress since I would prefer not to be put to the trouble of stripping you again to spank you."

Her mouth formed a surprised pout, but he did not care

to remain and further discuss his instructions. He had made his wishes plain and she had better do as she was told.

The sooner his bed-slave declared herself fully recovered from the birth and ready to perform all of her new duties, the better. His cock ached; he had to fuck her before much longer or he feared his balls might turn blue and shrivel.

He should have left her to make her lonely and cold bed on a pallet down his hall since it was torture to share his sleeping chamber with her and not plunge his cock into her.

What had he been thinking?

CHAPTER TEN

"No, I am not unwell. The Jarl told me to remain here until he returns." Mairead managed a tremulous smile for Aigneis when the woman lifted the curtain and appeared in the bedchamber.

"I see."

"I wonder, might I beg your help?" Mairead hugged the furs up to her chin, her bedraggled hair tumbling over her shoulders.

"Of course," replied Aigneis.

"Do you have a comb I might borrow? And... could you ensure that, when Gunnar returns, Donald is not within earshot. I am to be spanked, you see, and I fear I might cry out."

"Why?"

"Why...?"

"The spanking? Why?"

"Because I slept elsewhere. He came to seek me out in the night and brought me back here."

"I told you what his wishes were."

"I know, and you were right." Her voice trembled, just a little, but enough to alert the other woman.

"Are you afraid?"

"Yes, a little," Mairead acknowledged, though not so much so as she would have been had this been her first encounter with Gunnar's discipline.

Aigneis laid a soothing hand on Mairead's shoulder. "You have no need to be. He will not harm you. But you are right about the boy. There will be noise and he may not understand."

"And Tyra? Would you take care of her, too? I have just fed her."

"Aye. Tyra too. Meanwhile, I shall bring you food. I believe you will need it."

• • • • • • •

Gunnar returned just as Mairead finished her breakfast of porridge and honey. Donald perched on the edge of the bed, complaining about being confined to the longhouse for six more entire days.

"Seven days," corrected Gunnar as he entered. "Yesterday did not count."

"Yes, Jarl," acknowledged the boy, his face sullen but resigned. "Seven days."

"And you may start by collecting firewood," Aigneis called to Donald from the outer hall. "Come, be quick about it before the rain starts. You may bring your sister too and she can keep me company here by the fire while I spin."

Mairead helped Donald to cradle Tyra in his arms, then sent the boy off to deposit his burden with Aigneis. Gunnar lowered the curtain behind the boy and Mairead appreciated the small degree of seclusion it offered. She lowered her eyes, seized by a sudden and unexpected clenching within her lower abdomen. She wore nothing beneath the sark, and already her inner thighs were damp.

Had this Viking been correct in his outrageous suggestion? Did she actually enjoy a spanking?

She never had before, though in truth an angry backhanded slap across her face, a blow hard enough to send her slamming against the wall of their cottage and leave her lip bleeding bore no resemblance to the erotic sting of Gunnar's palm on her buttocks. Or she thought not, probably.

Would a spanking hurt as much as his belt had? Did he perhaps intend to use his belt again? He had not said, she simply assumed he would—

"Lie across my lap and lift up your sark."

He interrupted her musings with his curt instruction. Gunnar had seated himself on the edge of the bed, where just a few moments ago Donald had sat. The Viking regarded her over his shoulder, his eyes as dark as she had ever seen them and his expression stern.

She had questions, her head brimmed with them, but she supposed all would be answered soon enough. He kept his belt on, which was a relief she supposed. Mairead slipped from the bed and came around to stand before him.

"Shall I take this off?" She plucked at the fabric at the front of her undershirt.

"No. I want you to get in position then raise the sark for me. You will get yourself ready, bare your bottom for me to spank."

Oh, sweet Jesu. Something coiled and tingled between her legs, and she sensed a fluttering within that she could not quite name but she knew her most private places were dampening at his words. It would have been difficult to remove her clothing for him, but she had done it once and could manage again. This different approach of his was more intense, more humiliating. She was to aid in her own punishment by arranging herself just so.

"Mairead, do not keep me waiting."

"No, Jarl." She almost flung herself across his thighs, her head dangling down by his boot and her hair sweeping the floor. She dreaded what she must do next but wanted to get it over with so she reached back to grab the hem of her linen shirt and hastily pulled it up to her waist, then tucked the bulk of the material under her stomach to ensure it remained in place. She was horribly embarrassed, prayed that no one would see fit to open the curtain and see her thus. Had Aigneis managed to get Donald out of the longhouse in time?

"What are you thinking?" His tone was soft, and she took courage from that.

"I am afraid someone will hear, or come in."

"They might, but there is nothing you can do about any of that now. None of what is to happen to you is under your control so you might as well let it go. Relax, if you can, and surrender."

"I do not mean to fight you, Jarl. Or to struggle."

"I know that." He laid one warm, solid palm on her bottom and rubbed a large circle around her left cheek. "I was thinking more of what is happening in your head. You need only to feel this, not think overmuch about it."

"I... I will try, Jarl." Her voice fell to a breathy whisper. Her bottom was still tender from yesterday and as he pressed her delicate skin those sensations returned. How much more punishment could she take?

"You know why this is happening." It was a statement, not a question.

"I disobeyed you."

"Yes, though I now rather think you misunderstood my instruction rather than deliberately disobeyed. You should have checked, asked me to clarify."

"I will, Jarl. Next time."

"I shall make sure of it. So, are you ready?"

"Yes," she breathed. "Yes, I am ready."

The first volley of spanks were light, teasing almost. Gunnar rained slaps down on both her buttocks, covering the sensitive globes and causing her to clench and writhe on his lap, but not to cry out. It was painful, but not overly so and there was pleasure in it too, especially when he paused to caress her smarting skin. Now she moaned, but in startled delight rather than pain.

"You like that?"

She nodded, but then realised he may not have seen her. "Yes, Jarl."

"Will you spread your legs for me?"

"Of course." On one level, she had no choice, he would make her do as he wanted though he did phrase the command most politely. But on another this was exactly what she desired, what she had hoped for. Punishment, submission, sensuality—these were a heady mix and she no longer knew quite how to separate them, or even if she wished to. So she parted her thighs and lay still.

"So pretty, and so wet." He slid his hand between her thighs and stroked her soaking folds. Mairead tensed under the sudden wave of lust that seemed to engulf her. "Did I hurt you?" His voice was soft now, and achingly seductive.

"No, it was... more pleasant than I remembered."

"I see. And this?" Now he toyed with the pleasure nub he had awakened yesterday. Mairead stuffed her fist in her mouth in an attempt not to squeal out loud.

"Answer me. Is this nice?"

"Mmmmm."

Her muffled response clearly did not suffice. He dropped two hard slaps, one on each buttock. "I expect you to talk to me, to answer if I ask you a question. If you do not understand what I want of you, you may tell me that since I know our tongue is still new to you."

"It is very nice, Jarl." She blurted the reply out fast, fearing another onslaught of slaps and craving them at the same time.

"And this?" Now he circled her entrance with his fingertip.

"That too, Jarl. It feels so good..."

"This?" His finger entered her, just to the first knuckle she thought. "Any pain?"

"No, it feels wonderful. Perhaps you might... I mean, maybe a little more?"

"Can I trust you to tell me if I hurt you?"

"You have hurt me. You are spanking me, Jarl. It is

meant to hurt, is it not?"

"The spanking, yes. Not this." He swirled his finger between the swollen, sensitive lips. "You only gave birth a month ago."

"I am healed, truly I am. The birth was easy, and… oh! Ooooh." She let out a sob as he slid his whole finger into her.

"Tell me, Mairead. Is this painful?"

"No. No, it is… wonderful. Please do not stop."

"Greedy wench. You will take your spanking; then, if I am satisfied you have learnt better manners, I will give you what you desire."

"Please…"

She sighed as he withdrew his finger, then squealed when he resumed the spanking. This time he was not playing, not teasing her with gentle taps. He dropped one slap after another, alternating between her buttocks and even covering the backs of her thighs. The strokes where her thighs met the lower curves of her buttocks hurt the most and she could not stifle her anguished cries as the pain built, bloomed, burst across her tender flesh.

"Gunnar, Master, please. Please, I…"

He stopped frequently to rub her inflamed bottom, as though to work the pain right into her body. But it felt exquisite too, sensual and seductive as he caressed and soothed her, waiting until her cries subsided before picking up the spanking again.

"I am sorry. I will obey you, I swear I will. I never meant… Oh. Aaagh!" She begged, pleaded, sobbed against his shins but Gunnar did not let up. Neither did he pause to stroke and soothe any more. Her punishment was unrelenting and Mairead began to wonder if she truly could endure this.

And suddenly, he stopped. He rested his palm on her blazing, inflamed buttock and pressed gently. "What do you have to say to me, thrall?"

Mairead did not hesitate, she knew what was required

and could not get her words out fast enough. Her lack of familiarity with the Norse tongue did not hamper her as she begged for forgiveness.

"I will sleep in your bed, always, and I will obey you. I promise. I am sorry. I thought… I should have asked you, I know that now."

"You make a pretty apology, my slave. I believe spanking you when you require it will prove rewarding, and fruitful."

"Yes, Gunnar." She could think of no better response, though she hoped he would not find cause to repeat this exercise too frequently. Except… her private places were tingling, her inner thighs felt unusually moist. What was happening to her?

"Now, I believe I promised you a reward. It is time to further expand your knowledge of what transpires between men and women."

"Yes, Gunnar," she repeated. "Yes, please." She no longer claimed to possess such knowledge. Indeed, the depth of her prior ignorance became more apparent with every moment she passed in Gunnar's company. And her curiosity soared.

"Now you may remove your sark, and lie across my bed. On your back, your legs spread wide for me."

She obeyed, though not without a lingering wariness despite his promise not to hurt her. He had seemed unusually concerned at the prospect, in fact. The sark landed in a crumpled heap at his feet and she stepped around him to lie on the bed. Her legs, however, remained firmly closed. Twenty-five summers of deeply ingrained modesty were not shed overnight, however tempting and seductive the man.

She half expected that he would order her to spread for him, his tone assuming that iron core of authority that would tolerate no disobedience. He did not, though the wry smile he allowed himself suggested he had noted her reluctance. He leaned over her, his hands on either side of her shoulders, and she shivered in the knowledge that he remained fully clothed whilst she lay naked beneath him.

He curled his sensual mouth in a slight smile. His eyes were the colour of pitch, his hair blacker still as it fell forward to frame his strong features. He had never looked more handsome to her, nor more intimidating. She started to part her legs, then lost all sense of what she should be doing when he lowered his head further to brush his lips across hers.

It had been so long since a man had kissed her. Niall had, on occasion; Alred, never. And no grateful peck to express appreciation after a night of intimacy came close to the sweetly sensual caress of this dark Viking's lips on hers. His tongue teased the seam of her mouth and she parted her lips, then gasped when he plunged inside. Never, never had she experienced such as this before. She opened her mouth wider, intrigued as he stroked his tongue over hers, teasing her, playing with her, inviting her to join his sensual dance. She reached for him, cradled his jaw between her hands and lifted her shoulders from the mattress as she returned his kiss. He leaned in further, his elbows now on the bed as he deepened the kiss. Mairead was floating, grasping at him as though he were the one solid entity anchoring her to the earth.

She moaned when he at last broke the kiss, but arched her back as he licked and nipped his way down her throat and across her shoulder.

He did not stop there. Lower he went, to nudge her swollen nipple with his nose, then he opened his mouth and drew the turgid bud between his lips. It felt good, that sweet, sensuous tug as he pressed his tongue on the underside of the pebbled nub, the sensation at once familiar but quite unlike the greedy suckling of her baby. This was lazy, leisurely, playful, and transient as he ventured further down her body.

Gunnar paused to nibble at her belly button. It tickled, and she laughed out loud, wriggling as he held her steady for more.

Mercifully he did not linger long and soon resumed his

travels, this time pausing to kiss the nest of curls at the apex of her thighs. He would start back up soon, and perhaps kiss her mouth again as he had a few moments before. That would be nice.

"Oh. Oh!" Mairead yelped as he used his hands to part her thighs. This was unexpected, quite bizarre. What was he doing...?

"No. No, you must not!" His intent became obvious at last when he used his thumbs to part the lips of her sex. He was there, between her now widespread thighs, looking at her, gazing at that place that no one should ever see, expect perhaps in childbirth. But not like this, not as though he might like to—

"Oooh!" The breath left her in a whoosh when he lowered his head and drew his tongue along the length of her slit. "What are you doing? You should not..."

She abandoned her protests when he ignored her and did it again, then again. The sensation was exquisite, quite beyond description. Her body hummed with pleasure, despite the wickedness of this Viking's truly spectacular actions.

"Please," she moaned, though she was no longer certain what she pleaded for.

He lifted his head to look at her, meeting her eyes with that stern but steady gaze, that expression of utter confidence and authority that would brook no argument. "I have already explained that what is happening to you is not under your control. You are mine, you know this. I could tie you to the bed, but I prefer not to. You will lie still, and let me do with you as I will. Yes?"

She shook, her entire body trembling under the combined pressure of his will, and her longing for those feelings he had just evoked and that she wished to never end. She had no choice, he was right. And knowing this, she was released, absolved of all responsibility. She could submit, she *must* submit and he would give her everything she desired and more.

"Yes," she murmured. "Yes, I will be still."

He smiled. "I know you will," he agreed. "You will play the harlot for me because I ask it, and because you want it too. You want this…" He traced the outline of her entrance with the tip of his tongue. "And you want this…" He parted her lips with his fingers and plunged his tongue right inside her—in, then out, then in once more and swirled it around.

Mairead writhed on the mattress, failing completely to remain still. Her inner muscles clenched, something hot and greedy snaked from deep in her core to bring her hips thrusting up. She lifted her body, pressing harder against his mouth, his lips, his wicked, sensual tongue.

"Gunnar, please, I need to… oh… oh."

Her cries fell on deaf ears, or rather on ears that chose to ignore her strangled, incoherent mumblings. Gunnar continued to drive his tongue inside her, at the same time as his thumb found that needy little nubbin again and he rubbed.

She was close, her climax would soon be upon her and there was nothing she could do. What he was doing to her was wrong. It was decadent, dirty, and quite delightful and she could not get enough of it. Mairead's fingers were in his hair, twisting the soft, ebony locks around her digits as she sought to hang on to something, anything…

Her release drew a long, anguished moan from deep in her throat. Her body went rigid as waves of pleasure pulsed through her, then boneless as the delight ebbed and her muscles relaxed. He continued to lick and nuzzle and flick her nether lips with his tongue as her world tilted then reoriented itself. Only when she lay quite still did he raise his head to look at her again.

"That was perfect. You respond beautifully, my slave."

She had no answer for him. What *could* she say? It was not as though she might claim responsibility for her body's enthusiastic reaction, she could not help it. He made her feel things she had never so much as imagined and want things she could never have.

Or could she?

"Gunnar, please make love to me."

"Did I not just do so?"

"Inside me. I want you inside me. Your cock."

"Ah, now that would be nice. Are you quite certain this is what you want, my slave?"

"Yes, yes, *yes*!"

"I may not be gentle…"

"Despite what you say, I believe you will be gentle because you always are. In any case, I am not made of eggshells." She drew a long breath and sought to soften her impatient tone. He did not take issue with her impertinence, so she continued. "Please, Gunnar, I need you to… I need more."

"Then you shall have it, my demanding little slave." He rolled from the mattress, and in scant moments had shed his clothing. Mairead watched with undisguised interest, taking in the sculpted planes and hollows of his chest, the sprinkling of dark hair that arrowed down to the thicker thatch at his groin. She admired his corded muscles, the way they rippled beneath his skin. This dark Viking was a powerful man, strong, capable of terrifying violence as she had witnessed back in her homeland, but also capable of showing tenderness and caring. He had been kind to her from the start, he had protected her when she needed him, and he had been gentle with her children. This incongruous mix was proving to be a potent charm, evoking a lust and need within her that she had never experienced before and found herself uncertain as to how to handle it. Was she permitted to demand, to request, to just reach out and take as he would?

Gunnar approached the bed and Mairead abandoned any remaining inhibitions. As soon as he was beside her she wrapped her slender fingers around his cock and leaned forward to inhale the musky, masculine aroma of it. The head was shiny and smooth, glistening with the clear beads of moisture that dribbled from the very tip. Without thinking she smoothed the pad of her thumb across the crown and spread the wetness about, then leaned in to taste him.

Gunnar groaned and she withdrew at once, an apology springing to her lips.

"No, do not be afraid. That was glorious and you may be sure that I will appreciate more such attentions in the future. But now, I want only to fuck you. I need to be inside you."

"Yes, Master," she breathed.

He eased her down and onto her back. This time she spread her thighs wide without being instructed and gazed up at him, trusting him absolutely.

CHAPTER ELEVEN

By Odin's balls, this Celt is lovely. She possessed more than a mere prettiness, though his captive was without doubt a beauty. Gunnar paused to take in the glorious mane of amber curls and the mossy green of her eyes, the features that had first arrested his attention. He had more recently come to properly appreciate the soft swell of her lush breasts, the curve of her hips, the delicate contours of her long legs, her finely boned ankles. The sweet sight of her dainty fingers around his solid length had near enough unhinged him. Had she not begged for his cock he might have fallen to his knees himself.

She smiled at him and his erection lurched, his balls tightening in pained response. He had to have her. Now.

She was wet, ready for him. He positioned the glistening head of his cock at the entrance to her slick, tight channel and waited for several moments. Mairead gave an impatient mewl and shifted beneath him as though she would wait no longer and sought to somehow lift herself from the mattress and impale herself on his cock.

Maybe on another occasion he would permit that, but for now, this first time, he would control her. This was his way, his preference, she must submit.

Gunnar drove his cock forward, filling his slave in one long, smooth stroke. She gasped, quivered around his cock, but did not cry out. He remained motionless even so, scanning her features for any sign of distress. There was none. She returned his gaze, her emerald eyes dark with passion and need, her lips slack with lust.

He kissed her again, for no better reason than he felt like it. She tightened her sweet cunt around him, perhaps deliberately, perhaps not but he did not care. She gripped him, her channel hot and narrow and wrapped around his cock like the close-fitting leggings he favoured. He could no longer discern where he ended and she began.

"Mairead…" he growled. "This will not take long…"

"Then you may be required to do it all over again, Master." She lifted her hips, moving them in a seductive circle. There was no doubt she did so on purpose now.

"Impudent wench. You require further chastisement?"

"I require you to do what you have promised, Gunnar. Make love to me. Please. Do it hard, and… and…"

"Ah, lost for words at last? Thank all the gods for that." He withdrew his cock slowly, until he was almost completely out of her, only to drive it back again. He stroked in and out of her sweet channel, long and deep, and watched in wonder as her eyes widened. She lifted her legs and hooked her ankles in the small of his back, and grasped his shoulders with her slender fingers. She clung to him as though she feared he might slip away from her. She need have no fear of that.

He shortened his strokes now, jabbing his cock in and out of her entrance. She went wild beneath him, writhing, squeezing, her cunt convulsing around him. Leaning his weight on his left elbow he used his right hand to slip between their bodies and caress her swollen clitty, rubbing, pressing, pinching as she moaned her delighted pleasure.

"Come for me, little one. I want to feel your release on my cock."

"I cannot… I am not sure…"

He could not wait, it had to be now. "Come for me," he demanded. Gunnar rolled her clit between his finger and thumb at the same time as he buried his cock in her right to the root. It was enough, too much. She contracted around him, her entire body shivering as her climax crested.

His cock leapt within her warm, wet sheath. His aching balls twisted painfully within their sack and he roared as they expelled the first spurt of semen. The viscous fluid surged forth to fill her with his own hotness, pumping, gushing until he, too, was spent.

Gunnar collapsed onto the woman beneath him, only just managing to shift his weight in time to avoid crushing her. He pressed his face into the mattress beside her shoulder and groaned.

"Are you all right?" She sounded concerned. Gunnar would have laughed out loud if he thought for one moment he could spare the breath.

"Yes," he managed. "You?"

"I am well, thank you. You were very gentle, and I thank you for your consideration. Perhaps next time though, you might be a little less … restrained."

Gunnar gave serious consideration to the notion of restraining his impudent thrall, and possibly gagging her for good measure, but dismissed it. A far more appealing thought had taken root already and he would remain silent no longer.

"You are mine. You do not dispute this?"

"Jarl?"

"Do you dispute the matter, Mairead?"

"No, I do not. Have I displeased you? I merely thought—"

"Then you shall be my wife. I prefer that—to slave."

"You…? What? What did you say, Jarl?"

"We shall be wed. Soon. At once."

"But … why? I am… I mean, I thought…"

He turned his head to regard her startled features. She had never looked lovelier, or more desirable. Ah, yes, he would make her his wife and it would be among the best bargains he ever struck. He slung his arm across her shoulders and pulled her to him.

"Because I wish to, and because I can. Do you object to such an arrangement?" *And would it matter to him if she did?*

Mairead sat up, her beautiful breasts bobbing just above his eye level. Gunnar's mouth watered and his cock began to harden again, but the expression in her eyes now was serious, enough to give him pause. Something was amiss with his delightful slave turned bride-to-be.

"It is not that I object. As you say, I am yours, to do with as you decide."

"It is not quite so simple, and well you know it. I would not take your body by force, nor will I claim the rest of your life if you do not wish to give it. I believe you want me."

"I did. I do. But is not merely a matter of what I want. I have…responsibilities."

"And duties. To me." He was being unfair, demanding that to which he had no right. But she could not refuse him, he would not permit it.

Mairead straightened her body and stiffened her shoulders. She met his gaze, her expression one of grim determination. "Very well, I will marry you, but I have conditions. You must promise me that you will treat my children as you would your own. You must care for them and… and never shout. Not at them, not at me."

He glared at her, incredulous. "You would seek to bargain with me? Perhaps I should take a switch to you by way of a response to your terms."

Tears formed in her eyes and he wished he might bite back the sharp words. He had frightened her, and needlessly since he had not the slightest intention of hurting her, not over this. But he had terms of his own, and since she had raised the matter of her children…

"Tyra and Donald have no place in this discussion. It is between us, you and me."

"But—"

He raised his hand to lay a finger across her lips. "Be quiet, and listen to me. Heed me well on this, Mairead, because it matters that you understand my words." He furrowed his brow and waited for her nod of acknowledgement before he continued. "Tyra was fathered by another man, but she is mine now. The moment she slithered into my hands, covered in blood and began screaming fit to rouse the dead, she was mine. Nothing you may do, or not do, will alter that. Our child is not to be bargained with. Donald is more complicated. I know he does not wish for another stepfather but I believe he and I have now arrived at an understanding. I will continue to do what I may to help him grow into the man he can be, and again, I will do this whether you and I wed or not. He is my thrall; he lives in my house; he is my responsibility." Gunnar paused to let these matters take root between her beautiful ears before continuing. "You have managed to vex me on a number of occasions. Your lad, also. I do not recall ever shouting at either of you. I will raise my voice to my men, to urge them into battle, but that is not my way with my family."

She did not answer, Mairead just gazed at him, her eyes wide, her lips parted in stunned surprise.

"Do you have anything more to say on the subject of shouting, or might we move on to the matter of *your* wishes now?"

"My wishes…?"

"Do you wish to be my wife? It is a simple enough question."

"I… I had not thought to marry again. Alred was… not a pleasant companion, and—"

"I am not him. It will be different, between us. I have already shown you that, have I not?"

"Yes," she whispered. "You are a warrior, dark and perfectly terrifying, but I do not fear you as I did him."

"We have spoken enough of that man. Know that I will never raise my hand to you in anger, nor will I shout at you.

Know also that whatever might pass between us, I will not harm your children. I will protect them and you. I know you desire me, in time you will learn to love me, perhaps."

"Will you learn to love me?" she whispered.

He shook his head and gave her a wry smile. "No, little one. I will not need to for I already adore you. So, will you become my wife?"

She waited, eying him curiously before finally inclining her head in a studied nod. "You drive a hard bargain, Jarl, but I believe I might agree to your terms. If you will be so kind as to make love to me again…"

"Then we have arrived at an understanding." Gunnar rolled onto his back. "Though if you believe I shall allow you to become lazy whilst I do all the work in our bed then you are quite wrong. This time, you will ride me."

"I… oh…" She peered at him, her face a mask of confusion.

"Ah, have we stumbled upon yet another gap in your knowledge of that which transpires between a man and a woman?" He grinned at her and gestured with his fingers that she was to rise up onto her knees. "Now, you straddle me. Do you understand this word?"

"I believe that I do, Jarl." Mairead scrambled into position, one knee on either side of his waist.

"Excellent. Now you will shift back a little, and lower yourself onto my cock."

"Is that possible? I have never—"

"It is. Please proceed."

She shuffled back until her damp cunt hovered above his straining erection. Gunnar smiled at her again. "On this occasion, since you are new to this, you may use your hands to guide my cock into your body."

"How? Like this?" She took hold of his cock and carefully angled it so that the round, slick head rested between the lips of her pussy.

"Yes. Exactly like that," he breathed. "Now, lower yourself down. Slowly. Take all of it."

146

She chewed on her lower lip, her delicate features rapt in intense concentration as she sank onto his cock. She watched the place where their bodies joined, and stopped several times to glance back up at him as though seeking his approval. On each occasion he nodded, urging her on. At last she was fully seated, her bottom resting on his thighs. Her eyes were closed now, her lips slightly parted. "Did I do well, Jarl?"

"You did. You surely did. Are you comfortable?"

"I… I would not say that, exactly."

"Any pain?"

"No."

"In that case, you may move whenever it pleases you."

"How? What should I do?" She looked quite lost.

"Whatever feels good to you." He placed his hands on her hips and moved them in a circular motion and grinned as she let out a long, low moan. Next he lifted her a couple of inches, then allowed her to sink back onto him again. His reward was more moaning and a sensual sigh. "There, you get the idea now?" He released her hips and moved his hands around to the front to peel back the slick folds that barely covered her clitty. He laid the pad of his thumb on the engorged nub. "Rub against my thumb. Seek your release, do whatever you must to achieve it."

Her eyes popped open in sudden understanding of her own power to claim her pleasure, and his. She lifted her hips and lowered them again, this time using her inner muscles to increase the friction. Now it was Gunnar's turn to groan. He prayed she would find her climax soon for he could not stand much of this.

Mairead quickly eased into a sensual rhythm—lifting, lowering, rising, falling, all the while slowly rotating her hips in a manner calculated to drive him wild. She leaned forward, her plump breasts swaying before his eyes as she moved. Gunnar reached up to cup the soft mounds, testing their weight in his hands as he gently squeezed her deep pink nipples. He traced the outline of her aureole, admiring the contrast of dusky pink against the creaminess of her skin. Soon, when she was no longer feeding the infant, he might enjoy more sport here. And so might she if her contented expression was any indication.

"Gunnar, I need… Oh, yes, just like that. Yes, *yes*!" Her breathy moans were louder now, her demands more insistent. His own arousal built and threatened to crest soon. Too soon.

"Be still a moment. Allow me to help you…" He took over the action now, his fingers skimming her clitty as he gauged her response. He kept the pressure light at first, then increased the intensity of his caress until she cried out his name. Her features contorted in pleasure and her inner muscles convulsed about him. He bore the rippling caress as long as he could, then thrust up—hard. His shout was guttural as his own release surged forth again.

This woman would milk him dry, and he would love her all the more for it.

CHAPTER TWELVE

The wedding took place two weeks later. It was a quiet affair since Gunnar required no fuss, Mairead even less. There was no dynastic alliance to negotiate, no dowry to claim, just a few words spoken before his men and his followers and a feast for all at Gunnarsholm. If any considered the hasty marriage of a Viking Jarl to a Celtic thrall in any way worthy of comment, they did not share such a view publicly.

Tyra slept throughout the entire process. Donald sat beside his mother at the table in their hall, his face quite unreadable, as though the boy did not dare to express his fears. The boy's anxious features awakened a memory in Gunnar, one he had thought long buried, of being taken into his father's longhouse soon after the death of his mother. He had been a similar age then to Donald now, and just as scared though he would never have admitted as much. He was uncertain of his welcome, his place in this new home. Was he part of the family, or an outsider, a slave still?

His father, the Jarl, was always kind enough, though strict. Frey of Skarthveit treated his sons well, and expected much of them. He made no distinction between the legitimate one and the one born a bastard. But it was Solveig, his father's wife and Gunnar's new stepmother, or so he had always thought of her, who defined his childhood.

Solveig was an austere woman who ran their household with a rod of iron. All knew better than to disobey or rile her. In return, though Solveig was fierce, she loved her children dearly and this included Gunnar right from the moment he arrived, trembling at her table. He recalled that she set a bowl of broth before him, told him she was sorry for his loss, tousled his hair then bade him eat. When his stomach was filled she showed him where he was to sleep, in a warm spot right next to Ulfric.

Solveig offered little in the way of outward affection, not to any of them, but by her deeds Gunnar knew she cared for him every bit as much as for her natural born son. Her generosity to him was not effusive, but from that very first day he was never in any doubt of his welcome in her longhouse. She accepted him without question and he grew up under her stern, efficient care. Gunnar never forgot Solveig's understated kindness to a small, scared child and in return he became utterly devoted to her.

He knew of her affection for sure when, perhaps a year after entering her domain, he fell from a tree and broke his arm. He had climbed the massive Norwegian pine because Ulfric dared him, urging him to reach an osprey's nest that the older boy swore was up there. Solveig was furious with her son and whipped Ulfric for causing his brother to be hurt. She bound Gunnar's injured arm and took the smaller boy into the bed she shared with their father until he ceased crying with pain at night.

Solveig might appear cold, he could not deny that. Many considered her distant and aloof, but to him she had been there when he needed her, always utterly reliable. Although a grown man by then he had wept when she died, and he missed her still. Solveig had become his rock, and now this frightened little boy who shared his longhouse needed the same certainty he had been given.

Gunnar knew what he must do. He rose from the table and leaned down to speak into the lad's ear.

"Come with me, Donald."

The boy swivelled on the bench, his face white. Gunnar turned and strode for the door.

Outside, he waited for the boy to catch him up, then led the way to the stables. He was aware that Donald spent much of his time here since his punishment for the thefts had been completed. The boy was fascinated by horses, and Gunnar would use that now to his advantage. He entered the low building and approached the first stall, occupied by a dappled gelding he had acquired a few days previously. The animal was small and well-mannered and Gunnar had purchased him as a mount for his new bride.

"I have watched you grooming Knut. I had thought him a decent horse for your mother. What is your view, Donald?"

"He is very gentle, Jarl. She will like him, I think." The boy reached up to pat the horse's velvety muzzle.

"Do you like him?"

"Oh, yes. He is beautiful. I have been taking care of him. Will I still be allowed to do that?"

"You may. I believe your mother would appreciate your assistance as she is so often busy with Tyra, or helping Aigneis. I find though, that when we travel beyond Gunnarsholm I prefer her to ride with me. This little fellow will become fat if he is left in the stables overmuch."

"I… I will walk him. I will make sure he gets the exercise he needs."

"Better that you should ride him. A horse needs to gallop, not walk. I suspect a boy does, also. Certainly I always felt that it was so."

The boy's face fell. "I do not ride, Jarl. I am sorry."

"Then you must learn, and quick. I shall teach you. We start tomorrow."

"I have no horse." The lad looked bewildered.

"You do now. Knut shall be yours. I shall purchase

another mount for your mother."

"Mine? He is mine?" The lad moved closer to the horse, patting the silky neck.

"He is." Gunnar went down on his haunches to bring his eyes on a level with the small boy. "You were born a Celt, Donald, but you will grow up among Vikings. A Viking must ride, so he needs a horse. Now, you have one. Learn well, become a fine horseman and make me proud."

The boy gaped at him, open-mouthed. Gunnar winked and stood. "We should return to the feast. You will sit beside me?"

"Yes, sir." Donald trotted back across the settlement at Gunnar's side, chattering endlessly about his plans for Knut, his enthusiasm and excitement almost palpable as they resumed their seats in the hall.

Mairead glanced across at her son, frowning.

"Where have you been?" she whispered in Gunnar's ear. "And what have you done with my timid son?"

"We went to the stables. I have bribed him with a horse. And I told him how he could make me proud."

"You are a cunning man, Gunnar Freysson, and I love you."

"It is kind of you to say so, wife, particularly as the horse was to have been yours. I love you too." He reached for a steaming dish. "More carrots, my sweet?"

· · · · · · ·

Gunnar found married life very much to his liking. His habit had been to spend much time out of doors, or away on trading or hunting expeditions, but he found himself seeking to curtail such absences. He became inordinately fond of his hearth, or more accurately, his bed.

Aigneis was most obliging also in her willingness to whisk Tyra off on some domestic errand or other whenever Gunnar appeared in the longhouse doorway. As for the lad, he was invariably out of the house in any case, spending most of his waking hours in the stables. Donald was proving to be an adept pupil and had taken to the saddle with a natural ability. He had an easy way with horses, the boy's usual shyness dropping away when in their company. He had discovered his niche, he was happy. Gunnar was relieved; he had not expected that situation to be so easily resolved.

He lay on his back, a fur drawn across his abdomen to offer a cursory nod at modesty in case his servant might return. Mairead bustled about their chamber, seeking to restore her clothing to some semblance of order following a most pleasant half hour tumbling with him among the blankets.

"I must go to Hafrsfjord." He made his announcement to her back as she bent to poke at the glowing embers in the fire pit. "I have ewes which need to be taken to the market there, and we will need to purchase supplies for the winter. I have delayed the trip, but I cannot put it off much longer."

Mairead turned to regard him. "I see. Will you be away for long, Jarl?"

"A sennight, perhaps two. I was thinking I might make a detour to Skarthveit on the return journey."

"Skarthveit?" Mairead recalled Hafrsfjord, the bustling port where she and the other female slaves had been landed when they first arrived on these shores. Her memories of the cold, wet quayside were not pleasant ones, but that was behind her now. She did not recall mention of Skarthveit before.

"It is the homestead of my brother, Ulfric. You will have seen him. He prevented his slave master from killing your friend that day."

Mairead shuddered. She had never been so afraid in her life. "Yes, I remember. He had blond hair."

"Aye. He favours our father more than I. He does not know of our marriage yet so I should visit him and share the glad news."

"Oh."

"So, it would be best if you were to accompany me. You may make the acquaintance of your wider family. I have a sister, also, and a nephew."

"Oh." Now she stood and stared at him warily. "Are you sure?"

"Quite sure. I *do* have a nephew, and a sister. I would not make a mistake on such a matter."

"Fool. I mean, are you sure you want me there? What if they do not approve of your choice?"

"They will. Or more properly, they will not mind one way or the other. I am the bastard son of my father, a Freysson but not with any expectation of inheriting. Nor was it ever assumed I might marry in order to forge an alliance of any sort. Fine Viking families do not offer their daughters to bastards. I grew up in my father's house beside my brother and sister. I love them dearly and they love me. Our family is close, but I am on the outside, so my life is my own. Gunnarsholm is mine. I live as I please. I marry as I please."

"But…"

"You will be made welcome in my brother's longhouse, I promise you this. So will our children."

"They are to come too? Both of them?"

"Tyra is too young to be left behind, and Donald would, I suspect, take it amiss if he were not allowed to accompany us. So yes, both of them."

"When do you wish to go?"

"Soon, before the weather closes in for the winter. Within the next few days if we can manage it."

Mairead nodded, and he could tell that she was already planning the trip. "Very well. I shall talk to Aigneis about supplies for the journey."

CHAPTER THIRTEEN

The journey back to Hafrsfjord was considerably less arduous than the first time Mairead covered the route, not least because she was not expected to cover the distance on foot. She rode with Gunnar, or made use of one of the small wagons they took with them to carry supplies. Tyra was usually in her arms, or tucked within Gunnar's cloak. A delighted Donald rode his own small mount. Despite being new to horsemanship the boy sat the horse with a straight back and controlled the animal with an ease that appeared far more practised. Gunnar had told her of her son's prowess, now she saw for herself.

At night they slept under the stars, and she enjoyed the warmth of Gunnar's body as she snuggled up to him, Tyra nestling between them. They were on the road for three days before the roofs of the coastal town came into sight. As they neared the port Mairead scanned the boats moored in the harbour, seeking the one that had brought her to this land. She could not be sure if it was there, and perhaps that was for the best since those were not among her more pleasant memories.

"How long will we stay here?" she enquired of her husband, seated behind her in the saddle.

"The market takes place tomorrow. I am hoping to sell all our livestock within the day and acquire the goods we require. If I am successful we can leave for Skarthveit the following day if you wish. Or would you prefer to remain here for longer?"

"No, I am happy to leave as soon as our business is concluded." She did not wish to let Gunnar know how much she dreaded the coming meeting with her new family, but saw no merit in delaying the inevitable. She turned to gaze straight ahead as their party made their way down into the bustling port.

Gunnar's business was transacted with all the speed and efficiency he had hoped for and it was a well-satisfied Viking chief who ordered his men to load the newly purchased supplies onto their wagons and prepare to depart for Skarthveit. Mairead was startled to see a new slave among her husband's purchases.

"Gunnar, why have you purchased that poor wee lass? She looks quite terrified." The girl in question, aged about eighteen by Mairead's estimation, huddled among the sacks of grain on one of their wagons, her blue eyes wide with apprehension. She shrank away each time any of the Viking warriors approached the cart.

Gunnar glanced in the direction of the trembling girl.

"I find that my longhouse is suddenly full of children, and with a new mistress to serve also, Aigneis needs help. The wench will do well enough."

"But, I can assist Aigneis. We do not require more slaves."

"You would prefer I leave the lass here to take her chances? If you truly do not want her with us I shall put her back into the market, but I consider it best all round that she comes to Gunnarsholm."

"She is very pretty," observed Mairead doubtfully.

"Aye, Steinn has already pointed that out," agreed her husband. He turned to face her, cradling her face between his hands as he held her gaze. "Do you object to the wench?

I will not bring her to our home if you do."

Mairead shook her head. "No, I do not object. But, I am not comfortable that we should own slaves."

Gunnar merely shrugged. Although his memories of his natural mother were at best hazy, he had been very young when she died, Gunnar could never truly forget that he was himself born a thrall. As an adult, and a member of the ruling Jarl, this still tempered his attitude toward his slaves. He was not a man much given to personal reflection and rarely thought of his humble origins, but at some level he was aware that to do otherwise would be to dishonour the woman who gave him his life, and whose name was now carried by a child he loved.

"It is a name only. There is no difference at Gunnarsholm between thralls and karls. No one wears chains, all are fed equally, all are well housed, all must work. All must obey me as master."

"I know, but—"

He bent his head to kiss her mouth. "It is our way, sweetheart. The girl will fare well enough with us."

Mairead managed a small nod. "What is her name?"

"I do not know. She is a Saxon; that is all I can tell you. Perhaps you might go and speak with her, offer some reassurance that she is not about to be raped or beaten." He furrowed his handsome brow as he regarded the cowering wench. "By Thor's balls, she needs it."

"I know little of the English tongue but I shall do my best." Mairead returned her husband's kiss then started across the dirt track in the direction of their wagon. It never occurred to her to doubt Gunnar's assurance.

• • • • • • •

They had spent just two nights in Hafrsfjord, quite long enough as far as Mairead was concerned. She had learnt enough of the Norse tongue by now to understand most of the speech around her. She picked up on the muttered threats and sly looks her husband seemed to attract, especially from the followers of one Jarl in particular.

Gunnar appeared unconcerned, even when Olaf Bjarkesson barged right into him in the crowds at the market. Despite the teeming throng surrounding the stock pens Mairead believed the act to be deliberate, and she wondered at her husband's forbearance. Gunnar merely nodded to the other man and offered him a bright smile, which seemed to infuriate his adversary yet more. Bjarkesson disappeared into the crowd, his scowl fit to curdle milk.

"What was that about?" She tugged on her husband's sleeve to attract his attention.

Gunnar's expression was serious now, his feigned smile absent as he regarded her. "An old quarrel, aimed at my brother rather than me, though we are kin so…" He shrugged. "We had hoped this ill feeling would abate. Clearly, it has not."

"What did your brother do to him?"

"Olaf is of the opinion that Ulfric killed his sister and one of his brothers. He is wrong, but that is of little use to us now. The blood feud has gone on for years and, if anything, Olaf has become even more bitter as time has passed."

"His sister? And a brother?" Mairead clutched her baby to her as though she half-expected Olaf Bjarkesson to return and wreak his vengeance upon her child. "What happened?"

"Astrid Bjarkesson, Olaf's sister, was Ulfric's wife. She died, and Olaf is convinced Ulfric murdered her. It is nonsense; my sister-in-law died of a sudden illness. It could not be helped. Ulfric was not even present at the time but Olaf will not listen. The brother, Eirik, was betrothed to our sister. He met his end in a raid on a Celtic settlement on Orkney and Olaf blames Ulfric for the boy's loss because my brother led the attack. I was present also on that raid and can attest that Eirik made an ill-fated attempt to take on

158

four Celts wielding pitchforks whilst he himself was armed with nothing more than a short sword. The lad was a fool, a liability. He was young and stupid, but even so his death was a grievous loss to both families. Our sister mourns her betrothed still, and Olaf refuses to accept that there was little Ulfric could have done to prevent the tragedy."

"I can understand the man's grief, but..." Mairead was uncertain quite what to say. She harboured little sympathy for a Viking warrior who perished when seeking to attack innocent villagers. Perhaps if her own community had been handier with their pitchforks, she and the rest might not have been taken.

And she would not have become the wife of this darkly handsome Viking. Her children would still be fatherless, her little family would continue to eke out a living on the scraps handed out by others. No, she could not regret the events that had transformed her life.

Gunnar slung an arm about her shoulders and pulled her to him. "I believe we can all sympathise. The bonds of kinship are important, but Bjarkesson cannot see reason. There has been much muttering whilst we have been here, threats, murmurings of an attack planned upon my brother's settlement. Olaf goes too far."

"What will you do?"

"I shall warn my brother, certainly, and I will come to his aid if Olaf carries out his threats."

"Are we safe, at Gunnarsholm?"

"Yes, I am certain of that. My settlement is three days' ride away. Olaf is belligerent and vengeful, but he is also lazy. And his target is Ulfric, not me."

Mairead considered this reasoning and had to agree but still, she shuddered. Olaf Bjarkesson scared her.

• • • • • • •

"Tell me of your brother's home. What is it like?" Mairead again shared Gunnar's horse, Tyra sleeping quietly within her cloak.

Gunnar had sent the new slave, Edyth, and those men who could be spared straight back to Gunnarsholm so the party remaining with them was now much smaller. It did not do to descend on another settlement, however warm and genuine their welcome, unannounced and bringing many unnecessary mouths to be fed.

They were nearing the other Viking settlement, the place called Skarthveit where, Mairead assumed, most of the Celts taken with her would have ended up. The chief of her village, Taranc, was among those abducted along with his betrothed, Fiona. The last time she saw the daughter of the lord of Pennglas, the girl was lying injured beside the road. Mairead's own lowly status had meant that Taranc and Fiona were not among her friends, but she had come to like Fiona on the voyage over the North Sea and hoped she had fared well enough in her new circumstances. Though he had lived in the same village Taranc was a stranger to her, really, but she knew him to be a fine man and a good chief. He would not accept enslavement easily.

"Skarthveit is bigger than Gunnarsholm. It was built by our father and inherited by Ulfric on his death. There are more people there, many thralls and slaves as well as free Vikings or karls as we would call them. Ulfric is building a granary, and a harbour as he intends to keep his longships there."

"He has many ships?"

"Five dragon ships. Or perhaps six by now."

"He is engaged in much raiding, then?"

"Yes, but he trades also. And there is a small fishing fleet. The vessel you sailed on was a fishing boat."

"Why do you not live there? I know you and he are close."

"A village requires only one chief or Jarl, and I prefer to live a less rigid existence outside the confines of a Viking community. Even as the son of the chief, or nowadays the brother, my illegitimate status sets me apart. In my own settlement I can hunt, trade as I see fit, raid when I wish to. I answer to none, but Ulfric is my ally and my kinsman. We are the same blood and are bound together by that."

"And your sister? Are you close to her also?"

Gunnar seemed to hesitate before replying. Mairead turned to peer up at him.

"Yes," he answered at last, "yes, we are close enough I daresay."

It did not sound so, to Mairead. "Tell me about her. Has she married another, since her betrothed died on Orkney?"

"No, she has not. I wish she had."

Mairead did not comment, merely waited for her husband to elaborate. Eventually Gunnar obliged her.

"Brynhild never quite recovered from her loss, though I struggle to comprehend why. Eirik was a nice enough lad, but not exactly sharp-witted if you take my meaning. He would have made a piss-poor husband for her."

"Oh. You did not approve of the match?"

"No. Yes." He shrugged. "It was an agreement between our father and Olaf's uncle, the previous chief of their family so of course we all approved. But Brynhild would have trampled all over Eirik. She might have been younger but was ever the brightest among us as we were growing up, and would have soon become bored by Eirik's slowness. She would do better to wed a man who is her equal, a man she can respect, who might even have obedience from her. There are plenty such men about and she would have no trouble securing a husband for herself. She is a beauty, much sought after, with a fine dowry to offer. But Brynhild flatly refuses to so much as contemplate another marriage, declares herself heartbroken over her poor, lost Eirik."

"She must have loved him very much."

"Aye, you would think so, though she never showed much sign of it whilst he lived. She liked him well enough, we all did. She was happy with the match but the deep and abiding passion she now claims was never in evidence."

"So, what are you saying? That she feigned affection for

her betrothed?"

"I am saying that I am baffled. Whatever Brynhild might claim, her betrothal to Eirik Bjarkesson was not the love match she insists on reminiscing about, on her side or his. And now, she wastes her life keeping my brother's house for him and raising his son, our nephew. Brynhild adores the boy, and would make a fine mother herself but that will never be. Not whilst she continues to wallow in the past, awash with self-pity."

The exasperation in his tone was not to be mistaken.

"Perhaps your brother needs her, with his wife being dead—"

"Ulfric shares my view of the matter. He makes our sister welcome in his longhouse, of course, but would prefer to see her settled in her own. He has tried to persuade her to consider other potential husbands, would allow her to make her choice if there was someone she took a fancy to, but she digs in her heels."

"If she is happy—"

"Brynhild is many things, but happy is not to be numbered among them. Our sister is beautiful, talented, a fine homemaker, and a gifted weaver. She is also bitter, lonely, and angry, and in recent years has allowed her misery to eat her alive. If you behaved as she does, my love, your bottom would be ablaze and you would not sit for a week."

"It sounds as though she should be pitied, not punished."

"She is in need of both." He paused, then, "Brynhild does not lack for pity."

"Ulfric should punish her? Is that what you think?"

"It is what I would do to you. I should add that were you the object of my attention you would also be soundly fucked to ensure you properly understood that you were loved, desired, and mine."

Mairead swallowed hard. "I see. I shall bear that in mind."

"Do, little one. You do that." He bent to kiss the top of

her head. "Perhaps you need to be soundly fucked in any case. What do you think?"

"As ever, I defer to your judgement in the matter." She nestled against him, the sensitive folds between her thighs dampening at his words. "I wonder, might an opportunity present itself whilst we are at Skarthveit or shall I be obliged to wait until we return home?"

He chuckled and bent to nuzzle the tender spot beneath her ear. Mairead writhed in his arms and longed for the journey to be over.

• • • • • • •

"There. Do you see it? The cluster of buildings close to the shore. That is Skarthveit, where I grew up."

Seated now in one of the wagons where she had taken refuge to feed Tyra, Mairead's gaze followed the direction Gunnar indicated. She peered into the mid-afternoon sun and could pick out the settlement. It was considerably more extensive than Gunnarsholm, particularly if the acres of cultivated meadows ringing the village were also included. The place had an air of prosperity, of order, and of quiet calm.

Gunnar nudged his horse into a canter. "Come, let us surprise them. We should be in time for the *nattmal*."

At the mention of food Donald dug in his heels to urge his mount to keep pace. The boy was always hungry, it seemed to Mairead. The karl driving the wagon flicked his whip across the rumps of the two horses pulling it and they picked up the pace also. The group descended the hillside at a brisk jog, and were soon spotted by those in the settlement.

"They have recognised us. See, my brother comes to greet us himself."

Mairead could easily discern the tall, blond man at the head of the welcoming party and she remembered him with some unease. Despite her new status, he still scared her. All of these Vikings did. Under the deceptive veneer of civilisation, they still seemed to her to be wild, powerful, and above all, unpredictable. She trusted Gunnar, and Steinn perhaps since he seemed affable enough, but that was the extent of it. Her heart was in her mouth as they traversed the final meadow.

Gunnar slid from his horse to embrace his brother. The welcome seemed both warm and genuine, and the two men turned to pace back into the village, followed by Gunnar's men and the two wagons. Donald reined his horse in alongside the wagon in which Mairead rode and looked to her for guidance.

"We shall just follow Gunnar, and do as he says," she announced with a far greater degree of conviction than she actually felt. "These people are our family now."

Mairead accepted Steinn's proffered hand as she descended from the small cart. By the time she was on the ground Gunnar was already at the entrance to the largest and finest longhouse in the village, but he paused to look around before ducking his head to go inside. He met her doubtful gaze, smiled, and beckoned her to join him. Mairead reached for Donald's hand and stepped forward. She entered the longhouse a couple of paces behind her husband.

"Ah, Mairead, come in, come in." Gunnar beamed at her, and as she moved to stand at his side he took a now grizzling Tyra from her. The babe quieted at once. Gunnar usually had that effect. Her husband continued to smile at those gathered in the longhouse as though nothing at all out of the ordinary was afoot. "May I present Mairead, my wife. And this is our daughter, Tyra."

The tall blond Viking halted, eyes widening as he registered his brother's words. She had no doubt Ulfric realised the significance of the name they had chosen for the child. He met his brother's eyes with a knowing smile but did not remark upon it.

Mairead wished she could shrink sufficiently to crawl

beneath the table that filled the central aisle. The tall, stunningly beautiful blonde woman who had been fussing with the cauldron above the fire pit and who appeared to be mistress of this hall reacted more strenuously. She sank to the nearest bench, her face white with shock at this announcement.

Mairead lowered her gaze, suddenly finding intense fascination in the dusty toes of her stout leather boots.

"We are delighted to make your acquaintance, sister." Ulfric was the first to recover his manners and to Mairead's amazement he stepped forward. He kissed Mairead on each cheek, and even nudged his sister as though to urge her to do likewise, but with no effect. "Mairead, did you say?"

Mairead opened her mouth and would have tried to answer, but Gunnar seemed intent upon doing the talking for her. She was glad of his aid.

"Aye, Mairead, of Aikrig, in Scotland. You will recall my bride, I do not doubt. And the lad here, for you made a fair enough price on him." Gunner beckoned to a bewildered Donald who moved to stand by his side. She was pleased when Gunnar laid his hand on the top of her son's head, making his status apparent to all. He was one of them. "Come, Donald, and greet your family."

"But, she is a Celt." This from the woman, Brynhild, Mairead assumed. She appeared to have rediscovered her powers of speech and was clearly less than delighted to meet her brother's new bride.

"Aye, that she is," agreed Gunner, his tone hardening in a manner Mairead found both familiar and chilling. The warning was clear to all. "And now she is wife to a Viking."

"But, I do not understand. Why…?" Brynhild stood now and glared at her, distaste etched across her stunningly beautiful features.

Gunnar stiffened at her side and Mairead trembled. This was not going well. She should have known, should have convinced Gunnar not to bring them here unannounced. As she floundered, desperate to defuse the situation but with not the slightest idea how she might achieve that, help came from an unexpected quarter. It was Ulfric who stepped in to relieve the sudden tension that crackled between them.

"And a lovelier bride no Viking ever claimed." For such a large man he moved with enviable alacrity to place himself between Gunnar and Brynhild, at the same time ushering his visitors toward the table. "Welcome, Mairead. You must be tired after your journey, and your children will no doubt be hungry. Come, be seated…"

Dumbly, Mairead took the offered seat. She was grateful for the diversion and the refreshment, and relieved too when Fiona appeared from the back of the hall and embraced her.

"You are well?" Mairead whispered.

"Yes, very," assured the other Celt, and her ready smile appeared genuine enough.

"Fiona, you will entertain our guests. Hilla, Harald, fetch more food, more ale. Where is Njal?" Ulfric continued to direct the hospitality, calling upon his thralls to replenish the plates. At his summons a small boy came running in from outside.

"I am here," he yelled, making a beeline for his uncle. Gunnar laughed and caught the small, wriggling boy in his arms, hurling him up into the air as the lad shrieked with joy.

Ulfric's son looked to be perhaps the same age as Donald, maybe slightly younger. When Njal caught sight of the Celt boy hovering uncertainly beside Gunnar, he scowled at him with undisguised suspicion. "Who is that?" he demanded.

Again, Gunnar made the introductions. "That is Donald, my stepson. He is good with a sword and a fair enough shot with his dagger."

If the mention of a stepson struck Njal as odd he managed to hide it well enough. He was more interested in asserting his own superiority with the weapons mentioned and keen to demonstrate his prowess. Donald was having none of that and the two boys left the longhouse exchanging boasts, each determined on establishing the truth of the matter.

Ulfric drew Gunnar away. Mairead knew they had much to discuss, not least the threat posed by Olaf Bjarkesson, so she was not surprised when the men left the women alone. Her protectors gone, Mairead eyed Brynhild nervously, though the Viking woman seemed intent upon ignoring her presence in the longhouse. Brynhild strode around the hall, issued her instructions to the servants and went about her business as though two Celtic women were not ensconced at her table, eating her bread and cheese and supping her finest mead.

"Would you like to see the rest of the village? It is not quite dark outside."

Mairead interpreted Fiona's whispered invitation as a welcome opportunity to escape the icy silence emanating from their reluctant hostess. She nodded and gathered Tyra to her. Donald had yet to reappear but she supposed she would encounter him on her tour of the settlement.

As soon as they were out of earshot Fiona grasped Mairead's arm. "You are married then? To that Viking?" Fiona's expression was one of near disbelief. "How did that happen? I had assumed that he would... that he would...force you."

Mairead shook her head. "No, never. He has been kind, very gentle. I... I love him. And he loves me."

Fiona nodded slowly. "Yes, I can see that."

"You seem... saddened. Is Ulfric cruel to you? If he treats you badly I could speak with Gunnar. He might—"

"No! No, Ulfric is not cruel. He is not unlike Gunnar, by the sound of it—very persuasive in bed."

"You are required to sleep with him, then?"

"It is no hardship, but I am still his slave. He will never take a slave as his wife, so I suppose eventually... he will send me away. Or... or he will sell me."

Mairead reached for her new friend and hugged her. "I

do not believe Ulfric will do that. I do not know him well, but there is something about him, the way he looks at you, watches you. I believe he cares, but if he does decide to sell you I will ask Gunnar to buy you. You would be safe with us."

"If ever I lose Ulfric's favour I will need to leave here. Brynhild hates me, and would harm me if she could."

"Are you sure? She is hostile, certainly, but—"

"On my first night here she forced me to take a bath in icy cold water. She is not permitted to beat me, but will encourage Ulfric to do so at any opportunity. She constantly finds fault with me, nothing I do pleases her and I have ceased to try."

"She is a Viking, and you are a slave."

"It is more than that. She treats Hilla well, you saw that she does. And Harald. They are slaves too, Saxons, from England originally. Brynhild reserves her hatred for us Celts."

"Gunnar told me that her betrothed died in a raid on a Celtic village and that she has never recovered from the loss."

"Is it reasonable to hold all Celts responsible for the actions of a few? In any case, were those men not entitled to defend their homes? Their families?"

"Yes, of course. I know that. I was merely trying to understand. It is difficult for her…"

"And difficult, too, for those on the receiving end of her hatred," retorted Fiona bitterly.

They paused to lean on a low fence. In silence the pair of them gazed across the village at the two boys who were seated on the ground in front of the forge. Njal and Donald were engaged in a heated conversation but both were smiling. Mairead was glad. Her son had few enough friends and Njal would be his cousin, of sorts.

Fiona was her friend too, and like it or not, Brynhild was now her sister. Family was important, ultimately it was all they had. She knew this, and Gunnar had said as much too.

This intractable situation with Brynhild threatened all of them. It could not continue.

CHAPTER FOURTEEN

"There is a messenger from Skarthveit. It is bad news." Gunnar entered their chamber as Mairead was finishing feeding Tyra. She placed the child in her cradle and turned to face him.

"What has happened? Is it your brother? Is he attacked?"

Gunnar shook his head. "Not Ulfric. Brynhild. She has disappeared."

"Disappeared? But how…? Where…?"

"I do not know. The man sent by my brother has no information save that she was last seen three nights previously, checking their livestock in readiness for the coming night. In the morning, she was gone. A search has been mounted."

"This is terrible. How could such a thing happen? We must go to Skarthveit at once."

He laid his hands on her shoulders. "I would prefer if you were to stay here. I am to leave within the hour and we will be riding hard to reach Skarthveit quickly. I have no idea what has happened, though I cannot help but suspect Bjarkesson. Abducting a woman of another Viking family, even in the midst of a blood feud, is an audacious and singularly stupid act but I would not put it past him. If I am right, there might be danger. I will not risk your safety."

"But—"

"Please, heed me on this. I will go to help in the search, and I must leave at once. If we are to find my sister we must move swiftly. I shall take men with me, though I will leave enough here to ensure Gunnarsholm is safe. You will remain here, and I will send news as soon as I am able."

Her head still reeling from this awful turn of events, Mairead could but nod dumbly. Gunnar kissed her, then strode off to complete his preparations. Mairead scurried to assist, and within mere minutes it seemed to her, he and six of his men galloped from the settlement. Still stunned at the news, Mairead followed Aigneis back into the longhouse and sank onto a bench.

"Where can Brynhild be? What has happened? Poor woman… we were not friends, but I would not have wished her ill."

Aigneis placed a mug of mead beside her. "Fretting will not help. We must wait for word from the Jarl. And hope."

· · · · · · ·

Waiting and hoping proved fruitless. Gunnar returned after an absence of two weeks with nothing further to add. Brynhild had quite simply disappeared without a trace.

He and Ulfric had gone to the Bjarkesson stronghold to demand her return, but Olaf appeared as bewildered as they. Gunnar was inclined to believe the other chieftain when he claimed to know nothing of Brynhild's whereabouts, but this left them with no clues at all. They had no idea where to direct the search, although Ormarr's skills had been employed widely. He discovered no tracks, either left by the missing woman or by any wild beast that might have taken her. Had she been seized by wolves or even a bear there would have been some sign left behind. Brigands, too, would have left clues in their wake and in any case would have surely demanded a ransom.

Ulfric, Gunnar, and their combined forces had scoured the surrounding countryside, made enquiries in every town and settlement within a fifty-mile radius, searched barns, stables, even ships moored within the nearest ports. They found nothing, no sign at all. There had been no sightings of her, no talk of a woman answering Brynhild's description being seen, travelling on her own or in company. Brynhild had quite simply vanished.

Gunnar was at a loss. He sat on the end of their bed, his head in his hands. Mairead knelt on the floor before him and wondered how to offer comfort.

"We parted on angry words. I railed at her, for her prejudice, for her refusal to compromise or to put our family before her own irrational enmity. What if I never have any opportunity to set matters to rights between us? What if we never see our sister again?"

"We must hope she is alive and well. She may yet be restored to us."

"How? How can she be alive and well? If it was so, she would come home." He met her gaze, his expression anguished. "We would always fight, as children. She was the youngest, always quarrelsome, even then. But we loved each other. She would not leave us, ever. Something has happened to her. I know it, but I cannot help her and that is the worst part of all this. My sister needs me, and I am useless. Ulfric too. We have tried, we searched everywhere we could think of, asked everyone. We do not know where to go next."

"How… how is Ulfric?"

"Calmer than I, for once, but I can tell he is worried also."

"Of course. He must be. And Njal?"

"He is crying for his aunt. The poor lad lost his mother not so long ago, and now Brynhild. Ulfric's bed-slave is helping to care for him."

"Fiona? Is she…?"

"Relieved that her adversary is gone?" He shook his

head. "She would have cause to wish harm on Brynhild, and had Ulfric not been with her the entire night I would have suspected her of being involved. But Fiona had no opportunity, and seems genuinely upset by the entire business. Ulfric insists she is innocent, and I know of no reason to disagree other than the ill feeling which existed between them—and was mostly on Brynhild's part in truth. I am glad the boy has someone to care for him. And Ulfric."

"Njal could come here; perhaps he might enjoy spending some time with Donald."

Gunnar nodded. "I will suggest it, the next time I see my brother."

"So, what happens now? About Brynhild?"

Gunnar shook his head. "I wish I knew, sweetheart. I wish I knew."

• • • • • • •

"Will you take a bath with me, wife?"

"A bath? You mean in our chamber?"

Gunnar watched as Mairead laid aside the basket she had been using to collect sprigs of wild garlic ready to crush, no doubt for use in an infusion to aid digestion. He had been right to bring the Saxon wench into their household in order to lighten his new wife's work about the longhouse. Mairead now found much more time to devote to developing her range of herbal remedies and medicines. The settlement was glad of her skills and she was often sought out by those with ailments to treat. He was pleased to see his wife happy and so obviously content. She had found her niche and settled into it effortlessly.

And now, he must shatter her peace, it seemed. He cursed inwardly but knew he could not shirk the coming unpleasantness.

Seven-month-old Tyra sat on a rug at Mairead's feet. The baby had only just started to sit up and was fascinated with the expanded view of her surroundings this new skill offered. He could not help grinning when the little one held out her arms and chuntered incoherently at him. He stooped to pluck her from the ground.

"No, in the hot spring. We shall have it to ourselves." He managed a tight smile for his wife, despite the blackness of his mood.

"How so?" Mairead settled her basket on the ground, ready to accompany him. "Where is everyone today?" She glanced about her, scanning the wild meadow for the nearest servant. "I shall summon Edyth to care for Tyra, unless it is your intention that we should take her with us?"

Edyth, the wench he had acquired in Hafrsfjord, had settled in well. Gunnar had known she would. The girl was quick-witted and good with the children. She was also blossoming into a real beauty now that the haunted look of terror had dissipated from her features, a fact not lost on any of the males in his settlement. Which brought him back to his present predicament...

"I would prefer to have you to myself, Mairead. There is a matter I need to discuss with you. Edyth is... indisposed at present and Aigneis is busy so we will leave Tyra with Weylin."

"Indisposed? Why was I not told? I should see to her. Perhaps I—"

"Aigneis is with her." Gunnar glanced up as Weylin appeared, striding across the grassy hillside toward them. The man offered him an almost imperceptible nod as he drew near.

"What is happening? Something is wrong, I know it." Mairead looked from Gunnar to Weylin, her expression wary now.

"I will explain. Come." Gunnar handed the squirming baby to his servant. "See that we are not disturbed."

"Aye, Jarl," promised Weylin. He eyed his new charge with dismay. "Please... do not be long."

Gunnar bestowed an exasperated glower on the man and took Mairead by the hand. He towed her from the meadow before she could utter her next barrage of questions.

Although it was only a little after midday and the weather was unusually clement, the settlement lay eerily quiet as he strode though the outskirts of the village. Mairead could not fail to notice. He led her around the perimeter of his settlement in the direction of the wooded outcrop where their closest hot spring was located. It was a pleasant enough spot, secluded and a great favourite among his people. The proximity of the spring was one of the factors that had led him to select this precise place to build his home, and he was glad of it now. Difficult business was always best transacted in convivial surroundings.

They heard the water before they saw it. The hot spring at Gunnarsholm was located at the foot of a waterfall, creating an odd mix of freezing water cascading from above ground to meet the balmy current from beneath the earth. It was invigorating, inspiring, a truly unique sensation and one he always loved.

Gunnar released Mairead's hand and started to disrobe. In seconds he was naked and striding into the effervescent pool. He sank his shoulders under the water and leaned his head back to allow the frigid waters from the torrent above to pour over his hair. He slicked the dripping locks back and watched her from under lowered brows.

Mairead stood beside the pool, wringing her hands as she regarded him warily. "Have I displeased you, my husband?"

"No, not at all. Come, join me…" He extended his hand and forced a smile to his lips. "Please."

He watched as she undressed, the sight never failing to arouse him. His cock hardened as she stepped forward, picking her way with care across the flat rocks that surrounded the pool. As soon as she was close enough she grasped his outstretched hand and allowed him to assist her into the waters.

"This is good." She sighed and turned to lean her back against his chest. He brought his arms around her and revelled in the friction of his engorged cock against her smooth buttocks. Mairead did little to assuage his hunger as she rubbed against him.

"Little temptress," he murmured into her damp hair. "But sadly this must wait. Did I not say I wished to discuss a matter of some importance with you?"

"You said you wished to talk…" she twisted her neck to look back at him over her shoulder, "…and I surmise from your grim expression that it will not be a matter to my liking. Does… does this matter concern Edyth?"

"It does."

"And her… indisposition?"

"Yes. That."

Mairead turned to look him full in the face now. "Is she pregnant?"

Gunnar gaped at her, incredulous. Where did his normally level-headed wife get such a deluded notion from? "No! At least, I do not think so. How would I know?"

"You would know, if you… if you…"

"Oh, for fuck's sake." He glared at her as her meaning sank in. "You actually believe I have been fucking my little house slave?"

"No, no, I do not. At least I did not believe it, not until you started this. What am I supposed to think?"

"You are supposed to think that you are my wife. I adore you, and I want no other, least of all a skinny wench. Why would I even look at Edyth when I have you?"

"Because she is very lovely. Everyone can see that…"

"As are you. That is equally obvious."

"So, you are not about to tell me that you wish to set our marriage aside?"

Now Gunnar could only stare, open-mouthed. He had known he was handling this badly, but only now did the depth of his ineptitude become clear. Long moments passed before he regained his voice.

"No, I am not," he ground out. "You are my heart; that will never alter. I love you, I love our children…"

"*Our* children?"

He made no attempt to conceal his exasperation. "Your children, our children, what is the difference? We are a family and I have no desire to change that. Ever. Do I make myself clear, Mairead? I would not wish there to remain any lingering doubt between us on this matter."

She peered up at him, her eyelashes damp now. He suspected the waterfall was not wholly responsible. Her lip quivered as she sought her next words.

"I am sorry. I should have thought before I spoke..."

He flattened his mouth into a grim scowl. "Yes, you should. I have given you no reason to doubt me and you may be very certain that you *will* be sorry. I have had no cause to turn you across my knee these past months, but I consider it needful now, to demonstrate that I mean what I say. First though, I must address the real reason we are here."

"Yes, Jarl." She appeared contrite, though far from fearful at his promise to spank her. Maybe he had left such chastisement longer than was strictly wise. He could have found a reason to bare her bottom for a few well-placed slaps, had he cared to look. He gave his head a sharp shake in an attempt to clear it of such distractions and return to the matter at hand. He saw no merit in beating about the bush and opted to come straight out with it.

"I find I must whip Ferris again. I know that you found this distressing previously, but it is necessary. I wished you to know of my intention, and to understand the reasons for it."

Mairead's heart lurched. "Ferris? The man you flogged that first day I was here?"

"The same," confirmed Gunnar.

"He has been stealing again?" *Or worse? Had she been wrong to keep the slave's misguided threats to herself all these months?*

Gunnar shook his head. "Not to my knowledge, though it would not surprise me. He... he has attacked Edyth."

Now it was his wife's turn to appear incredulous.

Mairead stared at him, her emerald eyes wide. "Attacked? In what way has he attacked her? Is she hurt?"

"She will live, but yes, he did hurt her. Matters would have been considerably worse had Steinn and Weylin not heard her screams and intervened."

"Oh."

Gunnar watched his wife's features, saw her complexion pale as the implications of his account sank in. "He... he attempted to rape her?" Mairead's voice had dropped to a whisper.

"From what Steinn and Weylin have said I must conclude that he did. You understand I cannot allow this to go unpunished?"

"No, of course not." Gunnar was relieved that she appeared to agree with him, at least on the need to mete out justice. "What happened?" she demanded. "When..."

"This morning. Edyth was on an errand for Aigneis when she encountered Ferris returning from the lower meadow. It seems the man has been declaring his admiration for the wench since she first arrived here, but I am given to understand she does not return his interest. On this occasion, Ferris was not prepared to take no for an answer. There was an argument, then he dragged the girl into a stand of trees and attempted to take her by force. Luckily Weylin and Steinn were inspecting rabbit traps nearby and heard the commotion..."

"How... how far did he get?" His wife's voice was breathy, her shock clearly profound.

"Edyth's clothing was torn, and there is much bruising about her shoulders and breasts. Her face, too."

"He... he slapped her? Beat her?"

"Aye, it looks like it. By the time Steinn and Weylin came upon them she was on the ground and Ferris was lying on top of her. She had ceased to fight him. It is just as well my men were close enough to stop him in time."

"It is my fault..."

"Nay, love, it is Ferris' fault and he shall be made to pay."

"It is my fault," Mairead insisted. "I knew... I should have told you..."

"You knew? What did you know? That he lusted after Edyth? To be fair, most of the males in Gunnarsholm lust after the lass but Ferris was the only one who—"

"No. I knew what he was like. Ferris is a violent man who threatens women." She wriggled in his arms so that she was facing him. "He... he threatened me once."

"He did what?" Gunnar could not believe what he was hearing. "How did he threaten you? When?"

"S-soon after I arrived here. It was while you were away, chasing the raiders who stole your sheep." In short, stumbling bursts she confided to him the details of her conversations with Ferris. Gunnar grew more livid with each syllable.

"And why am I only now learning of this?" He had promised her a spanking for doubting his fidelity but this was worse. Much worse. By Odin she would not forget this day's punishment any time soon. "All these months you have been afraid of him?"

"No. No, I was not afraid. I... I thought him harmless, an embittered fool, full of threats but powerless to hurt anyone. It seems I was wrong."

"You were. You were wrong about Ferris and wrong to keep this from me. I would have ensured he could harm no one."

"With your whip?"

"Aye, with my whip. He deserves no less."

Mairead was silent, but he did not make the mistake of interpreting this as acquiescence. "There is more?"

She nodded.

"Tell me. Now."

"He wanted to kill you."

Gunnar snorted. "I daresay."

"He wanted me to help him."

"What?"

"He wanted me to murder you while you slept. He... he

thought I might because I was also a slave and by killing our master I would be showing loyalty to my people."

"I have to assume your loyalties were more complex than he believed." Or so Gunnar fervently hoped.

"Of course they were. You were never other than kind to me, and to my children. I would never lift a hand against you."

"Yet you kept that man's secrets, knowing what he plotted." He could not in those moments have explained to her the depth of his disappointment.

"I believed him powerless. He could never have harmed you without my aid—"

"Or that of another." Gunnar was baffled by her naivety if she truly believed the discontented thrall would be deterred simply because she refused to help him. "If Ferris sought to conspire with you, why not with others? He would likely have found an accomplice eventually."

Mairead's eyes widened as the truth of his words sank in.

"Oh, God," she moaned and buried her face in her hands. "I was a fool. You must hate me."

"Hate you? I am angry with you, more bloody angry than I can find words for right now, but I could never hate you. You are my wife, and I love you. Have we not already established that?"

"But, what about Ferris?"

"He will get what he deserves," growled Gunnar. And for himself he would find the entire business rather less distasteful than he had imagined. Ferris would come to bitterly regret his conduct here at Gunnarsholm.

Neither spoke for several minutes. Mairead's sobs subsided, as did Gunnar's temper, to be replaced by a deep sense of relief. Matters could have gone very differently, though Edyth might not share his satisfaction with the outcome.

Apparently Mairead thought so too. "Thank the sweet Saviour that Steinn and Weylin were close by and able to rescue poor Edyth. You are quite certain she will recover from her injuries?"

"Aye, I believe so, though she is very shocked and distressed."

"That is to be expected."

"Steinn wants her. Even now. I gather he has always wanted the lass but has been uncharacteristically slow to make his desires known. It might be best if they were to wed…"

"But, what if she does not feel as he does? Especially after… this."

"She would find safety in marriage. He is a good man."

"But she is still very young. And after such a dreadful experience… It is too soon, surely."

Gunnar shrugged.

"You would not force the issue? That would be cruel, and—"

"I have little interest in arranging marriages, apart from my own naturally, though I do believe it would be a good solution here. But I will not force anything. I leave that to you, my love. You shall decide what is best for the girl, and when. How does that suit?"

She craned her neck to regard her husband's deceptively fierce visage. "That would suit very well, Jarl. Thank you. And now, I must go to her. Perhaps I might help…"

She made as though to scramble from the pool but he tightened his arms about her. "Edyth will be glad of your ointments and such, I daresay. Right now, she is sleeping and Aigneis will remain with her until you return to the longhouse."

"I see… And Ferris? Where is he?"

"He is in the stocks at the back of the forge. He is going nowhere, at least, not yet."

"Not yet? What do you mean to do with him?"

"I would be within my rights to hang him, and I daresay the women of this land would be safer if I did so. Having heard what you have to say I might yet erect a scaffold."

"But you said he was to be whipped…?"

181

"Yes. Twenty lashes. That was the sentence he should have had last time but I curtailed it as he declared himself truly contrite. I will not be merciful again."

"No, I understand that. Rape... it is very serious."

Gunnar was no longer certain this was the worst of Ferris' crimes, but it was what seemed to most concern Mairead and he could hardly blame her. Women were vulnerable to the violence of men, and he knew enough of her past to realise she had faced her share.

"Yes. I appreciate that you might consider that we Vikings set little store by such niceties, and I do understand where that sentiment comes from. A Viking raid is never a pretty affair and whilst I do not personally care for needless violence against those who are defenceless I am aware that the women we conquer do not always fare well. But be under no illusion; here, in our homes, within our own community, we will not tolerate such lawlessness. I am chief here. It is my responsibility to maintain order, to mete out discipline and justice. Edyth is but a slave, but she belongs to me and must be protected also. She is entitled to expect no less. Had Ferris laid hands on a Viking karl, or even a woman of the Jarl, I would have hanged him, have no doubt on that. His plotting to murder me would merit his death, but I would have to call upon you to bear witness to it." Her rapid head-shake was not unexpected, and he resigned himself to the course he had already set out. "Very well then. One slave attacking another, this is less serious in Viking law but not without consequences. Ferris shall receive every one of his twenty lashes this time. They are well-deserved. Following his punishment he will be taken to Hafrsfjord and sold. I will not have him here, endangering the women of Gunnarsholm. Or me for that matter, since I doubt his hatred will abate as a result of what I plan for him. His new master will be informed of his crime, and can take such precautions as he sees fit."

"Where will Ferris end up?"

"My guess? As an oar-slave on a dragon ship. He will

have no further opportunity to molest women or plot against his master."

"That… that sounds like a hard life."

"Yes, and invariably a short one, too. The dangers are extreme. He has brought this on himself though, and I want you to understand why I must deal with him harshly. I hope that you can agree with my decision, despite your having sought to protect him from a whipping all these months, but I must tell you, it is final."

Mairead met his gaze, her own expression steady. "Good. I am deeply sorry I kept his secrets."

She would be, he promised himself.

"Good? You are at ease with all of this then?"

"I underestimated him, did not take seriously the danger he presented and Edyth was hurt. I now realise that he would have hurt me if he could, if he ever had a chance. You too. He cannot stay here and… and I know you must make an example of him. I… will you insist that I watch the whipping?"

"Under Viking law a trial is always public, and so is the punishment for a crime. I could add the charges you have made, his threats to you, his conspiring to murder me, but I prefer not to. I see no merit in giving his deranged ideas more credence that is absolutely necessary, and neither do I wish to insist that you bear witness. Unless you want to?"

She shook her head again.

"Very well. Just the attempted rape, then. All may witness the proceedings, but I will not compel you to do so. Nor Donald."

"Thank you. I prefer not to. When will it…?"

"Soon. As soon as Edyth is sufficiently recovered to accuse Ferris. There is enough evidence against him with just the testimony of Weylin and Steinn, and I myself saw her injuries. But the victim is entitled to see justice done so I shall delay until Edyth is ready."

"I see. And, Edyth is sleeping now, you say."

"Yes, that is right."

"She is not in danger? She has no need of my assistance at this moment?"

"I think not."

"Then we have a little time to ourselves. There is no pressing rush to get on with matters."

Gunnar tilted his head to one side, considering her statement. "No pressing rush, as far as I am aware."

"In that case, it would be a pity to waste this rare opportunity to take advantage of the waters. I... I would like to atone for my earlier ill-chosen words, and for... everything else."

"You intend to drape yourself across my lap then, and offer up your beautiful bottom for suitable punishment? Perhaps I should seek out a bundle of switches."

"Yes, if you wish me to. I deserve no less. But I was thinking rather of an act of worship."

"Worship?" He furrowed his brow. "What do you—?"

He was silenced by the grip of her small hand around his solid cock. His balls contracted and his shaft lurched in her fist.

"My husband, if you would perhaps lift yourself up a little, perhaps be seated on the edge of the pool...?"

"Ah." He could find no objection to her suggestion and soon adjusted his position accordingly. His cock jutted straight up, droplets of moisture already dribbling from the tip. As he watched, Mairead rubbed the pad of her thumb around the crown, spreading the wetness about. She moved closer and knelt before him in the pool, his erection at eye level to her. With a slow smile she tilted her head back to look up at him. The naughty little wench actually licked her lips...

"Mairead, I... oh, fuck..." He let out an oath as she opened her mouth and took his cock between her lips. He closed his eyes, leaned back on his hands and allowed his head to drop back, savouring the sensations as her tongue curled around the smooth head, then traced the ridge on the underside. Encouraged, she lifted herself higher and inched more of his cock into the wet warmth of her mouth. Her teeth grazed his shaft, her tongue lapped at his head, her cheeks hollowed as she applied just a little suction.

"Wife, you will be the death of me," he warned, without conviction.

Her response was a low hum, which sent delicious tingles the length of his erection. *By Thor's balls, where did she learn such a trick?*

Gunnar reached for her, grasped a handful of her wet hair in his fist but did not pull. He merely held her there, her face perfectly positioned for him to fuck should he choose to take control. Gunnar saw no immediate need for that. Instead he allowed her to continue her game, hissing as she took more of his length, then more still. She angled her head to use the pocket of her inner cheek, and he permitted this. In time, she would let him have her throat, but for now, her ministrations were bliss enough.

He sat upright again and watched her through heavily lidded eyes. She was beautiful, this fiery-haired Celt he had become obsessed with and taken first as his slave, then his wife. He had been right, she was perfect and never more so than when her lush lips were stretched tight around his cock. Her cheeks worked, her throat rippled. He watched as she drew in a breath through her nose, and his balls twisted painfully. It would not be long.

"I will spend in your mouth and you shall swallow it. All of it." He lifted one brow as though to ask if this plan was quite to her liking, though in truth he was ready to insist.

There was no need. She nodded, just a little, but enough to leave him in no doubt. He sank his other hand into her hair and now he did twist the flaming locks between his fingers. Her eyes widened. He knew he was hurting her, but equally he was aware that she did not want him to stop. One small hand cupped his aching balls, the other rested on the top of his thigh and squeezed his taut flesh. She caressed his balls and dipped her head a fraction more, took as much of him as she possibly could and she sucked hard.

His release exploded from deep within his aching nuts. Semen rushed to fill the hot cavern of her mouth and he saw her throat work hard to clear it. There was more, spurt after spurt gushed forth and still she fought to swallow all of it, as he had instructed. A trickle of the pale, milky liquid escaped from the corner of her mouth and he reached to catch it on the tip of his middle finger. All the while Mairead maintained eye contact with him and lapped at his turgid, demanding cock.

Only when the final tremors of his climax had passed did he loosen his remaining hold on her hair. He relaxed and settled back again, though he continued to watch her as she sat back on her heels. His cock bobbed free again and she managed a tremulous smile.

"You lost a bit." He offered her his finger to lick, the stray droplets still balanced there.

Mairead wrapped her tongue around his digit and cleaned it thoroughly. He stroked her cheek, then her hair and knew he had the most ridiculous smirk on his face but it did not matter. "I love you," he murmured.

"I love you too, my husband," came the reply.

Now he smiled in earnest. "In that case, there only remains the matter of your earlier ridiculous outburst and your utterly regrettable lapse in judgement."

"You mean to take a switch to me." Her features betrayed her apprehension, but Gunnar was never a man to shy from administering discipline when required.

"Ah, you thought to distract me with your delightful mouth? Alas, it has not worked though I do thank you for your efforts, my sweet. I have no switch to hand but I shall treat you to a spanking, and believe me when I tell you, you will not sit easily for a week. Then I shall fuck you. I consider it best."

"As you say, Jarl. Should I…?" She glanced about, as though seeking a suitable location for her spanking. She need not bother.

"You should clamber up here and lie across my lap,

wench. Be quick about it."

"But, it is cold, out of the water…"

He flexed his shoulders, now quite dry since he had been out of the warming confines of the pool for some time. "You will become accustomed to it, though I grant you it is all the more reason not to delay. Do you require my assistance?"

"I believe I can manage." She poked with her toes at the floor of the pool until she found a solid footing, then stood up with care. She stepped forward, leaning on his shoulder for balance and lifted her foot up onto the ledge beside her.

Gunnar almost missed it. The subtle, barely perceptible gesture very nearly escaped him. Mairead slipped, lost her balance momentarily before he grabbed at her waist to steady her. She tightened her grip on his shoulder, and brought her other hand to her abdomen where she spread her fingers protectively over her flat stomach. He helped her from the pool, then held his silence as she draped her slim body over his thighs. He took a few moments to admire the plump curves of her bottom, then laid his hand on the fleshiest part.

"When were you intending to tell me?"

"Tell you?" She twisted her body around to look up at him. "Tell you what?"

"When were you going to tell me about the baby?"

Her face paled. "How did you know?"

"I am the one asking questions. You, my sweet, are the one tipped up ready for a hard spanking. So, when?" He dropped a gentle slap onto her upturned buttock by way of encouragement.

"Soon. I… I only became sure myself a day or so ago. It is very early…"

"Is it too early? After Tyra?"

"I do not believe so. I am well, and strong. And, if it has happened, then…"

"Quite. So, I shall need to extend my longhouse at this rate."

"I am sorry, my husband. Perhaps it would have been preferable to delay, but—"

"But that is not in your control, or mine, really. The gods have a way of determining these things, we mortals must accept our fate."

"I… I suppose so."

"Accept our fate, but we should not tempt it."

"What do you mean?"

"I mean, my love, that I am not minded to seriously spank a pregnant woman, however deserving you might be of such attention. I will not risk harm to you, or our baby, so I shall have to devise an alternative means of punishing you. Your current situation does lend itself to various possibilities, though." Again he dropped a soft spank onto her unprotected buttock. "I wonder, could I ask you to reach back and spread the cheeks of your bottom for me?"

"What? What did you say?" She made as though to squirm from his lap but he was quicker and anchored her in place with his arm.

"You heard me. I can manage without your aid, of course, but the experience will be less daunting for you if you cooperate."

"What experience?" she squeaked. "What do you mean to do to me?"

"I intend to bury my fingers in your arse, my love. One at first, then two, then a third. By that stage I expect you will be ready to take my cock."

"Your cock? You cannot mean to… to…"

"To fuck your arse? I assure you, Mairead, that is exactly what I do mean. So, is it to be with your cooperation or without it? Your choice."

CHAPTER FIFTEEN

Mairead lay motionless across Gunnar's thighs, shocked into silence. Surely what he had threatened was impossible. She had never heard of such a thing.

No one would ever… Would they?

"So, which is it to be?" His tone was low, seductive even. Despite her stunned reaction to his perfectly wicked intention, Mairead could not fail to be aroused by him even so.

"This is a cruel punishment. I spoke without thinking, but—"

"Not cruel, sweetheart. It will require a lot of trust, but I will not harm you. You know that. Nothing I am about to do offers risk to you, or our baby."

"But, you said…"

"I know what I said, what I am going to do. And you will let me, will you not? You might even help me…?"

"I do not know how," she croaked, close to tears.

"I told you. All you must do is reach back and spread your bottom cheeks for me. Show me your rear hole and ask me to fill it for you."

"Ask you…? I could never—"

"Then do not ask. I shall fill it in any case, first with my fingers, then my cock. And you, my sweet, will soon get over your current shock and outrage. I believe you will love what I am about to do, if you let yourself."

Mairead could not comprehend such a possibility and actually entertained the notion that her husband had become temporarily deranged. She resumed her wriggling and squirming, quite determined to escape. "Please, do not do this. Let me go back to our house. I swear I will never speak rudely to you again, never doubt you again."

Gunnar handled her with ease. He allowed her to go nowhere, just held her until she quieted again, then he leaned down to murmur in her ear.

"Trust me, that is all I ask. One finger. You can manage that. You know you can."

"One finger? But you said three. Then your cock."

"Aye, all of that, in time. But we do this in easy stages. So, just one finger, to start with. Will you agree to that?"

Mairead considered her husband's bizarre request. One finger. It did not sound quite so bad, and if this would appease him, perhaps he would be satisfied with that. Even as she formulated her response she knew he would not stop at one finger, but she saw no other option.

"Very well, Gunnar. I will try."

He kissed the back of her head. "Good. I am proud of you. So, will you help as I asked?"

Mairead drew in a long breath, then exhaled. She dragged in another deep lungful of purifying air then, thus fortified, she reached back. First her left hand, then her right. She grasped the fleshy cheeks of her bottom and pulled them apart. The act itself was mortifying. His gaze on her felt physical, as though he actually touched her, her most private place exposed for his perusal.

"You are so beautiful, Mairead, and never more than when you submit to me in this way." He spoke softly, little above a whisper. Mairead's belly twisted and something warm began to unfurl. How was it possible he could arouse her even in this manner?

"Will it hurt?" she whimpered.

"Maybe, a little, but never more than you can bear. I must stretch you, but we will go slowly and I will wait if you ask me to. You will have all the time you need."

"Th-thank you," she managed, pitifully grateful for this apparent concession.

"You are most welcome, my love. Now, could I seek your further assistance? Would you be so good as to lick my finger? You must ensure that you wet it all over as this will aid in lubricating the way."

Oh. *Dear sweet Lord.* Mairead swallowed, at once conscious of the dryness in her mouth. The one time she could wish for moisture and she had failed already.

"I cannot," she wailed. "My mouth is like sawdust."

"This will not do." Gunnar lifted her so that she was perched up on his knee then leaned to one side and extended his left arm to cup his hand under the cascade of cool water streaming down the rock face behind him. He brought the refreshing, sparkling water to her mouth. "Drink," he commanded, tipping the cool liquid over her parched lips.

Mairead relished the sensation of the frigid water in her throat. She licked her lips and Gunnar soon brought more water to her mouth. Only after the third drink from his cupped hand did she thank him again and declare herself sated.

"Ah, then perhaps now you might oblige me..." He presented the middle finger of his right hand, his requirement clear.

Mairead opened her mouth and poked out her tongue. She took several seconds to thoroughly lick the extended digit, then sat back. "Is that enough?" she asked.

"We shall soon see." He tilted his chin in a gesture to indicate she should resume her earlier position. Mairead obeyed, and in moments lay across his thighs once more. She reached back and parted her cheeks without being asked again.

Gunnar was gentle, she could not deny that. He circled her tight hole with the tip of his moist finger, teasing and pressing, and were it not for the decadent intimacy of his touch she might have thought he played a game with her. There was nothing of the urgent in his caress. Rather he tempted and tantalised, he sought, claimed perhaps, but never demanded. Despite herself, despite her fear and apprehension, Mairead relaxed under his delicate touch. He soothed her, reassured, calmed, and eventually she sighed as the tip of his finger entered her.

He paused, waited for her to adjust, to accept what was happening, then he started to circle again. Now, though, he was inside her, easing her puckered entrance to loosen, to open for him. She still held her cheeks apart but she found it harder to maintain her grip now. Her hands were boneless, her fingers feeble.

"You may let go now, if you wish."

Mairead was thankful for the reprieve and tucked her hands beneath her. She closed her eyes and allowed her muscles to soften, her thoughts to drift as her husband worked his wicked magic. She was aware that he pressed harder, eased first one knuckle past her entrance, then the next. It felt odd, not quite pleasant, but maybe something oddly similar to that. It was not painful, certainly, and perhaps there was a hint of sensuality. Were she pressed to name it, Mairead's overwhelming response was one of utter humiliation. Her husband was exerting his absolute power over her. She knew it, he knew it, and she found that realisation quite breath-taking and utterly erotic.

"Gunnar," she breathed. "Please…"

"Am I hurting you?"

"No. It is… not unpleasant."

"Ah," he acknowledged. "Then perhaps we might venture to add a second finger now."

"Will you require me to lick it?"

"No, not this time. I find you have quite sufficient wetness here to ease the way for us."

Mairead gasped as he withdrew his finger, then slid his entire hand over and through her soft folds. He rubbed the tip of her most sensitive nubbin as he passed and she writhed in sudden arousal.

"Oh. Oh, my goodness, that is... oh!"

"You like this part?" He continued to stroke and caress, gathering up her juices on his deft fingers.

"You know that I do, Gunnar."

"In that case, turn around and lean on the rocks. Lift your bottom up high and spread your legs wide for me."

Mairead was past the point where she might have questioned anything he instructed her to do. Her obedience was instant and soon she was on all fours on the edge of the pond, her husband behind her in the water. He had a perfect view of her quivering cunny, but she found she no longer cared. Gone entirely were her earlier feelings of vulnerability. Her inhibitions were shattered and it mattered not that what he was doing was so wicked. All that concerned her now was how he might make her feel.

"Gunnar, please..."

"Patience, my sweet. I promised you two fingers next, so you shall have them. Two in here..." he drove the digits of his left hand into her cunt, and slid the middle finger on his other hand back into her arse. He drew it in and out several times, "...and two in here." He inserted a second digit into her straining rear hole.

The sensation of fullness was powerful, almost overwhelming. Mairead squealed, and could not stop herself from flinching.

"Too much, too fast. We go slower, then." He curled the fingers in her cunny to caress that spot inside that he knew would drive her into a frenzy of need. She was so preoccupied with the powerful sensations rippling through her inner walls that she almost did not notice when he started to twist and rotate his fingers in her arse.

Almost, but not quite. There was no pain though, just a feeling of being stretched and impossibly full. The double penetration both thrilled and scared her, but she could not help squeezing around his exploring digits.

"Ah, you are liking this a little more now, I suspect. Am I right, Mairead?"

"It… it is peculiar. But, yes, I do like it. I think."

"And this?" He withdrew his fingers from her cunt to replace them with his thumb. His fingers were now able to reach her most sensitive pleasure nubbin and he went to work there, rubbing, pressing, squeezing. Mairead could not quite comprehend what hit her. Arousal burst from deep within her core, shards of shimmering, whispering light seemed to shoot to her fingers and toes, to the very ends of her hair. Her climax was upon her, almost instantaneous, powerful, gripping and scrambling her senses. Her rear hole stretched further. There was a pinch of pain and she knew he was inserting that third finger, but she no longer cared. Awash with pleasure, drowning in sensual delight, she was utterly relaxed. He could do with her as he pleased.

Mairead moaned when he withdrew his fingers from her arse, almost pulling them right out of her before driving them deep again. He kept the strokes slow and even, and she felt every brush of friction against her inner walls.

"Please, do not… No… yes. Oh, yes, there. That feels…"

Mairead was near incoherent with lust by the time he pulled his fingers out entirely. His right thumb was still nestling within her cunny and he swept his fingertips over her clit as he positioned his cock at her now loosened rear entrance.

"Please, I need my release again. Just once more…"

"Ah, but once would never be enough. I believe we can do better than that. Come for me now, my little wife. Show me how well you obey my commands."

"I… I…"

"Now, Mairead." He scratched the very tip of her clitty with his fingernail and she was lost. As she trembled and shuddered with the force of another powerful release, he drove his cock into her waiting arse. Mairead was conscious of everything that was happening to her, but nothing mattered any more save the need to experience the sensual delights he showered upon her. Every touch, every press and squeeze, every intimate stroke and wicked caress sent tingles of pure delight to her very core. As his cock filled her, as he sheathed himself right to the hilt within her tight channel, she let out a scream of pure ecstasy. Her body convulsed and shook, her arse quivering about him as she managed to actually squeeze down and grip him inside her.

"Ah, you feel so good, so hot and tight and... oh, yes. Yes!"

Mairead was climaxing again, and she knew that Gunnar was with her this time. He leaned forward, his chest against her back as his cock lurched and leapt within the confines of her body. It was beyond good, beyond delight. The sensation was quite sublime and Mairead believed that if it was possible to expire from pure pleasure she would meet her Maker in the next few moments.

She did not. As the waves of ecstasy receded, as her world righted itself and her senses returned to a state where she could scrape together something resembling coherent thought, she found she was still very much alive. Her husband's cock was still embedded in her arse and she believed she had never felt better in her entire existence.

"Mairead? Sweetheart? Are you all right?" Gunnar sounded concerned as he withdrew his erection from her arse and rolled to lay beside her. "Look at me. Talk to me."

She turned her head, a faint and probably idiotic smile plastered across her features. "Husband?"

"Wife?" He sounded uncertain, apprehensive even.

Mairead prised her eyelids open and managed to focus on the handsome, dark features so close to her face. "I am well, I think." She paused, considered a few more moments, then, "Am I supposed to be well? That was a punishment, was it not?"

"I believe I prefer you to be well, punishment or no."

He sat up and pulled her into his lap. Mairead was content to lay her cheek against his bare chest and listen to the rhythmic beat of his heart. Life was good, she mused, and full of unexpected twists. His life, her life, the life of the tiny scrap of humanity just quivering into existence inside her.

"We should go. Back to the house. Tyra will be hungry. And Edyth…"

"Soon. Aigneis will feed our baby if need be, and Edyth is in good hands. First, we shall finish our bath."

"What? But—"

Mairead managed to take one breath as he tilted forward and toppled the pair of them into the warm, tingling caress of the hot spring. Mairead went limp in his arms and he held her against him as he trod water, then quickly found his footing. He kissed her dripping locks as he settled the pair of them in the invigorating foam.

"Soon enough, my love. Soon, we will go home and deal with what must be done. But for now, this is our time."

• • • • • • •

"It is done."

Mairead set aside the hank of sheep's wool she was combing in readiness for spinning and lifted her gaze to meet that of her husband. Gunnar remained just inside the entrance to their longhouse, still bare-chested from his exertions in administering Ferris' whipping. He raised one eyebrow as though seeking her reaction.

"I see. Would you care for a mug of ale?" She forced her voice to remain calm, though she had found the entire episode harrowing. Whilst she had not witnessed the punishment herself, she could not fail to hear the sounds of it, even buried indoors. Ferris had been most vocal, at least at first. Mairead did not dispute the justification for what had just taken place in the open square at the rear of their longhouse, but she would not pretend to be at ease with it. In fairness, Gunnar did not ask her to approve, merely that she should accept the necessity.

"Perhaps later." He came to seat himself opposite her. "Are we all right, sweetheart? Do you think me a brute?"

Her response was quick and certain. "I think you a man of honour who does not shirk his duty." She paused, then, "Where is Ferris now?"

"With Weylin. He will be taken care of, and should be fit to travel to Hafrsfjord in a few days."

"I see. Would you object if I were to attend him? I have ointments which might ease his suffering."

"His suffering is entirely of his own making, but if you wish to offer aid I will not prevent it. You will not be alone with him, though. I do insist on that."

"Of course. I shall accompany Weylin."

"Fine." He settled back to regard her for several moments. "And how are you this day? You look pale. Were you ill again this morning?"

"A little, but it soon passes. It was the same with Tyra, and with Donald. In a couple more months this sickness in the mornings will ease."

"You are not to overtax yourself. Edyth is able to help again now, and if need be I could purchase another servant when I sell Ferris."

"Thank you, but no. That will not be necessary."

He grinned at her. "You will never be comfortable that I buy and sell slaves, will you?"

"I fear not, my husband. In fact, would you take it amiss if I were not to come with you to Hafrsfjord on this occasion?"

"No, I understand your reluctance. You may remain here if you prefer. In fact, that would be better since I intend not to return at once after my business at the market is concluded. I shall visit Skarthveit to find out if there is any further news on my sister." He fixed her with a level gaze. "People do not simply disappear."

Mairead did not entirely agree. She had lost one husband at sea, and had herself been abducted from her home.

People did vanish without trace, especially when Vikings were involved, but she had to agree that Brynhild's mysterious disappearance some months before was out of the ordinary.

"Ulfric would have sent word if there was news, surely."

Gunnar inclined his head in acknowledgement. "You are probably right, but I will not cease to hope. Brynhild was a difficult woman. I know she was rude to you and treated Fiona badly, but even so she is my sister. It pains me that my last words to her were spoken in anger and I would wish things to be right between us."

"I do understand that. She is your family and I hope she will be found soon, safe and well."

He nodded, but his tight expression told another story. Neither of them would voice their fears, but no one really expected the missing woman to return after all these months. "I am minded to seek my brother's leave to take one of his longships moored at Hafrsfjord and mount an excursion to the Shetland Isles."

"You are going raiding again?" Mairead could not keep the shock from her tone, or, probably, the disappointment. Most of all, though, she was gripped by fear that her husband might one day not return from one of his Viking raids. "Please, must you do this?"

He smiled at her, but his expression was determined. "It is in my blood, sweetheart. I cannot settle to a different life and neither can my men. I will be gone for perhaps a month. Six weeks at the most. You will be safe here, and I will return as soon as I can. I have much to draw me back home again and will not wish to stay away too long."

"But—"

He reached across the table to lay his finger across her lips. "Let us not discuss this further for we will not agree. Instead, I would prefer to take advantage of Edyth and Aigneis' absence in the meadows. Is Tyra asleep?"

"Yes. In our chamber."

"Ah, good. It is rare that we have the longhouse to

ourselves, especially not in the middle of the day."

She smiled behind his quieting finger. "Not that you would ever let such inconveniences prevent you doing just as you wish, Gunnar."

"I am chief here, am I not? If I wish to fuck my wife on the table in my own hall I shall do so."

"Indeed. None would dispute your right. Might I suggest you bolt the door first, though?"

"You may lock it if you insist, but first you will stand up and remove your clothing for me. I find I wish to inspect what is mine."

CHAPTER SIXTEEN

"Attacked? But, this is not possible. Who would dare…?"

"It is an old enemy, lady. A blood feud. Olaf Bjarkesson…" The messenger from Skarthveit sat at her table, answering her questions around a mouthful of her finest bread and Aigneis' cheese. "When will the Jarl be back? We need his aid."

"I do not know. A month at least. He left here a sennight ago. I had expected him to make a detour to Skarthveit on his way to Hafrsfjord. Did he not arrive there?"

"No, lady. He must have set to sea at once. A month, you say?"

"Yes, but you shall have all assistance that may be mustered here. My husband left men to guard his home and his family. They are at Ulfric's disposal."

"We would not wish to—"

"Gunnar would do this if he were here. We shall leave within the hour."

"Ulfric would not expect you to come yourself, lady."

"I shall do so anyway. I may be able to help, if there are people injured…" Mairead bustled about her longhouse collecting necessities for a hasty departure. "Aigneis, you will remain behind and take care of Tyra. Donald too."

"I want to come," protested the boy who had been listening intently to the exchange. "I have been learning swordplay, I can help to fight."

"No," insisted Mairead. "You are too young still, though I know you are quite courageous enough. You will be needed here, with all the men gone."

Donald raised himself to his full height, his shoulders back and his back straight. "I promised Gunnar, before he left, that I would take care of you. I cannot do that if I remain here. I have to come with you if I am to make him proud."

Mairead steeled herself to insist, but one look at her son's determined face convinced her otherwise. Gunnar's attention and almost casual kindness had brought about a profound effect on the boy. She would not be the one to undermine Donald's newfound confidence and sense of duty. "Very well. But be quick. We must leave at once." The lad managed one beaming smile before he sprinted outside.

Mairead hoped she had made the right decision, but it was too late to go back on it now. She had her own preparations to make if they were to depart for Skarthveit with sufficient daylight left to cover several miles before they must make camp for the night.

• • • • • • •

"You managed to fight the attackers off? Thank the sweet Lord that you were victorious." Mairead dismounted in front of the longhouse at Skarthveit and acceded to Donald's pleas that he be permitted to run off at once and seek out Njal. She returned Fiona's hug. "Is there anything I can do, now that we are here?"

"We have a few injured who might appreciate your aid. But none too serious. We were lucky."

"We were not so much lucky as inspired. At least, one of us was." Ulfric had sauntered up behind Mairead and now bent to kiss Fiona's upturned face. "Welcome, sister. Is my brother not with you?"

"Gunnar is away. He has gone raiding, I suspect making use of your longships, Jarl. He would have come at once had he been at home when your messenger arrived. As it is, I thought to offer such assistance as we could."

"It is appreciated." Her brother-in-law's smile was broad. "Come inside, take some food with us and I shall allow Fiona to tell you of her heroic exploits in leading my Celtic thralls to aid in our victory. I find she is quite the warlike little savage beneath that meek exterior."

"She is?" Mairead peered anew at Fiona but could discern no obvious difference since last she saw the woman.

"He is jesting. I merely advised that we should make use of all forces at our disposal, which included the slaves. In return for their freedom, they agreed to join the Viking force and defend Skarthveit when Bjarkesson attacked us. Please, come inside..." Fiona led a bemused Mairead into the longhouse and called for one of the servants to bring food and ale.

Mairead sank into the seat offered, and took a deep draught of the ale that had appeared by her hand. She glanced about as Fiona addressed the domestic mundanities associated with entertaining unexpected guests. Beds were required, extra food for a feast that evening, a plump young ewe was to be slaughtered. Fiona dealt with all of it, every inch the chatelaine of this home.

"So, Ulfric has freed his slaves?" Mairead offered the question when Fiona at last took a seat beside her. "All of them?" Her gaze was directed pointedly at Fiona's ankle. The last time she had seen the other woman, Fiona still wore the shackle.

"All of them. I was freed some months ago."

"I see. So, you have remained here by your own choice?"

"Yes, I have. I... I love Ulfric. And I believe that he loves me."

"I know that. I knew it that last time, when we visited

here, before Brynhild disappeared."

"It was so obvious?"

Mairead merely nodded. "I am pleased for you, if you are happy here."

"I am happy. I just..."

Mairead studied her new friend. "You miss your father? Others left behind?"

"My father, mainly. And of course Brynhild. For all her faults, I would not have wished harm on her."

"Ah, yes. Is there still no news of Brynhild? No clue at all?"

"Nothing. We are baffled. Njal does not speak of her so much anymore, and Ulfric neither. But I cannot settle, cannot rest until we know."

"Gunnar is the same. He bitterly regrets the angry words he exchanged with his sister, the last time they spoke. They quarrelled because of me, because I am a Celt."

"Brynhild hated Celts. She despised all of us. There was no reasoning with her."

"Even so, it pains Gunnar that the last words between them were of anger and hatred."

"I can understand that, though most of the words I exchanged with Brynhild were angry ones, particularly by the end. I could not in honesty say that I miss her but for Ulfric's sake I would do anything to help find out what happened."

"As would we all." The two women sat in silence for several moments, remembering their shared adversary. Mairead patted Fiona's hand. "But now, you must tell me what Ulfric meant by one person being inspired. You were actually involved in the battle? You fought alongside the Vikings?" Mairead could not hide her astonishment. She was very impressed.

"I did, though as I have said, my fighting was done from a distance."

"You are magnificent. Ulfric clearly thinks so too."

"I am not entirely sure what Ulfric thinks."

"How can you not be? He is proud of you, and utterly devoted. It is obvious…"

"To you, perhaps. I think so too, but at times I am not so certain." Fiona got to her feet and straightened her skirts, clearly ready to change the subject. "Shall I take you to our injured now? There is one man who has a fractured arm. It has been set, but still pains him a great deal. Perhaps you can ease his suffering."

Mairead followed the other woman, ready to do what she could.

The conversation may be over, but she had heard sufficient to form a view of what was going on here. The sooner that oaf Ulfric got his house in order, the better, in Mairead's opinion. Gunnar and Ulfric might be brothers but it seemed to Mairead that these Freysson Vikings had little in common when it came to their dealings with the women who loved them. She much preferred Gunnar's approach.

· · · · · · ·

Mairead was not certain whether or not to share the news of her pregnancy, but she was sorely tempted. These people were her family now. She had a sister in Fiona, or so she thought of the other woman, and sisters shared such confidences, did they not? Thus fortified, she whispered her news as they sat together for the night's feasting. As was usual in large Viking gatherings, most of the folk gathered to share in their meal ate from their laps and sat on the many beds, benches, and upturned buckets that had been brought into Ulfric's dwelling, the largest longhouse in the settlement, to accommodate everyone.

Fiona let out an excited squeal and hugged her hard. "I am so pleased for you. And for Gunnar. You must be sure and tell him so."

"I shall," promised Mairead.

"What is this? Are you seeking to conceal your news from me, little sister?" Ulfric was seated on Fiona's other side. He leaned back to eye Mairead over Fiona's shoulders. "Tell my brother I wish him well, and that I will only excuse his borrowing my longship without my permission if he brings his new family to visit us soon."

"I shall pass that message on, Jarl."

He grinned and waved to summon one of his servants. "Bring more food for our guest. She has need of sustenance if she is to breed fine, strong Viking sons for my brother." Mairead might have preferred a more discreet response, but accepted the proffered plate of marinated whale meat, a delicacy for which she had yet to develop a particular taste.

Whatever the circumstances that had brought them all here, these people were her family now and she harboured no doubt at all that she belonged with them. She had only to glance across the room at Donald, seated beside his friend Njal and laughing at the antics of an excited puppy, and she knew she had been right to place her faith in Gunnar Freysson.

• • • • • • •

Mairead arrived back at Gunnarsholm three days later. She barely had time to unpack her belongings and feed Tyra before another delegation from Skarthveit was at her door. She had been shocked enough at the news of the attack by the Bjarkessons, but she was utterly stunned by the tidings that had now arrived.

"They are leaving? All of them? All of Ulfric's family, every one of his people?" Mairead gaped at the messenger

"Aye, lady. Skarthveit is to be abandoned, left to Olaf Bjarkesson if he wants it so badly. The Jarl is minded to seek a more peaceful home elsewhere."

"But…" Mairead could make no sense of this, none at all. No one had breathed a word of this plan while she was there, but a few scant days previously. Indeed, Ulfric had insisted that Gunnar was to visit them at Skarthveit, with his expanding family. "Are you quite certain? There must be some mistake."

"No mistake, lady. All who wish to do so will go with Ulfric, and for those who choose to remain in their native land, our Jarl seeks a place for them with his brother. Gunnar Freysson has need of strong, loyal men, perhaps?"

"Yes. No. I mean, of course, anyone from Skarthveit would be welcome here. But surely…"

"I shall return then, and tell my Jarl that this is so."

"You will do no such thing until you have explained to me just what is behind this mad scheme. Ulfric would never turn and run. Gunnar will be back soon and he will lend his aid to defend his brother's stronghold. Why would Ulfric decide to simply capitulate in this manner?"

"He did not tell me, lady, not exactly. But his lady did. She said that you would ask, that you would have many questions."

"His lady? You mean Fiona?"

"Aye. The Jarl is to wed her. Today, I believe."

"Today?" Mairead reeled under this latest news. At least, though, this was something she had seen coming and could welcome, though she would have loved to be present at the feasting. Still, if Fiona had seen fit to offer some sort of explanation for this latest twist of events she was glad of it. "Never mind the wedding. Tell me what Fiona said."

"She said that the Jarl seeks a place of safety for his family. He has no appetite for a prolonged and bloody feud with Olaf Bjarkesson and fears that this war will not end until all are dead and our lives in ruin. He wishes to avoid that outcome, and has decided that might best be achieved by moving somewhere else."

"He is letting Bjarkesson win?"

The man shrugged. "There are those among us who see it that way, though most agree with the Jarl. It is a senseless quarrel, not worth the sacrifice of all we have. Another place might be better for us. And if we can find a place to settle where the winters are not quite so long, the nights not quite so dark…"

"You are leaving the Norseland?"

The man nodded. "We are, lady. The Jarl does not know where we shall end up, but he will send word when we are settled."

• • • • • • •

Her husband returned to Gunnarsholm just a few days after the astonishing news from Skarthveit. Mairead had been torn between the urge to rush back to Ulfric's settlement to find out exactly what was happening, and the need to wait at home for Gunnar's return. She had opted to remain where she was, not least because she doubted her husband would be best pleased to learn she had made another headlong dash across the countryside in the early stages of her pregnancy. Better sense had prevailed and she had stayed put.

Mairead had not expected him for another week at least, so was delighted to spot the group of Vikings galloping across the hillside in the direction of their village. She recognised Gunnar at once by his dark leather attire and the huge black stallion he always rode. Something warm and soft unfurled in the pit of her stomach, and for once it had nothing whatsoever to do with the usual inconveniences of pregnancy.

She had missed him, in their bed most of all.

"Quick, we shall have feasting this night. Aigneis, Weylin, we must make ready. The Jarl is back."

There was barely time for the roasting fires to be stoked before the men of Gunnarsholm clattered into the village, their smiles and shouts of welcome suggesting a successful trip. Mairead cringed; she really did not wish to hear tales of conquered peasants robbed of their possessions, their food stolen, their crops and homes wrecked. Marriage to a Viking was not without its complications, but she could not resist throwing herself into Gunnar's arms the moment he dismounted.

"What is this, my sweet? Am I to think you may have missed me? Shall I go away more often if it earns me a welcome such as this?"

"No, you should not. I prefer you to stay here with me." She reached up to whisper in his ear, "An empty bed is much too cold at nights for my liking."

"Then I shall have to warm it for you. Shall I do that now or might we unsaddle our mounts and perhaps eat a bite or two first?"

"The bed must wait, I fear. I... I have much to tell you."

At once the smile faded from his features. "Is all well with you? The babe...?"

"Yes. Yes, we are fine, all of us. The news is from Skarthveit."

"What has happened? My brother...?"

"He is well, they all are."

"There is news of Brynhild?"

"Sadly, no. Please, come inside and be seated and I will tell you all."

• • • • • • •

Gunnar listened in near silence as she recounted what she knew of Ulfric's decision, his displeasure visibly mounting. As soon as she finished her account he stood and paced the hall, his expression stony.

"So, he has gone, with not so much as a word to me."

"He did send word, Gunnar."

"Send word." Her husband's derisive snort told her what he thought of that. "He should have come here himself, discussed his worries with me. We could have sorted matters out with Bjarkesson, somehow."

"I do believe he has done what he felt was the best, for his people, his family."

Gunnar whirled on his heel and slammed his fist into one of the central props that supported the roof. "I am his family. He should have waited until he could speak to me."

Mairead cringed at his thunderous tone. "I am sorry. I only—"

Her husband ceased his railing at once and reached her in two strides. He took her face between his hands. "Sweetheart, it is I who should apologise. I did not mean to shout at you. I swore to you that I would not." He gritted his teeth. "I am just so fucking angry with my fool of a brother. This makes no sense. What was he thinking?"

Similar questions had regaled Mairead since she had heard of Ulfric's intentions and she was no closer to answers now than she had been at the beginning. "I do not know. But, there are likely to be people from Skarthveit arriving here soon. Not everyone wished to go with Ulfric and I said they would be welcomed here. Perhaps we will better understand when we have spoken with those remaining behind."

Gunnar nodded, and since he appeared slightly calmer now Mairead ventured on. "It did sound to me that there was general support for his plans. I think, for the most part, your brother's people were glad enough to follow him."

"I daresay, but it makes no difference. He should have waited until he could speak to me."

Privately Mairead agreed, but there was no point in dwelling on that. "It is done now. We must wait for word from him. Your brother will let us know where he has settled, I am sure. You *will* see him again."

Gunnar regarded her, his features more pained than she had ever seen them. The scar on his cheek glowed, livid in the firelight. "I hope so, even if it is only to knock some sense back into him. I have already lost my sister, by all the gods I will not lose my brother too!"

"My husband, please come to bed."

"What?"

"Or perhaps you might prefer to remain here. That is quite all right." An idea was forming. Mairead stepped to the outer door and closed it, then dropped the bar on the inside to ensure no one entered. She moved to stand before her husband, then slowly lowered herself to her knees at his feet.

"Mairead, what are you doing?" Gunnar glared at her, his brow furrowing ominously.

She reached for the fastenings on his leather breeches. "It is obvious, is it not? I wish to welcome you home."

"Wife," he growled, "there is no need... Oh, fuck."

He ceased his protests when Mairead freed his cock from within his breeches and wrapped both her hands around it. She stroked the length of his shaft from root to tip, cradling his erection between her palms. She paused to glance up at him.

Gunnar's features had softened, his eyes articulating his need. It was all the encouragement she required.

Mairead leaned forward, the tip of her tongue extended. Delicately, she licked the crown of her husband's cock, as though to test and savour the musky tang of the juices leaking from the slit at the end. He possessed a flavour all his own, she was sure of it. He tasted salty and rich and utterly masculine, an aroma that spoke to her of leather, the saddle, and the tall, swaying pines that covered this cold land she now called home.

Gunnar groaned and wound strands of her hair about his fingers. "Open your mouth wider, Mairead. Let me fuck you there."

She may have started this, but it was clear that she was not to remain in control. As though to press his point, he tightened his grip on her locks to the point of pain. She parted her lips wider, her jaw stretching to allow him access. Gunnar began to thrust, short and shallow initially but his strokes soon lengthened. When she might have angled her head to direct his length into her inner cheek Gunnar held her in place, each stroke driving his cock deeper. He hit the back of her mouth and she gagged. He paused and Mairead swallowed hard, regaining control of her reflexes. She raised her eyes to meet his, saw his eyebrow lift as though seeking her permission to continue. If she were to struggle, to attempt to pull away she knew he would not force her, but she had no desire to do so. She wanted to do this, was determined to offer her mouth if he wanted that.

There was nothing she would not give this dark Viking of hers, were he to ask.

She slowly closed her eyes, the gesture one of contentment, of permission, of acceptance. He caressed her cheek gently, then seized her hair again and drove his cock right to the back of her mouth. Mairead's throat opened to accept the intrusion. She breathed through her nose as he filled her throat with his solid cock, her head bobbing back and forth with the power of his thrusts.

Mairead was utterly passive now, perfectly submissive as she yielded to her husband's sensual demands. He fucked her mouth hard, each driving stroke demanding surrender, acceptance, deference to his will. Mairead gave without question, welcoming his dominance and the security it offered.

Gunnar's cock leapt in her mouth. He swore, the sound more akin to a growl than human speech. He plunged deep again, then held still as his semen surged forth to fill her throat. There was so much, gushing again and again. She tried but could not swallow it all. Some escaped to slide down her chin. Mairead ignored that and fought to clear her airway, dragging in ragged breaths through her nose as and when she could. It was enough. She remained still, his cock lodged against the back of her tongue as the final dribbles of his seed slid down her throat. Satisfied and spent, he released her hair and allowed her to relax and move back. Only then did she at last manage to fill her lungs completely

Mairead flexed her jaw, only now realising how much she ached from forcing her lips wide. She swiped her hand across her chin, felt the stickiness there and gathered what she could on her fingers.

"Do you need a cloth? Some water?" His tone was soft now, heavy with sated lust.

She shook her head and started to lick her fingers, each

caress of her tongue deliberate and leisurely as though she would take the utmost care not to lose so much as a drop of the precious essence.

He dropped down onto his haunches to meet her eyes. "Such a temptress, my sweet little wife. Who would have thought you had such a wicked way about you?"

She smiled at him, her expression one of secrets shared and intimacies exchanged. "I knew *you* to be a wicked and dangerous man, my husband, the first moment I saw you." She lifted her hand to caress his scarred cheek. "So dark and forbidding, but I always knew that you concealed a softness within."

He turned his face to kiss the centre of her palm. "Ah, but are you glad of my wickedness, Mairead? Perhaps just a little?"

"More than a little, my Viking, though I do value your gentler core."

"That is reserved for you, sweetheart. And for our little ones, of course." He lowered his hand and laid his palm over her still perfectly flat belly. "I find I love you even more when you are pregnant, though I would not have believed that possible."

"Do you have matters demanding your attention, Jarl, or might we find a little time to warm our bed together?"

He grinned at her. "Ah, so demanding but I do not blame you. I believe I may be beholden to you now and I could not settle to my other tasks knowing my wife remained unsated." He rose to his feet and offered her his hand. "Come, we shall find all the time we need. I recall you possessed the foresight to bolt the door…"

CHAPTER SEVENTEEN

"Jarl, may I speak with you."

Gunnar turned to regard the smaller man who had sidled up to him as he crossed his settlement. He had spent a hard but productive morning drilling his men, including young Donald who was coming along very well, and he was now rather looking forward to spending a few quiet minutes with his wife if she was to be found anywhere about their longhouse. He really did not have time for this.

"Could it wait?" His tone was more brusque than he intended, but sadly Dagr did not bring out the best in Gunnar. The Viking chief well recalled the man's careless cruelty to both Mairead and Fiona all those months ago when the female Celts first arrived in the Norseland. Dagr had arrived at Gunnarsholm, along with half a dozen others and their families some twelve or so weeks previously and Gunnar wished the man had not been among the karls from Skarthveit who had opted not to follow Ulfric into his self-imposed exile. He did not feel it right to pick and choose who he would permit to stay, however, so all the newcomers had been welcomed and work was going on to construct the additional longhouses required to house them.

Dagr shrugged at the rebuttal, nodded and turned to

leave him.

"Wait." Gunnar halted his stride. "Is it a matter of importance?"

"Aye, Jarl, it is. But not urgent."

Something in the man's demeanour set Gunnar's senses jangling. He did not particularly like the man himself, but Dagr had enjoyed his brother's trust so that at least entitled him to a hearing. "Come with me," commanded Gunnar, and continued on toward his longhouse.

Dagr followed him through the low doorway, then stood awkwardly on the threshold when he caught sight of Mairead tending the ever-present cooking pot that was suspended over the fire pit.

Gunnar kissed Mairead, then bent to pluck Tyra from the cradle on the floor. The baby was asleep, but he still enjoyed the way her little body felt as she snuggled in his arms. His love for this small child remained a source of some wonder to him and he gazed fondly at the tiny features before gesturing Dagr to be seated.

"Would you like a mug of ale? I am sure we have some about…"

"Of course." Mairead moved to fetch the required refreshment.

"No, I am fine. Thank you, Jarl. Lady." Dagr inclined his head to Mairead, then turned to regard his new overlord once more. "This is a matter of some… sensitivity, Jarl. Is there somewhere private…?"

Gunnar frowned, not caring at all for the man's attitude. "This is sufficiently private. My wife is privy to any matter concerning me. You may state your business."

"It… it is about your brother. A family matter, Jarl…" Dagr fairly squirmed under Gunnar's intense and decidedly hostile scrutiny. It did him no good whatsoever.

"My family are about me. Get on with whatever you have to say, or leave us to our meal."

"Perhaps another time…" Dagr made as though to rise from the stool he had sunk onto at his Jarl's invitation.

Gunnar's patience was at an end. He had commanded the man to speak freely before Mairead, he had damned well better do so or face his Jarl's wrath.

"Sit down, and fucking speak. Now." He glared at the nervous karl, but the outcome was inevitable. Mairead moved to stand behind him, her small hand upon his shoulder in a welcome display of unity and marital bliss.

"Very well." Dagr shifted in his seat and found something of much fascination to study an inch or so beyond the toe of his left boot. "It... it concerns your brother, Ulfric and ... your sister, the lady Brynhild."

"My sister?" breathed Gunnar.

"There is news of Brynhild?" Mairead gasped behind him. "Is she found?"

"Yes. I mean, no. No, she is not found. But neither is she truly lost."

Gunnar lowered his tone, the menace clear. "You are speaking in riddles, man, and I find I do not care for it. What do you know of my sister?"

Dagr drew in a deep breath, raised his eyes to meet Gunnar's angry gaze, and opted to ignore Mairead entirely. He commenced his tale. "At his wedding feast, on the eve of his departure from our shores, Ulfric took me aside and bade me bring you a message. He knew that I was among those who did not choose to sail with him, and that I would be coming here to Gunnarsholm. He was most particular that I should wait until no less than three new moons had passed before speaking with you, but that I should repeat his words accurately and fully. It... it is quite a story, Jarl."

"Then please do not let me interrupt the telling of it." Gunnar handed the still sleeping baby to Mairead then leaned forward, his elbows on his knees. Dagr had his undivided attention.

"You are aware, I understand, that there was enmity between Lady Brynhild and the slave, Fiona. And that Ulfric favoured his bed-slave. He... he valued her highly."

Gunnar nodded slowly when Dagr paused but offered

no comment.

"There was… there was an incident, soon after you visited Skarthveit with your new wife. Ulfric went to Bjarkesholm to attempt to negotiate a truce with Olaf. He was away for several hours and during his absence lady Brynhild attempted to murder your brother's bed-slave." The words tumbled over each other, as though Dagr could not blurt out his message fast enough.

"No!" Gunnar soared to his feet to tower over the man. "You are a liar! You will regret peddling this falsehood, I can promise you…"

Dagr remained where he was, but his expression took on a more defiant air. "Jarl, I know how dreadful this sounds, but I am repeating exactly what Ulfric said to me, I swear it."

"You swear? Do not think to make this worse. I—"

"Husband, we should hear him out."

Mairead's voice, soft but firm, caused Gunnar to cease his tirade. He glared at her instead. "You believe this… this rubbish? You actually think my sister would stoop so low? Or that my brother would trust such a tale to his slave master?"

She stood firm, her chin tilted up. "I believe it could be true. Fiona herself told me that she feared for her life, that Brynhild would do her harm if she could. Perhaps an opportunity did present itself, and Brynhild took it."

"Fiona said that? To you? But… why?"

"Because she was afraid. I know that much was true, Gunnar. I saw that for myself."

He stared at her, speechless. *Could there after all be some merit in this bizarre tale?*

Mairead continued. "We were not there, husband. We did not see, but Fiona told me that Brynhild hated her, that your sister was cruel and vengeful, that she made her life a misery in many small ways and would have done far worse had Ulfric not forbidden it. We should hear more of what your brother told Dagr." She turned to the man, still seated before them. "There *is* more, I assume?"

"Yes, lady. There is more." Dagr cleared his throat and waited as his Jarl resumed his seat. "So, Ulfric returned from Bjarkesholm earlier than expected, in time to prevent his sister from completing her plan. The slave had been in danger, but survived her ordeal."

"What did Brynhild do to her?" Mairead asked the question, but had she not, it was on Gunnar's lips to do so.

"Lady Brynhild had the slave fastened in the stocks, and would have left her outside the entire night had our Jarl not returned, found her half dead with the cold and freed her in time."

"That is a cruel fate," observed Mairead softly.

"There must be some mistake," protested Gunnar. "Brynhild would not have done that. She had a temper, certainly, but such calculated malice—that was not her way."

Mairead did not respond, though it took but one look into her grave face for Gunnar to know that his wife did not see this matter as he did. He scowled at her, unwilling to allow this madness to take root. Surely there was some other explanation for whatever had taken place at his brother's settlement.

"Could it have been an accident? Perhaps Fiona misunderstood..." He was clutching at straws.

"The thrall did not fasten herself into the stocks, Jarl." Dagr's remark was reasonable enough, but Gunnar was sorely tempted to boot him into the nearest ditch, even so.

Mairead again laid her hand on his shoulder, then she took up the questioning of the karl. "So, Ulfric returned and freed Fiona. What happened then? How does this link to Brynhild's disappearance? I assume there is a link?"

"Aye, Lady. Ulfric knew what Lady Brynhild had done, and why. She hated Fiona, and he realised that he was unable to protect his slave and allow Brynhild to remain in his longhouse. So... he arranged for her to be taken away."

Dagr fell silent. Gunnar and Mairead were speechless

also. Gunnar got to his feet and raked his fingers through his hair. He could not take this in. He took a couple of paces toward the door, then swung back to face the karl

"What do you mean, 'he arranged for her to be taken away'?"

"One of the other thralls, a man called Taranc. A good worker, strong… He escaped the same night that the lady disappeared and neither have been seen since. It seemed too much of a coincidence, many questioned it, but the Jarl insisted that there was no connection. However, on the night of his wedding he told me a different tale. Ulfric told me he struck a deal with Taranc. Our Jarl offered to aid him in his escape, even provided him with a boat to return to his homeland, on condition that he take the lady Brynhild with him. The slave accepted the deal, and he abducted your sister."

"You are saying that Ulfric knew of this. All along, he has known where Brynhild was and did nothing to rescue her?" Gunnar was incredulous.

"Aye, he knew. Or at least, he knew who she was with. As to her whereabouts, I do not believe he was certain, but it had been his assumption that the slave Taranc would seek to return to his home in the land of the Celts. Since Ulfric arranged it, he would have seen no cause to rescue his sister. Lady Brynhild was exactly where he wanted her to be, where he put her, even, and she has been all along."

"Taranc took Brynhild to Aikrig?" Mairead's delicate features were ashen, her eyes a deep green in the flickering firelight.

"Where?" Gunnar peered at her. "Where did you say?"

"Aikrig. The village where I used to live, before I was… taken. Taranc was our chief there. That is his home."

"By Thor's balls and his silver hammer, I will kill my brother for this. I shall disembowel him with my own hands. He had our sister abducted by savages. All the time he knew where to look for her and he told no one. He let her suffer…" Gunnar paced the floor of his longhouse, and only lowered his voice when Tyra began to wail. He continued to prowl to and fro, uttering his curses and dire intentions for dealing with the brother who had so dishonoured their family. "How could he do this? What was he thinking? And to deceive us, all of us, all these months. He saw how we grieved, how desperately we searched for her…"

"My husband, please be calm. Consider your brother's reasons." Mairead gestured to Dagr to leave them alone, but muttered to him that he was to remain close in case they needed to question him further on any aspect of his account. The man was quick to do her bidding, clearly reluctant to remain in Gunnar's company if that could be avoided.

As soon as the door closed behind the retreating karl, Gunnar turned on Mairead. "Do not even think about trying to defend him. Ulfric has betrayed us, abandoned his family for… for what? A slave?"

"He loves her. He has married her. Fiona is more to him than a mere slave. You of all men should understand that."

"Me? I understand none of this. I would never betray my kin."

"You have not been called upon to make such a choice. You are fortunate. Your brother was faced with a difficult decision. You heard Dagr—Brynhild tried to *kill* Fiona. Perhaps Ulfric feared she would make another attempt and the next time she might succeed. I believe he did what he considered the best for all."

"How could this have been best for Brynhild? She might be dead, or living a life of abject misery, the prisoner of a savage brute who has reason to hate her because he was himself taken as a slave by our people."

"Taranc is neither a savage nor a brute. He is a good man. I know this, and I believe Ulfric knew it also or he would not have sought his aid."

"A good man does not abduct a helpless female," protested Gunnar.

Mairead merely smiled. "No? You have a short memory,

husband."

"That was different. I never meant to harm you. Ulfric never intended harm to Fiona either, for that matter."

Mairead smiled again, and nodded. "Taranc is a good man," she repeated. "If Brynhild is with him, she will be safe."

•••••••

Two days after the revelation of Ulfric's part in the mysterious disappearance of his sister, Gunnar arrived at a decision. He had wrestled with the facts as he understood them for hours upon hours, considered every possible angle and permutation, analysed the information he had and quizzed Dagr closely for every last detail he could wring from the man. Improbable though it had seemed initially, he now accepted that Ulfric had been faced with a difficult, nay, impossible choice. If he knew his brother, Ulfric would have been racked with doubts ever since. Gunnar was guessing now, but it would not surprise him to learn that the compulsion to go after his sister, to see for himself that she was well and cared for, could have been a factor in Ulfric's seemingly absurd decision to abandon his homestead and set sail for the land of the Celts. He was convinced that was where his brother had gone. Nowhere else made any sense.

And now, he knew what he must do.

Mairead had taken Tyra with her and they were at the river washing clothes with Aigneis and other women from the settlement. Gunnar set off to seek her out, his pace measured and unhurried as he strode across the meadow to where the women laughed and chattered in the chilly shallows. Mairead saw him coming and came to greet him, Tyra in her arms.

She linked her arm with his and they strolled for a few paces. "I had not thought you to harbour an interest in laundry, my husband."

"I have an interest in talking with you. Are you busy?"

"No, the clothes can wait. I believe Aigneis will do better without us hindering her in any case." She fell into step beside him. "This is about Ulfric? And Brynhild?"

She knew him so well. He nodded. "I must go there. I must see for myself that she is well, and bring her home where she belongs."

"Of course. That is the right thing to do."

"You agree with me? Even though I may have to kill this Taranc to accomplish my aim?"

"I do not believe that will be necessary. And despite what you may believe, Taranc is not a weak man. He could not singlehandedly fight off a horde of Vikings all armed to the teeth, but we will not take him by surprise this time. We will talk with him, and the outcome will be different. There are more ways to settle a matter than with a sword."

Gunnar allowed himself a derisive snort. He would put his faith in good, hard steel every time, but was not about to be deflected. Her choice of words had not escaped him. "What is this 'we'? I shall go, not you. And I have every intention of taking this Celtic chief by surprise. There will be no negotiating. I am going to bring my sister home."

Mairead stopped and turned to face him. He recognised that determined glint in her mossy eyes and groaned to himself.

"If you go to Aikrig, I shall come with you. We go there to talk, not fight, and I will be of assistance. I know Taranc, he will be more likely to listen and negotiate if I am there."

"If there is any listening to be done he will listen to me, or face the consequences."

Mairead rounded on him. He could not recall ever seeing her more fierce. "No! No more senseless bloodshed. They are my people, and I will not stay here quietly and allow you to go there with murder in your mind. I can help, I can assist you in achieving what you want without harming innocent people. You must do it my way."

"I must? I think you forget who is master here, my sweet." His tone was deceptively quiet, but Mairead did not appear impressed.

"You cannot be master if you are not here, *Jarl*. And know this, if you go off alone to do this thing your way, *I* shall not be here when you return."

"Mairead…" He sharpened his voice, intending to quell this rebellion before it took hold, but to no avail.

"You may threaten me, beat me, have Weylin attempt to lock me in your longhouse, but it will not work. By the time you return from this foolish quest I *will* be gone. I am asking you, for once, to listen and to do this my way. Why must you be so pig-headed, and so bloodthirsty?"

"For fuck's sake," muttered Gunnar, exasperated. *Might Weylin manage to secure her in their longhouse?* He could not see it, not really.

"Please, do not curse in front of Tyra. She is starting to repeat things."

Gunnar was about to apologise, but caught himself in time. Here was his salvation, though. "You cannot come. What about the children? And, you are pregnant."

"Donald and Tyra will come with us. And it is still the summer, in the coming weeks the weather will be as calm as it is ever likely to be, the crossing should not be arduous. I was far more heavily pregnant when I first made the trip and you offered no objection then."

"It might be dangerous. I would not have harm come to you—or them."

"If Brynhild and Taranc are at Aikrig, we shall talk. If they are not, we shall come away. That is not dangerous."

"I do not think—"

"We are going to Aikrig. All of us. It is settled. How soon can we be ready to leave?"

He really should not allow her to always have the last word, Gunnar reflected, as they ascended the slight incline back up to their village. It had become something of a habit, sadly, and now he had another problem to contend with.

What if, when Mairead found herself again on her native soil and surrounded by her own people, his beautiful wife and their little family did not wish to return with him to the Norseland? Could he force her all over again?

Gunnar rather thought he could not.

Shit!

CHAPTER EIGHTEEN

"Jarl, there are dragon ships already on the beach."

Gunnar strode to the prow of the longship to stand beside Steinn, the lookout. "You are right." He shielded his eyes with his hand. "Odin's teeth, I believe they are my brother's."

"Aye, looks like it," agreed the young Viking. "We are in the right place, then."

Gunnar growled his agreement, already contemplating the coming confrontation with Ulfric. This would not be pretty.

"Set a course to come up on the beach close by, but ensure we have water enough to launch again in a hurry if we need to. And make plenty of noise. We want them to know we are coming this time." Whether the impending encounter was to be with his brother, or the Celtic chief, Taranc, or even both, Gunnar would much prefer to get it over with early.

And it would not hurt to have his dragon ship at his back and a ready means of escape.

Mairead stood beside him as the bow of the longship scraped over sand and the vessel juddered to a halt. They had already agreed that Tyra was to remain on the longship with Weylin, who had requested leave to accompany their expedition. Gunnar was the first to leap over the side into the shallows. He turned and held up his arms for Mairead, and managed to keep her out of the frothing waves and deposit her on the damp sand.

"Welcome home, my sweet. Now, let us see what sort of reception awaits." He took her hand and together they advanced up the beach, their men thronging at their back.

They had not taken many paces forward before a lone figure emerged from the shadow of the trees ringing the cove. A familiar, tall, lean silhouette clad in Viking tunic and leggings and a heavy cloak of blue wool confronted them from the top of the rise, blond hair flowing loose about his shoulders. His eyes were a deep and compelling blue, wary and alert. He looked every inch the conquering hero, ready to defend his land to his last breath.

Gunnar signalled to all in his party to halt, then continued on alone. He confronted his brother and the two circled each other cautiously.

"Ulfric? You look well."

"You too, brother. I see you managed not to sink my dragon ship. I am relieved, though it would have been courteous to have sought my permission before taking it."

"Just as you showed me the courtesy of seeking my opinion before you banished our sister to fend for herself among our enemies?"

"Ah, yes. About that…"

"Do you really want to know what I think about that?"

"I believe I can hazard a guess."

"Do not trouble yourself. Let me make the matter plain."

Gunnar was reasonably certain his brother never saw the punch coming. His fist connected with his brother's jaw, there was a sickening crunch and Ulfric staggered back. The man did not fall, though, damn him. He did not even crumple to his knees, unconscious, as any decent adversary should. Instead, Ulfric shook his head, his wild, golden mane shimmering in the breeze, and he flew at Gunnar like a man possessed.

Even though he had initiated the attack, Gunnar was taken by surprise at the ferocity of Ulfric's response. The pair rolled along the sandy ground, each doing his utmost to deliver kicks, punches, blows to the head and body. Gunnar took a particularly vicious punch in his kidneys, and another just missed his balls. His brother always did fight dirty.

He managed to retaliate with a decent upper cut to Ulfric's temple, then tried to bring his knee up in his brother's groin. He was dimly aware of Mairead's voice as she exhorted them to stop, to not hurt each other, to talk about this.

He might talk later. For now, he would settle for killing his brother, or at the very least beating the faithless bastard senseless.

Gunnar had the upper hand, at last. He rolled on top of Ulfric and managed to deliver a couple more punches to that chiselled jaw. He chose to ignore the several punishing blows he had already taken and the very real probability that he had lost a least a couple of teeth and his jaw might be broken. He raised his fist to complete the job, then roared in shocked fury as a torrent of icy water caught him full in the face.

Gunnar barely had time to gasp in a startled breath and turn his head when another onslaught hit him. The freezing water this time doused his hair and shoulders. He could see his brother had fared no better and was also gasping and wheezing like a beached eel, his pale hair plastered against his scalp.

"Get up, the pair of you. Do you never learn? Grown men, brothers, brawling in the sand like a pair of rabid dogs."

Gunnar turned his head in the direction of the angry female tone. It was a voice he remembered well.

"Ah, Brynhild. I was hoping to run into you."

"Were you? Well, now you have, and you can at least do me the honour of standing to greet me properly."

Gunnar eased himself painfully to his feet. He had forgotten how vicious Ulfric could be in a fight and he now hugged his ribs gingerly. Mairead appeared at his side, solicitous as ever.

"Are you hurt? I can prepare a poultice for you if you like. And for you too, of course, Ulfric."

"Thank you, little sister, that would be most welcome." Ulfric had also clambered to his feet and now had the audacity to greet Gunnar's wife with a lopsided smile. "May I bid you welcome to our new home. I had not expected you to join us quite so soon, but it is good to see you. Was it really necessary to bring him, though?"

Gunnar had no time to form the required pithy retort.

"Shut up, the pair of you. Come with me." Brynhild glared from Gunnar to Ulfric, offered a brief nod to Mairead, then turned and made her way up the beach. She disappeared into the trees, and the battered Freysson brothers had no option but to follow in her wake.

• • • • • • •

"Where are we going?" whispered Mairead as they passed the entrance to the track leading down to Aikrig.

"Pennglas. The manor house," clarified Ulfric. "Fiona is there, and her father. And Taranc."

Gunnar clenched his jaw but said nothing. He looked forward to at last meeting the infamous Taranc.

"The village is about a mile inland. I daresay you remember the route, brother."

"Well enough," agreed Gunnar. Mairead slipped her hand into his and he gripped it hard. He was glad, despite all his protestations, that she was here.

The rest of the walk up to Pennglas was completed in silence, each lost in their own thoughts and memories. The remaining Vikings who had accompanied Gunnar trailed behind them, though no one unsheathed their swords. Gunnar had issued strict instructions, at Mairead's urging, that there must be no bloodshed if that could be helped.

He supposed bloodying his brother's nose did not count.

Brynhild remained in view as they made their way through the thick woodland, then across the clearing where the village lay. Gunnar studied her and had to admit she looked well enough. She was still the tall, slender, stunningly beautiful woman he remembered, though she appeared different somehow. There was a more knowing air about her, and a hint of maturity that he now realised had been lacking. Her experiences over the last year or so had changed her, whether for the better remained to be established.

Pennglas was much as he remembered it: a cluster of dwellings, mostly constructed of stone and wood with thatch roofs, and each cottage surrounded by pens for livestock. It was not unlike a Viking homestead, apart from the rough manor house that dominated the village.

Gunnar remembered this place well, and in particular he recalled the hot-headed youth who had rushed headlong from the doors of the manor house on that fateful day that seemed so long ago now. The young man had bellowed battle cries as he rushed to meet the invading Vikings armed with just a shovel. Gunnar had found himself with little option but to stop him and had slain the lad on the steps of his home while an older man, presumably the lad's father, looked on. With a sinking feeling, Gunnar began to appreciate that the coming encounter would be even more difficult than he had expected. It was not as though the old man might not recognise him. He was distinctive enough.

"Fuck," he muttered. *Why could things never be simple?*

• • • • • • •

Brynhild led them right up to the manor house. She paused at the foot of the imposing stars leading to the main door and turned to face both her brothers.

"I trust you can manage to behave with a degree of respect whilst you are guests in another's home? Lord Dughall has always been most kind to me and I would not have him upset. He has not been well, of late."

Gunnar narrowed his eyes. He could not imagine the old man's health benefiting greatly from a visit by the man who he had witnessed killing his son, but there seemed to be no way of avoiding the confrontation. "I daresay we shall manage," was the best he could offer and he gestured to his sister to lead the way in.

The entrance led straight into the main hall, lit by just one window. The only other illumination was provided by the fire in the huge grate at one end of the structure, and torches fastened to the walls. At first sight it appeared to be the home of a prosperous man, one who enjoyed his comforts if the padded settle and benches were anything to go by. A large table was situated at the end of the room close to the fire, and another at right angles to it covered most of the length of the hall.

An elderly man sat in the centre of the high table, Fiona beside him on his right. Njal occupied the seat next to her. The boy leapt up as soon as he spotted Gunnar and ran to greet him.

"Uncle! I knew it must be you. I told you, I told you, Mama, that it was my uncle."

Mama?

Njal flung himself against Gunnar's leather-clad legs and hugged him, only now catching sight of Mairead. "Is Donald here too?"

"He is, somewhere…" Gunnar turned to peer into the group of Vikings who had gathered at the foot of the steps behind them. "Ah, there he is. Donald, come and greet your cousin."

His stepson bobbed forward eagerly and the boys soon disappeared into the crowd, the Viking ranks having been swelled by a gaggle of curious villagers.

"Will he be all right?" fretted Mairead.

Gunnar privately felt that the boy was not the one to be most worried about, but saw no merit in sharing this. "Aye, he will be fine," he assured her. "So, shall we get on with this talking you were so keen on?"

Gunnar turned to regard his sister. Brynhild stood at the end of the table, her hands folded at her waist. She appeared perfectly calm, though the slight quiver in the muscle at the corner of her left eye betrayed her agitation. None but he and perhaps Ulfric would recognise the sign though.

He cleared his throat. "Brynhild, I am glad to find you well. And relieved. I had feared for you. We all did, though I am given to understand that perhaps the matter of your disappearance was not quite the mystery we first assumed." He spared a glower in the direction of his brother, who had taken the seat at the table beside his wife recently vacated by Njal. His brother's eye was swollen and he moved with obvious discomfort. Gunnar took some measure of satisfaction from these observations. He turned to face his sister once more. "No matter, I am here to take you home."

Brynhild tilted her chin at him, her eyes narrowing in an expression of belligerent disdain he had seen more times than he cared to recall as he grew up. She glared at him, as though considering carefully what her response might be. At last, she spoke.

"Thank you, my brother. Your concern is noted and I am sincerely glad of it. However, your aid is not needed. Had I desired to return to my homeland, I am quite certain that my husband would have taken me there."

"Husband?" Gunnar wondered if he might choke on his tonsils. What the fuck else had been going on whilst he languished in Gunnarsholm in total ignorance?

"Yes, my husband. Ah, heré he is…" She turned to face the outer portal, where the assembled Vikings and villagers parted to make way for a man striding through their ranks. "Taranc, come and greet my brother. You will remember Gunnar, I am sure?"

"I do, yes." The tall, brown-haired Celt approached their assembled group to take his place beside Brynhild. He slung an arm across her shoulders and she turned to offer him a quick kiss. Never particularly demonstrative, this was the most overt display of affection Gunnar could remember his sister ever exhibiting. Taranc's smile was warm as he returned her kiss. "I am sorry I could not be here to greet our guests earlier, but as soon as I learnt of their arrival I made all haste to join you. Needless to say, Morvyn was not cooperative." He passed the squirming bundle he held in his spare arm to Brynhild. "Our son is demanding his next meal, my love."

Son? Gunnar gaped, open-mouthed as Brynhild calmly accepted the baby and sat down to feed him. He remained too astonished to do other than accept Taranc's outstretched hand and allow the other man to greet him properly.

"I expect you have questions. Ah, I see you and Ulfric have already started your own discussions." Taranc winced as he eyed Gunnar's bruised features. "Never mind. Shall we be seated and perhaps we can deal with the rest over a mug of ale and some food. Fiona, do we have the makings of a feast to welcome our visitors?"

"We do, of course." Fiona trotted off in the direction of what Gunnar assumed must be the kitchens. She spared her husband a warning glance before she left. Ulfric responded with a shrug.

For want of a better plan at that precise moment Gunnar stepped forward to accept Taranc's offer of a seat. As he passed before the older man who had thus far remained silent, Dughall of Pennglas rose painfully to his feet. Gunnar paused before him.

Dughall peered intently at the tall Viking, his eyes dimmed by the cloudiness that so often afflicted the old. Gunnar began to wonder if, perhaps…

"You. I recognise you." The old man pointed directly at him and Gunnar bowed his head politely.

"Lord Dughall." He bowed respectfully and scrabbled about for something polite to say. "I must thank you for your kindness to my sister whilst she has been here."

"Brynhild is most dear to me," replied the Celtic noble. With slow, unsteady steps he made his way around the table to stand in front of Gunnar. Once there he tipped his head back to look up into the Viking's face as though studying every detail of his features. "You were here before, that other time, on the steps of this very house."

"I—"

"Aagh!" Gunnar's response to his elderly accuser was cut off by a scream from his wife. Mairead bent double and clutched her belly. Gunnar was at once by her side.

"My love? Is it the baby…?" He pulled her into his arms where she grabbed at his tunic and groaned loudly.

"I do not know. I feel… Oh, I need to lie down. Is there somewhere…?"

Gunnar snatched her up into his arms. "My wife is indisposed. She is pregnant, and—"

"This way." Brynhild stood and beckoned her brother to follow. "She may rest in the solar." Without waiting for his response Brynhild marched across the hall in the direction of a doorway in the far corner, her baby still at her breast.

Gunnar strode after her, his wife cradled in his arms. Mairead continued to moan with dramatic, and to Gunnar, quite terrifying, effect.

"Ask Lady Fiona to come at once." It was the old man's voice Gunnar heard as he exited the great hall, issuing instructions to a hovering servant. "And tell her to bring refreshments for the lady."

Brynhild led him through the lord's private sitting room into the master bedchamber where Gunnar deposited his now less vocal wife on the bed. He crouched beside her.

"I should never have brought you here. I knew it was too much, too soon…"

Mairead glanced past him, to the door. Only Brynhild had accompanied them. Seemingly satisfied that they were in private, or as near as made no difference, she smiled at him.

"Hush, my husband. I am quite all right. I merely thought a short diversion would be helpful. A moment to collect our thoughts, and perhaps for you to speak with your sister privately for a few moments."

"What? You are not ill? The baby…?" After the revelations of the day Gunnar had thought not much else would surprise him. He was wrong, clearly.

"As I said, I am perfectly fine." She pushed herself up into a sitting position and reached out her hand to her sister-in-law. Brynhild, too, was peering at her suspiciously as though not quite able to comprehend this latest twist of events. "It is so pleasant to see you again, Brynhild. And what a lovely child. He is a fine, strong boy, I see. Is he not, Gunnar?"

"Er, yes. Very strong," agreed Gunnar, never taking his eyes from Mairead. "And you, wife, are a cunning, scheming woman who deserves a spanking. You may be sure, I am keeping count. I believe you just shaved a good ten years off my life with that stunt."

"My apologies. And to you too, Brynhild. I meant no ill, just—"

"What has happened?" Fiona burst through the door, a jug in her hand. "I brought mead, and we have some good wine if that might help." She rushed to the bed, set down her pitcher, and reached for her friend.

Mairead grinned at her from the bed. "I simply suffered a momentary upset. I am quite all right now, thank you. But since we are all here, perhaps you two can aid me in convincing my husband that there is no immediate cause to further sully his reputation with Lord Dughall by shedding yet more blood on the steps of his manor house. Are we to gather that you have arrived at an understanding with Taranc, Brynhild?"

"An understanding? 'Tis more than an understanding has produced this outcome." Gunnar gestured to the baby.

The little one had now sated his appetite and was beginning to fret for further attention. Brynhild set him on the bed beside Mairead and sat beside him.

"Yes, Taranc and I have been able to settle our differences. We are wed and… I am happy."

"Happy?" Gunnar could not contain his exasperation. "But how can this be? He abducted you, did he not? Or so we were informed."

"He did," Brynhild acknowledged, "but that was … a misunderstanding. It is all cleared up now and we have a good life here. I… I have a new family, and—"

"A new family?" prompted Mairead. "You mean Dughall? And Fiona?"

"Yes, and Taranc of course. And my little Morvyn. He is a great joy to me."

"Of course. Children are such a blessing, do you not agree, my husband?"

She knew exactly where to wound him, Gunnar reflected as he regarded the gurgling infant. His nephew kicked his feet and offered a toothless grin as Mairead picked him up and nestled him to her chest.

Mairead crooned at the squirming child. "Morvyn and our little Tyra will be playmates, perhaps. Just as Njal and Donald are…"

"That will be nice," agreed Fiona. "You will be remaining with us for a while, then?"

"I am not entirely sure. Your father…" Gunnar knew he must resume the conversation with Dughall before much longer. "I would not wish my presence here to disrupt your peace." He hesitated, then, "It *is* peaceful, I take it? Between you two." He had not forgotten where their current predicament originated. He eyed Fiona and Brynhild with some disquiet.

"Aye, I hope so," his sister murmured. "I have apologised, and explained what happened. I hope we understand each other better now, and we are friends I believe."

Brynhild looked to Fiona, who bowed her head in agreement. "Yes, we are friends."

"No more talk, then, of attempted murder?" Gunnar's tone had hardened. "Of thralls being left in the stocks to freeze to death?"

Brynhild coloured. "That was a mistake, a misunderstanding... I did not intend—"

"I know that you did not." Fiona took her hand and levelled a calm stare at Gunnar. "It is done with. We will speak of it no more."

Gunnar held her gaze, considering this latest turn of events.

He would have the full story of the incident with the stocks, he promised himself, but not today. It was sufficient that Fiona and Brynhild seemed at ease together. Which only left the somewhat awkward question of his new brother-in-law, and of course his brother. He grimaced. He'd be damned if he was going to apologise to Ulfric this side of Valhalla. The elder Freysson had a lot to answer for and a pummelling in the sand was no less than he deserved.

"I shall leave you women to become reacquainted," he announced, with a lopsided grin. "I suppose I should return to the hall and let everyone know of your swift recovery, my love. They will be relieved, I am quite sure. And I expect your husband..." he nodded at Brynhild, "and your father..." he tipped his head at Fiona, "have much they wish to say to me."

"You will talk? Not fight?" Mairead bestowed her sternest expression upon him.

"Aye, on this occasion, I shall do as you suggest. It appears to have worked thus far." He dropped a kiss on his wife's forehead and strode to the door.

• • • • • • •

Only Taranc and Ulfric remained at the table when Gunnar emerged from the solar, each nursing a mug of frothing ale. Ulfric laughed out loud at some remark of the Celt's. The rest of the throng of Vikings and villagers had dispersed, and Dughall, too, was nowhere to be seen. On catching sight of Gunnar, Ulfric stopped laughing and glared at his brother. Taranc's expression was somewhat warmer. He reached for a pitcher of ale that stood on the table and poured a third mug.

Gunnar drew in a fortifying breath and stepped toward the table, accepting the Celt's silent invitation to join them. He paused in midstride as Donald came hurtling through the outer door and charged down the hall toward him. Gunnar bent to catch the lad as he rushed toward the solar.

"Whoa there. What's the hurry?"

"My mother," panted the boy, eyes glistening. "I heard… I mean, they said she was ill. Is she… is she dead? She is not dead, is she?"

"No!" Gunnar placed his hands on his stepson's narrow shoulders. "Of course not. She is absolutely fine. A minor upset, that is all."

"Oh. I thought… Oh." Donald was clearly fighting back tears.

Gunnar cursed himself. He should have remembered to send word to the lad. Instead he hugged him. "All is well. You can go and see her if you like, or you can go back and find Njal."

Donald did neither. He simply stood, ashen-faced, his shock and fear still evident. Gunnar was reminded of his wedding feast. He had had cause then to offer the lad reassurance and it seemed he must do so again. His jug of ale would have to wait.

"Come with me a moment, Donald." He steered the boy into the alcove by the window and the pair sat on the stone seat inlaid into the thick wall. Gunnar leaned forward so he could look Donald in the eye. "I understand why you were worried. I love your mother too and would not wish her ill. We have that in common, you and I."

"Yes, sir," muttered the boy.

"We have much else in common also. Your little sister, we both love her, do we not? And our home across the North Sea? We both love horses too. There is much to bind you and me together, which is how it should be, in a family. Would you not agree?"

"I… I suppose so, yes."

"And soon you will have another brother. Or perhaps a sister."

"A brother," corrected Donald firmly. "It must be a brother."

"I see. We will both love him, also."

"Yes, sir."

"In a family, we take care of each other. Whatever might happen to your mother, you will still be mine. I will take care of you, you may rely on it."

"Because you own me. You b-bought me."

Gunnar smiled at him. "I had a good bargain, that day. And now you have the means to buy yourself." He tugged at the length of leather cord still slung about the boy's neck. The medallion, he knew, lay within his tunic, never far from Donald's heart. "But no, not because of that. The truth is simpler. It is because I love you. You are as my son, just as you are your mother's son. As Tyra is mine, and our new baby will be."

"You are not my father." Donald turned to face him fully.

"No, but I have decided to love you anyway."

"You have?"

"Aye. So, we understand each other?"

"I… I think so."

From the bemused expression on the boy's face Gunnar thought he was far from properly comprehending the significance of this conversation, but it was a start. "Do you want to see your mother now?"

Donald thought for a moment, then shook his head. "No. If you say she is well, then I do not need to see. I shall go back to Njal."

"Very well." Gunnar stood. "I will be here, if you need me."

Donald just nodded and took a few steps toward the door. Suddenly he stopped, turned, and ran back to Gunnar to fling his arms about his waist. No more words were said, none were needed. As quickly as he had embraced him the lad released his Viking stepfather and ran from the hall without another backward glance.

EPILOGUE

One month later

"You have been avoiding me."

Gunnar looked up from polishing his sword in the great hall to find Dughall of Pennglas standing behind him. For an elderly man, and one who was almost blind, the lord of Pennglas moved with astonishing alacrity when he chose to. Gunnar stood and bowed to the Celtic lord.

"I trust I find you well," he started, uncertain how to properly address a man whose son he had slain right before his eyes. "Would you prefer me to leave you?"

Dughall ignored the question. "I am well enough. These old bones feel the onset of winter keenly though. It comes early this year." He eased himself into his usual chair at the head of the huge table.

"Aye, so I understand." Gunnar sheathed his sword. "I will ask Fiona to bring you a warming draught."

Dughall waved his hand in dismissal. "I do not need anything, not just yet." He fixed his keen but near enough sightless gaze upon Gunnar. "You will not be able to return to your homeland until the spring."

"I prefer not to," agreed Gunnar, "given my wife's

condition. She is enjoying her visit to her old home."

"A fine woman. I do recall seeing her here, from time to time, in the old days. Before…"

"Yes. Before." Gunnar met the old man's gaze, but could find nothing more to say to him. 'Sorry' seemed hardly enough, and in any case, he was not truly repentant. Had he not slain the youth, Adair, it would have been Gunnar's own life blood spilt that day. He was a warrior, a Viking. He had done what he must, though he had thought it a waste at the time and was minded to say that much at least. "I would have wished that day had ended differently. I did not seek his death." He had no need to say more. They both know who and what he referred to.

"I know that. My eyes are bad now, but not so much then. I watched. I saw that you gave Adair time, time to surrender, to drop his weapon. I, too, pleaded with him to do so but he was always hot-headed, my boy. Always one to rush in and think later. Fiona too, come to think of it. They both take after their mother."

"I expect she was a fine woman," offered Gunnar. It was little enough by way of mollification, but he would take what he might find. "You have not told Fiona that her brother died at my hand."

It was a statement, not a question. Gunnar had spent the first few days in Pennglas fully expecting to be confronted by a vengeful Fiona demanding retribution for the death of her brother. Ulfric would not oblige her, he knew that, but it would be awkward. Gunnar would feel compelled to leave the village. The fact that Fiona had not mentioned the matter could only be explained by her ignorance of it. He had thought back to that day and realised that apart from Dughall himself, no one else witnessed Adair's death. Even Mairead did not know. For reasons known only to the old man, Dughall had not shared the information.

"I have not," agreed Dughall. He paused, then, "You may choose to, but I leave that decision to you, when you consider the time to be right."

"I do not understand," began Gunnar.

"You might, if you live as long as I have. I have concluded that in old age we see things differently. Perhaps it is the knowledge that we shall not share the time to come which compels us to do what we may to influence future events while we still can."

Gunnar was still at a loss. The old man grinned at him and patted his arm.

"Lad, if hating you would restore my son to me I would do it, make no mistake on that. But it will not, and I see nothing to be gained by using what I know to drive a wedge between my remaining child and the husband she loves and who clearly loves her. Ulfric is your brother, and I would not compel him to defend you against his wife's grief and anger. Whether I like it or not you are a part of this family. I hope you will prove yourself worthy of it." He paused then grinned in wry amusement. "You have done well."

"I beg your pardon."

"This is a small enough place. You have done well to evade me, despite my failing eyesight."

Gunnar suspected it had been the other way around in truth and that the old man had chosen to shun his company until he was ready to speak to him. It would seem Dughall had now chosen his moment. What was more, he had plenty still to say.

Dughall leaned forward to plant his elbows on the table before him. "I hated you, at first. You and all your kind. Murderers. Robbers. Abductors of our women, and of our fine young men. Your raids brought death and hunger to our villages, enslaved our people."

"I know. I…"

"Do not apologise," snapped the old man. "Not unless you truly mean it. What is past is past."

"Yes." On this much at least, Gunnar could agree.

"I was listening, that day."

"Lord Dughall…?" Gunnar found himself at a loss.

"The day you arrived here. After the onset of your wife's

241

sudden malady. I was pleased to see her much improved so quickly."

"Yes, just a brief disorder, mercifully."

"Indeed. I was at the foot of the stairs, close to the window alcove, when you spoke with your son that day. You did not see me."

"No, sir. I did not." Gunnar remembered the conversation with Donald. "The boy was upset and I sought to reassure him."

"You are a good man."

This was not even remotely what Gunnar had expected to hear from Dughall. He regarded the older man warily. "My family is important to me. More so than anything else, I find."

"And to me. For all his faults, I loved my son and you killed him. No, do not protest. We both know what happened, and how it came about. The situation will not improve for discussing it further so let us leave it where it is. I prefer to look to the future now, to the future of my family. My first grandchild is due in a few months, and will be half Viking. Your sister has become like a second daughter to me now, and she is a Viking too. It seems our futures are linked, the families we both prize are intertwined, so we must find a way to get along together."

"I admire your wisdom, Lord Dughall, and your farsightedness."

"If that is so, then I find myself wondering why you do not emulate it."

"I beg your pardon."

"Your brother. You must make your peace with him."

"I have. We—"

"You no longer seek to murder one another on our shore, but there is not peace between you. You are angry with him."

"Have I not the right? My sister—"

"Your sister has found her own happiness. She has forgiven Ulfric for his actions. Can you not do so?"

Gunnar shook his head, his jaw flexing. "He should have spoken to me. He should have sought my help. Brynhild could have come to Gunnarsholm…"

"Perhaps," agreed the older man. "But he did what he thought best."

"We are brothers. He should have trusted me. I could have helped…"

"Have you said this to your brother?"

"He knows."

"I suspect he does not. Your anger is rooted not so much in Ulfric's actions but in your disappointment, in Ulfric's failure to seek your aid. You blame him for what he did *not* do."

"What does it matter now?"

Dughall shrugged. "As I have said, 'twill be a long winter."

"You believe I should talk to him."

"As do you. You know that you must."

Gunnar gave a mirthless laugh. "You and my wife have much in common. She also sets great store by talking."

"A wise young woman. You chose well." The old man set his bony fingers on the arms of his chair and made to rise. Gunnar stepped forward to offer his hand. Dughall took it and hauled himself to his feet. "My thanks, young man. And now, I believe I might seek the comfort of my solar. I believe your brother is in the stables should you wish to seek him out."

"Perhaps I will." Gunnar bowed to the older man. "I thank you for your wise counsel. And for your generosity to my kinsfolk."

"As I appreciate yours. Donald is a Celt, as is your wife. You have been generous to them, and I gather you showed kindness to my daughter during the early days of her captivity. We may not forget the past, we may not forgive, but we can attempt to live together in peace and try to fashion a future. That is what I want, for my children, my grandchildren. I have arrived at an understanding with your brother, my son-in-law, and I confess it has not been easy. You will do no less, I am sure. Now I wish to make my peace with you and ask that you continue to care for those we both love."

Gunnar bowed his head. "I can promise you that much, sir."

"Then we are done here." Dughall started toward the door to his solar. "I believe I would like that warming draught now, if my daughter is anywhere about."

THE END

Made in the USA
Middletown, DE
30 September 2020